INFERNO

THE KINDRED SERIES, BOOK 4

ERICA STEVENS

Inferno (Book 4)

Phoenix Rising (Book 5)

The Ravening Series

Ravenous (Book 1)

Taken Over (Book 2)

Reclamation (Book 3)

The Survivor Chronicles

Book 1: The Upheaval

Book 2: The Divide

Book 3: The Forsaken

Book 4: The Risen

Books written under the pen name
Brenda K. Davies

The Alliance Series

Eternally Bound (Book 1)

Hell on Earth Series

Hell on Earth (Book 1)

Coming August 2017

The Road to Hell Series

Good Intentions (Book 1)

Carved (Book 2)

The Road (Book 3)

Into Hell (Book 4)

The Vampire Awakenings Series

Awakened (Book 1)

Destined (Book 2)

Untamed (Book 3)

Enraptured (Book 4)

Undone (Book 5)

Fractured (Book 6)

Historical Romance

A Stolen Heart

CHAPTER ONE

"THIS IS THE CENTER OF TOWN?" Melissa inquired, disbelief evident in her tone of voice.

Devon stared at the small buildings as they drove past at a snail's pace. There was a tiny post office with two mailboxes out front, a barber shop, tailor, dry cleaner, a bank, and a rather large general store he suspected passed as their grocery store too. He turned down a side road and passed by a Catholic church, a synagogue, and a Lutheran church. The road spilt at the end and headed toward the woods and side roads or back toward the center of town.

Though a few cars lined the roadsides, they were all in parking spaces. They hadn't been abandoned but placed there by their owners. Even the homes they drove by still had cars waiting expectantly in their driveway, just hoping their owners would come out and take them for one final spin. Devon knew that wasn't going to happen.

"Go back," Chris said.

Devon tried to get a sense of the place as he tried to figure out if there were still people living within the small array of homes. "Do you sense anything?" he asked Chris.

Chris's hand clenched on the back of Devon's seat as he leaned forward. "No, nothing. But just because there appears to be no one left in these homes, doesn't mean there still aren't people in homes elsewhere in the town."

"Go further down there," Luther instructed as he pointed ahead of Devon.

He kept to the left and headed down a small road lined with woods, but speckled with antique stores, a couple of bookstores, another dark gas station, and one log cabin that sold honey. "There's a school about a mile down, but I don't think that will do us any good," Luther stated as he watched the GPS. "We're going to have to find a place to stay soon."

Devon made another left toward the main strip. "We can return to the hotel; I don't think they would go back there after exhausting their prey, but I don't know for sure. Daylight will offer us no protection either, some Halflings can go out during the day; they are still part human after all."

Melissa shuddered and shook her head as she wrapped her arms around herself. "Absolutely not, I am *not* going back to the hotel. That room was awful, just awful."

"Maybe we can find a house to hole up in," Liam suggested.

"You mean one of the homes where the people have either disappeared, or are splattered all over the walls?" Melissa demanded.

"We have to stay somewhere," Liam responded as the voice of reason. "And we all have to eat eventually."

Melissa's dark eyes scanned the night as she bit on her bottom lip. It was apparent she didn't like the idea of staying in this town, but there was no way Devon was leaving it. Though he had no proof Cassie was here, it was the closest they had come to finding anything since she'd disappeared. None of them wanted to be in this godforsaken town, but they wouldn't leave it until he knew what was going on.

Devon drove through the main street again. "Did Halflings kill all of these people?" Chris inquired.

Devon shook his head as he gripped the wheel tighter. "No, they couldn't have. There would have to be at least a hundred of them to kill all of these people before the neighbors noticed. I don't know what is going on here, but *no* one would be crazy enough to allow that many Halflings to roam the earth." Though he said the words, he wasn't completely convinced of them.

"Do you think something else happened to them?" Melissa inquired.

"There's no way to know right now," Annabelle answered.

"If I start trying to eat your brains, you have my permission to cut my head off," Chris said.

"Excuse me?" Liam blurted.

"You know the zombie movies where no one ever knows how, but all the people start to go crazy and try to eat everyone's brains," Chris explained patiently.

Liam stared back at him, his nearly silver eyes questioning and thoughtful. His shaggy brown hair fell in disarray around his handsome face as he shook his head. "That is why I don't watch TV."

"Seriously?" Chris looked as if he believed the zombie story more than Liam's statement.

"Really," Liam stated. "I prefer to read. Remember, I was born in a time before electronics."

"You drive this big Caddy with a GPS and every new technological device in it, but you don't watch TV?"

Liam shrugged again; Chris glanced toward Annabelle who

lifted her dainty shoulders in response. Her normally lively sea green eyes were dull and flat, exhaustion and stress had taken their toll on her. "I like the Caddy and technology," she told Chris. "Liam still prefers horseback."

Chris chuckled as he slapped Liam on the back. "Oh man, I have so many great things to show you! Once this mess is over, I'm gonna introduce you to the fantastic world of the twenty-first century!"

"Yes, and until then, can we leave the TV talk till later," Devon said.

Everyone within the vehicle became silent as he drove down another road, discovering the small firehouse and police station. They passed an ice cream stand, boarded up for the winter, and a tiny movie theatre with no showings listed. Though they passed a few more houses, Devon still couldn't pick up any hint of human life.

"Go back to town Devon. The General Store will probably be the best place for us to hole up for a bit. It should have supplies, and maybe even some weapons," Luther said.

Melissa's dark hair spilled around her as she hugged her knees to her chest. Chris rested a hand on her arm as he sought to give her comfort. Though she hadn't seen the inside of the manager's office with his broken, bloodied body, the vision she'd received of it had shaken her greatly. "Can't we just stay in the car?" she whispered.

"Melissa, we need a place where we can relax, move about, eat, go to the bathroom, maybe even sleep," Annabelle said quietly. "And we can't keep the car running all day, we don't know if we can get gas out of the station pumps."

"We can siphon it out of other cars."

Annabelle leaned forward to grasp hold of Melissa's arm. "We'll stay in the car for now," she conceded. "But we can't stay in it forever, and we have to stay in this town for at least another day. There may be survivors out there that need our help, and we have to know what is going on here."

Melissa chewed on her bottom lip before nodding. Her shoulders went back as resolve settled over her pretty features. "Ok."

Devon wound his way back through town. "I'm not so sure I want to know what is going on here," Chris mumbled.

Devon agreed, but he wasn't leaving this town until he knew for sure Cassie wasn't somehow caught up in the oddity that was this town. Chris suddenly bolted upright, his hand slammed down on the back of Devon's seat. "Stop the car! Stop the car!"

"What is it?" Melissa cried as Devon slammed on the brakes and jolted everyone forward.

"Is it Cassie?" Devon demanded.

"No." Chris's voice was tinged with an odd sense of disbelief. Devon's hope plummeted; he had to fight the urge to rip the wheel free of the car. "It's Julian."

Devon's mouth dropped as Chris's words sank in. "What?" Annabelle gasped in disbelief. "Are you sure?"

Chris's forehead furrowed in confusion as he frowned. "I'm sure it's him, but it's different. He *feels* different."

"What do you mean?" Devon growled.

It made no sense, what could Julian possibly be doing *here*? Though Devon didn't trust him, he knew Julian wouldn't have created the monsters running loose here. Julian knew better than that; he knew what kind of havoc and death such creatures could render. Julian loved mayhem and murder more than most, but even he wouldn't take the risk of having the vampire population exposed to the outer world and terrified humans who would only choose to destroy their race.

Chris shook his head again; he rubbed the bridge of his nose as he tried to sort through the emotions Julian was emitting. "I don't know Devon. It *is* Julian, I'm certain of it, but he's not the same. He's not as angry or something, he's not as… he's not as…" Chris broke off, at a loss for words as he stared at Devon helplessly. "He's not as filled with hatred."

Devon frowned over Chris's odd statement. What was going on here? "How far is he from here?"

Chris stared out at the dark road, and then pointed ahead of him. "Ahead of us somewhere, not far, I don't think."

"You don't think?" Devon grated.

"Devon, just drive," Annabelle said. "We'll find him."

Excitement thrummed over Devon's skin and electrified his body. His knuckles were white upon the steering wheel as he started forward once more. Hope filled him; anticipation consumed him. They had been looking for Cassie, and had somehow managed to stumble upon the one person who could truly help them find her. He didn't linger on thoughts of what Julian could possibly be doing here; he only thought about finding him.

"Dani," Chris whispered.

"Excuse me?" Anger narrowed Melissa's onyx eyes as she whipped around to face Chris.

"Dani is with him," Chris said distantly.

The world turned into a fiery haze of red that blurred Devon's vision. Dani and Julian were together! Had Julian helped Dani and The Commission, take Cassie from him? If he had, Devon was going to rip Julian limb from limb. Luther leaned away from him; his eyes were wide as his mouth parted. Chris seized hold of his shoulder and clenched down. "You have to calm down Devon; I can't feel them over your emotions," he said in a choked voice.

Devon tried to calm himself, but the fiery storm building

inside him was shaking him to the very core of his being. He had to compose himself; he had to get a hold of his emotions. They had to find Julian. It may be the only chance they had of finding Cassie, and he couldn't risk losing it. He shuddered as he tried to keep himself from completely unraveling, but he had never suspected Julian may be in on all of this too. That Julian may have helped Dani in taking Cassie away from him, that Julian may have *hurt* her.

"Stop!"

The shout, issued from Melissa, caused him to slam the brakes on again. He jerked against the steering wheel as Luther bounced against the dash. Liam cursed loudly as he shoved himself off the back of the passenger seat.

"Look!" Melissa leaned forward and thrust a finger at the woods. "I know I saw something. *There!*"

Devon strained to see through the woods on his left, and then he saw it. The headlights illuminated a flash of red eyes as one of the Halflings scurried into some thick underbrush and scurried out of view once more. "It's coming for *us*." There was a small hitch in her voice.

"Yes," Devon agreed. He was spoiling for a fight, spoiling to get rid of some of the rage and confusion coursing through him. But there was no time for it right now. Not when they were this close to finally getting some answers.

He was shifting into drive when a flurry of motion about a hundred feet up and to the right, caught his attention. He turned toward it as three figures burst out of the woods. They stumbled up an embankment before staggering onto the road. Devon's mouth dropped, his chest constricted as they turned toward the vehicle.

Cassie's golden hair shimmered as vibrantly as the sun in the splash of the car's beams. It was the balm he'd been seeking; the miracle he'd been searching for. The sight of her instantly calmed the furious monster raging inside of him. It brought back the warmth and joy he'd been missing for the past couple of weeks.

The scrubs she wore were torn, bloodied, and wet from the snow covered branches of the forest. Her bare feet were bloodied and raw looking, but she was still the most magnificent thing he'd ever seen.

She stared at them unblinkingly; her red eyes vibrant against the white pallor of her face. The red eyes terrified him most. Had he lost her? Was she gone? Had she become one of the things that had devastated this town? And just what was she doing with Julian and Dani?

Her mouth parted as she took a startled step away from the vehicle. Julian was the first to react as he began to forcefully pull her toward the other side of the road. Devon's eyes latched onto their entwined hands as Cassie scurried after Julian with Dani close behind. It was the spectacle of those hands that drove him into action. He would *not* lose her like this, and he wasn't going to let her disappear again.

He couldn't survive it if he lost her again.

Throwing the door of the SUV open he plunged into the cold. "Cassie!" he bellowed as they slipped down the hillside of the road and back into the woods.

Cassie stumbled as Julian pulled her onward after she'd stopped abruptly. Her head whipped toward him, her hair billowed around her as the wind caught hold of it. Her eyes met his and tears bloomed within their vivid ruby depths. Even from their distance, and above the howl of the wind, he heard her pant his name.

"Devon!" she broke free of Julian's hold. Using her hands,

she scrambled through the shifting rocks that skittered under her feet as she pulled herself up the embankment. "Devon!"

He was still too astonished by her sudden arrival to move. Her reddened eyes suggested she was something different, someone else, but her reaction to him was what he would have expected from *his* Cassie. The one who had loved him whole-heartedly and *never* would have been holding hands with Julian. Her voice rang with pure joy, her face lit with the radiance of love as she reached the road.

He didn't know what was going on, and he didn't care. Releasing the car door, he raced toward her, needing to hold her and touch her again. "Cassie look out!"

It was Julian's shout that alerted him to the threat he had forgotten about in his astonishment at seeing her. The blur moved from the woods and emerged just feet from her as it raced across the road. It was hunched over as it used its hands and feet like an ape to run.

Cassie's mouth dropped as it barreled toward her. "Cassie!" Devon shouted. The thing was closer to her than he was, closer than Julian, who had raced out of the woods after her. Devon was startled by the strange certainty filling him that Julian would protect her from the thing.

Cassie darted to the side as the thing launched itself at her; its clawed hands outstretched with deadly intent. Twisting to the side, she seized the creature by the collar of the tattered shirt it wore, though the thing was clearly nothing close to resembling human anymore. She spun to the side as she flung it away from her. Devon was startled by the strength and speed she displayed, but his surprise didn't slow him as the creature rebounded to its feet. It screamed as it raced back at her. She was braced for the attack, but Devon raced past her and seized hold of the creature before it got to her.

His hand constricted around its throat as he slammed it onto the roadway and smashed its head off the asphalt. It howled as it squirmed beneath Devon and clawed at his hand. Disgust curved his upper lip as he crushed the creature's windpipe with a sickening pop.

The squeals and grunts were silenced, but the monster continued to fight to break free. He glanced up at Cassie, horrified to find her watching as he gradually decapitated the pathetic thing. Julian arrived at her side and grasped hold of Cassie's shoulders to spin her away.

"Julian don't!" she protested as she tried to wiggle out of his grasp. Julian held her firm though, refusing to let her turn back around, something Devon was infinitely grateful for. "Let me go!"

Julian's gaze was insolent and cold as he remained focused on Devon. Fresh wrath tore through Devon as he took note of Julian's hands resting so comfortably, *possessively*, upon her. He twisted the creature's head to the side and savagely yanked it back. Its head gave way with a sickening crunch and a horrendous tearing sound.

Devon tossed the head aside as he leapt to his feet. Julian stared back at him with his chin tilted proudly and a sneer curving his upper lip. Devon took a step toward them, prepared to kill Julian if it came down to it. Julian's eyes warmed as he glanced at Cassie, squeezed her shoulder, and reluctantly released her.

Then, Cassie turned toward him. She stared up at him, her eyes searching, as tears simmered in her ruby colored eyes. Her lower lip trembled when she stretched a shaky hand toward him, seemingly afraid he might disappear. He knew exactly how she felt. This was far too dreamlike to be real, far too unexpected after the weeks of uncertainty and terror. He was scared if he touched her she would vanish like smoke and all of this would prove to be some sort of torturous dream. He didn't think he could take that if it happened.

Yet, he couldn't stop himself; he had to touch her. He had to know if she was *real*. Unable to take one more second of their separation, he seized hold of her shaking fingers. Relief and awe pooled through him; the knot in his chest eased as he savored the silken, solid feel of her skin. Her fingers clenched upon him, her nails dug into his skin, but he didn't care. He didn't care about anything now that he'd found her again and was touching her again. A small sob escaped her as he pulled her forward a step.

"Cassie," he breathed her name reverently.

Wrapping his arms around her, he pulled her against him. Awe filled him as his hand threaded through her tangled hair. She was so warm, and alive, and in his arms again where she belonged, where she would *always* belong. He fought back the tears of relief threatening to fall. More tears escaped her as her small fingers dug into his back. She was the most magnificent thing he had ever felt. Closing his eyes, he buried his face in her silky hair.

"Cassie," he groaned as her sobs increased and she tried to burrow closer to him.

"I was beginning to fear I would never see you again!" she cried, her slender frame shaking with the force of her tears.

He pulled back to simply look at her again, but the minute he saw her cherished face, he knew he couldn't stop himself. He cupped her face and wiped the tears from her cheeks as he bent his head to hers. A small moan of pleasure escaped her as he took ardent possession of her mouth.

Her arms wrapped around his neck, her fingers entangled in his hair as she melded against him. He had never forgotten how right it felt to take her in his arms, but the memories of their last touch paled in comparison to actually holding her again. Her tongue entwined eagerly with his as he tasted her in deep, forceful thrusts that made his body thrum with passion. He lifted her up, crushing her against him as he cradled the back of her head and savored everything about her.

He wanted more of her, *needed* more of her. He'd nearly lost her; he'd been without her for so long he was on the brink of losing complete control now that he had her again. He was closer to completely snapping and changing her than he'd ever been before. If he changed her, he would never have to part from her again. He would be able to find her anywhere, and she would be immortal, safe from death, and far stronger than she was now. Abruptly he pulled away from her. His head dropped into the hollow of her neck as he struggled to keep his riotously swaying emotions, and body, under control.

He didn't care they were standing in a road, in the middle of nowhere. He didn't care that at his back was the man who had once been his best friend, but was now his greatest enemy. He didn't even care there was an unknown amount of monsters in the woods around them. All he cared about was holding her, touching her, possessing her. All he craved was to taste her again, to savor her blood, and to feel her in every possible way.

Her fingers slid over his cheeks as she pulled him from her neck. Her supple lips teased his as she tried to ease the tension within him. She'd always known when the beast inside was on the verge of taking control, always known how to soothe him as she did so now. "I love you," she whispered. "So very much."

"I love you."

His body pulsed with excitement as she opened her eyes to his. They were the spectacular violet blue color he remembered and loved so dearly. "Your eyes aren't red anymore," he told her, baffled by the sudden change.

She grinned up at him as he wiped a few streaks of blood from her delicate cheeks. Even filthy and disheveled she was the most exquisite thing he'd ever seen. "Neither are yours."

It had been almost two weeks since his eyes had been normal, since he'd had enough control over himself to keep the demon inside securely locked away. Her presence made the man in him stronger than the demon constantly lurking just beneath the surface. Perhaps his presence helped to do the same thing for her. But why were her eyes red when she had still been in complete control of herself, and her body wasn't trying to turn into something else? What had been done to her? Where had she been? He could only hope she hadn't been changed beyond repair.

He didn't know what had been done to her, but from the looks of her now, she'd been put through the ringer. Anger spiked through him as he caught the scent of her blood. It wasn't the same sweet scent he remembered. There was something different about it, something tangy and wrong. And beneath it all, he could smell Julian.

He tried to control his emotions, tried to keep them hidden from her, but envy was eating at him. What had they done to her in there? What had they given her to cause her blood to smell so abnormal, and her eyes to change without losing control of herself? Why did he smell *Julian* on her? Was it because they had been together, or had something more been done?

His attention turned to Julian. His face was a mask of indifference, but Devon could sense the underlying tension and anguish running through him. Julian was trying to be stoic, but it was obvious that whatever had happened to them, Julian had also been changed by it.

Cassie's fingers drew his attention back to her as she stroked his cheeks. She smiled at him so beautifully that he forgot all about the strange scent clinging to her. All he could do was hope he could ease whatever torment she had been through, and that she could forgive him for losing her in the first place.

"We should probably get off the street," she murmured.

He couldn't help but grin at her as he pulled her close and kissed her nose. "Yes."

He wrapped his arms around her before stooping to effortlessly pick her up. She didn't make a sound as she entwined her arms around his neck and snuggled closer. Her breath was warm on his skin, her body fit perfectly against his as she buried her face in his neck.

Devon turned back to the group standing outside the SUV. Luther's arm was wrapped around Melissa as she wept silently. Liam and Annabelle were standing with their arms around each other. Chris had moved forward, his mouth hung open. Devon didn't like the confusion he saw on Chris's face. It only served to heighten his own doubts and concerns about Cassie and Julian and where they'd been.

Cassie lifted her head from his shoulder and blinked tiredly. He could feel the exhaustion radiating from her. "You are coming with us," she said to Julian.

Devon tensed, his hands tensed upon her. "Cassie…"

"He's coming with us Devon," she said forcefully. "He is my friend. I will *not* leave him here."

Devon couldn't stop the bolt of jealousy and confusion ripping through him. What had happened between them, and *to* them, for her to want Julian to stay with her? "I'm coming," Julian replied firmly.

Cassie may think they were "friends", but the look in Julian's eyes said he thought more, or at least *yearned* for more. Devon shifted her away from Julian. Then Julian looked up at him, and though Devon sensed jealousy in him, he didn't sense any malice. Not like there used to be.

"And her?" Devon inquired as he nodded at Dani.

Cassie's lip curled as she moved to look around him. "She's coming too, we're going to get some answers," Julian retorted bitterly.

Apprehension was evident in Dani's gold streaked hazel eyes as she studied all of them. Then she looked toward the woods and took a step closer to Julian. "I'm coming with you."

"You didn't have a choice," Julian assured her flatly.

"Be nice," Cassie told him. "She did get us out of there."

"She also helped to put us *in* there."

Cassie bit on her bottom lip as she nodded. "Can we go please?"

"Anything you desire," Devon assured her as he strode past the two of them.

CHAPTER TWO

CASSIE REFUSED to release Devon as she sat in his lap. She was exhausted, but she was afraid to go to sleep. She was petrified this would all turn out to be a dream, and she would awaken in that cramped cell again. She shifted on Devon's lap; her hand curled into his shirt as she pressed against him, trying to assure herself he was real.

His chest was solid beneath her hand and slightly cooler under his shirt. His lean muscles rippled as his hand entangled in her hair, and he held her close. She glanced up at the rigid contour of his jaw, taking note of the dark bristles lining it. He'd always been clean shaven, but now sported a few days worth of growth.

He was just as magnificent and handsome as she remembered. His presence filled the hole that had been present since she'd been ripped away from him and placed in that horrendous cell. He made her complete. He was everything good and right and just within her.

His beautiful emerald eyes warmed with love as he pulled her closer against him and dropped a kiss on her forehead. Cassie met his lips for a brief kiss she wished was so much more. She longed to be out of this cramped vehicle, and to have some time alone with Devon.

Not that she wasn't grateful to see her friends too. Especially Chris and Annabelle, as she'd feared Dani had done something awful to them, but they were here before her, alive and healthy. Tears filled her eyes as she stared at the back of Chris's blond head. He'd always been her best friend, her anchor in the world, but it was Devon she needed now, and in a way she never had before. She'd been kidnapped, tortured, brutalized and changed in ways she didn't even know. She needed his caring and uncondditional love more than anything right now. Trailing a finger under his jaw, she relished the feel of his coarse hair against her skin. She admired the way his black hair fell across his face and outlined the gorgeous contours of his refined features.

Reluctantly she turned her attention away from him as the SUV made a right hand turn onto a strangely deserted street. Though it was still dark out the sun would be coming up soon, there should be at least a few people moving around. Some lights should be on in the windows as people brewed their morning coffee, showered, and dressed for work.

"What is going on around here?" she asked as they drove down another deserted street.

"We don't know," Chris answered. His sapphire gaze was troubled and questioning as he turned toward her. Cassie frowned at him. He had been staring at her strangely ever since she'd gotten into the vehicle. He had hugged her, had even shed a few tears, but he hadn't stopped looking at her as if he didn't understand her, or even know who she was.

"Where are we going?"

"The General store," Melissa answered with a small quiver in her voice.

"We're staying here? We're staying in *this* town?" she was unable to keep the tremble of alarm from her voice.

"It will be ok." Devon rubbed her arms as he tried to calm her.

Her heart hammered as she turned back to him. "No, those people and those *things* are in this town! They'll take us back there, if they find us! We can't go back in there!"

She was nearly shrieking by the time she was done, and shaking so fiercely her teeth were chattered together. "Cassie…"

"No!" A sense of impending doom settled over her; she wheezed as she tried to get air into her tortured lungs.

Devon kept hold of her as she tried to get free of the vehicle and the pressing weight on her chest. Julian leaned over him, grasped hold of her chin, and forcefully pulled her head toward him. "Enough, Princess!" He told her as Devon released a ferocious growl that caused the hair on the back of her neck to stand on end.

"Get your hand off of her!" Devon spat.

Julian chose to ignore him as he continued to hold onto her. "I promise you, we are *never* going back in there. They will *never* touch you again. You have to keep yourself under control because we have got to figure out what is going on here. We have to know what they were trying to do to us down there, and what they *have* done to this town."

Cassie fought back the wave of tears filling her eyes. "Or what they *did* do to us," she whispered as her thoughts turned to her red eyes and the strange control she'd had over herself earlier. She recalled the shots they'd injected her with that had turned her veins a different color.

"Yes." Cassie tried to breathe through the pressure in her chest.

Julian's full mouth twisted into a small smile. "You survived down there, you *will* survive this."

Cassie nodded, a single tear slid down her face as she set her shoulders in resolve. "You're right," she whispered. "And don't call me Princess!"

He grinned at her and squeezed her chin before retreating to the far back of the vehicle. Everyone stared at her in bewildered silence, and then their gazes flitted toward Julian. She could sense their confusion and uncertainty, sense the questions in their minds, but no one said a word. She squeezed Devon's hand as she tried to reassure him, but she wasn't sure she succeeded.

Devon was her heart, but he was going to have to accept that Julian had become her friend and they had forged a strong bond while imprisoned together. Their bond had become so strong that she considered Julian as good of a friend as Chris and Melissa.

The fact Julian had kissed her was a detail she decided best left between her and Julian for now. There was no reason to burden Devon with it at this point. He would destroy Julian if he learned about it, and she couldn't allow that to happen, especially since she'd allowed the kiss to happen. She'd been confused about her feelings toward Julian. She knew Devon possessed her heart and soul, but Julian had become a big part of her life, and she loved him. She could never love him like she loved Devon, she had doubted that, but Julian never had.

She thought back to Julian's words after he had kissed her. "I know, Princess, I know. I just needed this."

At the time she hadn't known what he meant, she understood now. She'd been lost and confused, but Julian had known she would always choose Devon over him. Julian had understood she did love him, but Devon was the only one for her. Though it had happened once, they both knew it would never happen again.

Tears clogged her throat as she pressed closer to Devon. It wasn't a secret she would always keep from him, and one day she *would* tell him, but she couldn't do so now. Devon had to learn to trust Julian as much as she did. She couldn't lose Julian now; she needed him to help get her through all of this. She would always need him she realized.

Devon had to realize Julian was different and wasn't their enemy, or the same murderous monster who had once been Devon's best friend. No, this Julian was evolving, becoming someone different, someone good and trustworthy. He was learning to care for someone other than himself; he was becoming more human again and less of a monster. He had become someone who would do anything to keep her safe, and she would also do the same for him.

Even if the person she had to keep him safe from right now was Devon.

Cassie squeezed Devon's hand again, seeking reassurance as she leaned her head against his chest to savor the scent of him. His hand entangled in her hair, crushing her to him with a desperation that left her breathless and on the verge of tears. She ached for the loss and confusion he had gone through, and still seemed to be going through. He bent his head to her, his lips pressed against her forehead and cheek, before finally resting against her neck.

She felt the rapid increase of tension and hunger coursing through him. Closing her eyes, her body tingled with excitement as she felt the hot press of his fangs against her skin. She wished they weren't here, that they weren't trapped in this unending nightmare, and they were alone so she could truly enjoy his love and strength.

Cassie's eyes flew open as the vehicle came to a stop. She *had* to be strong now. Taking a deep breath, she reluctantly pulled away. He kept hold of her hand as she rose up to look at the large red general store. "Why are we here?" Dani inquired.

"Supplies," Luther answered briskly.

"Julian and I will go in first."

They had just found each other again; she wasn't ready to part with him yet. "I'm coming with you."

"Cassie..."

She shook her head and brushed aside the strands of hair that fell across her eyes. "No, I'm coming with you."

Devon glanced warily at the store then back at her. "She'll be fine; she's been through far worse than this. Now let's get going, the sun is coming up," Julian said briskly. "Luther, open the back door."

Cassie found herself staring back at them with her chin tilted up. She knew she wasn't the same Cassie they'd known before her kidnapping, but she was really getting tired of their questioning looks. She may be tougher now, but at heart she was still the same person. Mostly, there were a few changes that were unsettling. Changes she wasn't sure she would ever understand.

Luther sighed before leaning forward to push the button that opened the back door. Julian slid out the back and slammed the door down behind him. Devon hesitated, but Cassie continued to hold onto his hand, unwilling to let go. "Ok," he relented.

"I'm coming too," Liam said as he shoved open the door and plunged into the brisk predawn air.

Cassie shivered in response. When they had fled their prison, she had been too hyped up on adrenaline to really feel the cold, but now it seemed to pierce her to her bones. Devon slid out of the car and helped her out behind him. Cassie winced as her brutalized bare feet hit the ground. She absently noted she'd somehow lost the nail on her right pinky toe. Shuddering in revulsion she quickly looked away from the bloodied mess of her feet.

"Are you ok?" Devon demanded as he studied her soiled and bloody feet.

She managed a feeble smile as she nodded. "I heal fast, remember?"

A small smile curved his full mouth but his eyes remained hard. "I remember. I'll carry you."

He bent to pick her up, but Cassie quickly shook her head and held up her hand to ward him off. "We're both going to have to be ready in case something happens. I'm fine Devon, really."

"The door is open." Cassie glanced over at Julian as he slipped through the darkened doorway. A moment of panic descended over her as he disappeared from view.

"Stay by me," Devon ordered in a low voice.

Cassie nodded as they entered the dark store. Her eyes instantly found Julian amongst the shadows as he surveyed the building. The store smelled tantalizingly of oats, honey, corn, sweet feed, and leather. The sweet scent of food caused Cassie's stomach to rumble. Liam searched for a light switch, but Julian seized hold of his arm. "They'll see the light if you do that."

"You don't think they haven't already seen the headlights?" Liam retorted.

"The lights stay off," Devon told him.

They moved into the store cautiously. Although it was dark, her eyes picked up most of the details. She kept her ears trained for any hint of movement, any furtive sound that might signal the impending attack of one of the monsters haunting this town.

The wooden floor boards squeaked under their feet as they

crept forward. They passed by the glass countertop with a cash register placed at the end of it. Oddly enough, inside the countertop was an array of jewelry neatly tucked next to some brutal looking hunting knives. Next to the counter was a large display of penny candy with even more candy bars set up on the wall behind it.

"Those will come in handy," Julian's eyes were latched onto a foot long bowie knife.

"Good thing this is a hunting community," Liam muttered as he focused on the back row of the store.

Hung on the back wall was a vast assortment of crossbows and long bows. A thrill of excitement shot through her; she itched to get her hands on one of those crossbows. It had always been her favorite weapon, and she excelled at it. Devon pulled her to the side and led her past rows of brown Carhartt jackets, pants and coveralls. Across from the outdoor gear was a row of sweaters, sweatshirts, and long johns.

Devon paused to pull a jacket from the hanger. He slipped it around her shoulders and tugged it into place. She hadn't realized she'd been shivering until the warm material encircled her and drew her attention to the goose bumps covering her skin. The sleeves were too big but Devon rolled them back and snugged them into place.

Love filled her as he brushed the hair back from her face. "There's some food over here," Liam announced.

Cassie's hand easily slid into Devon's as they moved further down the aisles. Liam and Julian were standing in the far left aisle that ran the length of the store. Freezers full of soda, ice cream, and frozen goods filled the wall. A row of canned foods, bagged foods, and junk food lined the shelves on her right.

Julian's ice blue eyes gleamed in the glow from the coolers as he strode toward the back of the store. Broad double doors opened into a large room packed nearly to the ceiling with bags of animal feed. There was food for dogs and cats, but most of it consisted of cow and horse feed, with a stack of grain in the back for chickens, goats, and sheep.

"Everything you could possibly require in one little store," Liam muttered.

Cassie walked over to the back wall of windows. The room was held up by stilts, and the backyard sloped down a steep rock and dirt hill. Staring out the window, she wasn't surprised to find a mixture of tractors, mowers, trailers, and other assorted equipment in the back. There were also a few chicken coops and dog pens. Nausea twisted through her, bile rose up her throat at the carnage of what remained of the animals that had once lived within those pens.

Devon rested his hands on her shoulders as he pulled her away. Julian shook his head as his lip curled. "Disgusting, vile creatures," he muttered. "There is one thing we don't have in this little store."

"Blood," Cassie answered for him.

"Yes."

The three living dead stared at each other. Cassie was uncomfortably aware she was the only morsel in front of them. "Let's gather some supplies and get out of here," she said.

"We're going to be here for a while." Julian pointed out the window to the rays breaking over the horizon. "Not all of us are lucky enough to withstand its rays."

Cassie winced as she recalled what had been done to Julian while they'd been prisoners. Cassie could still see the remnants of a burn at the edge of his platinum blond hair. "Aren't we?" Devon inquired.

Cassie shot Devon a stern look. He couldn't know what had happened to Julian in there, but there was no reason to provoke him. Julian quirked an eyebrow in amusement, though it did little to cover the tension thrumming through him. "I may have been on this earth for hundreds of years, but that is one trick I haven't managed to master. Let's get the others."

He turned away and glided gracefully back down the aisles. Cassie started to follow him, but Devon held her back. "Cassie I don't know what has happened to you, or to Julian, over the past couple of weeks. I don't know why the three of you are together." He broke off as he studied her. Cassie knew he'd like an explanation, but she wasn't ready to relive that awfulness right now. "I know you feel we can trust him, but…"

"I *do* trust him," she interrupted. "I know it's asking a lot of you Devon, but you must trust *me* on this. Julian will not do *anything* to harm me."

A strange look crossed his face, a flicker of hurt and apprehension flashed through his eyes. "Fine" he relented. "If you trust him around your friends, I will also. For now."

"I do, Devon. I trust him completely."

She knew her words baffled him, but she couldn't help it. There was no time to explain now, and he had to stop provoking Julian. "Then let's go."

She followed him back to the front of the store and outside. Annabelle was standing by the SUV rapidly searching the surrounding area. "We'll be staying here for now," Julian announced.

Annabelle's shoulders slouched in relief as she nodded briskly. She turned to the vehicle and threw open the driver's side door. "Come on," she called into it.

CHAPTER THREE

CASSIE WAITED IMPATIENTLY for the microwave to beep. The plate her frozen pizza was on bumped every once in a while against the sides of the machine. Her mouth watered as the scent of the bubbling cheese filled the air. Turning away, before she drove herself crazy with hunger, Cassie looked around the small room they had discovered behind the row of candy bars.

Inside were a coffee pot, small mini fridge, and microwave. There was also a little TV and radio. Devon was fiddling with the old TV, trying to find a channel, but receiving nothing. He slammed his hands off the side of it; a loud curse escaped him as he switched it off.

"Beating on it won't make the cable come back on."

Cassie glanced over her shoulder as Julian appeared in the doorway and smiled in wry amusement. His platinum hair was still damp and disheveled from washing it in the same sink Cassie had used to clean herself up. He had slipped on a pair of jeans and a flannel shirt that looked completely out of place on him. Yet, he still somehow managed to look gorgeous and at ease. She shook her head at him as Devon scowled ferociously.

"Thanks for the info. Have any more little tidbits of advice for me?" Devon sneered.

"Now, now, no reason to be snippy," Julian replied flippantly.

Devon's scowl deepened as he rose to his feet. Cassie glanced rapidly between the two of them. Julian still appeared casual, but beneath his calm exterior she sensed a rising tension inside of him. "Stop it," Cassie said and stepped between the two of them.

Devon was the first one to back down when the microwave beeped. Cassie's mouth watered as he pulled the plate out and eyed Julian as he handed it to her. Cassie eagerly seized hold of the plate as she chose to ignore them for the time being. "We found a storage area," Julian informed them. "In the cellar."

Cassie blew on her steaming pizza. She was very tempted to start eating it now, and to hell with the burnt mouth, but Julian's words enticed her almost as much as the pizza did. "There's a cellar?" she inquired.

"Yes, come on."

Cassie glanced at Devon before following Julian from the room and toward the back of the store. A large mat had been pulled back to reveal the wooden planks of the floor. In the middle of the planks was an open trap door with a single metal ring at the end of it. Everyone had gathered around the trapdoor to peer into the darkness below.

Cassie forgot about her pizza as she stepped next to Chris. The harsh scent of mildew wafted up, but nothing stirred within the dark recesses of the empty room. "I don't sense anything down there," Chris told them.

"I don't smell any humans," Liam added. "There are rats though."

Cassie's nose wrinkled at the thought, her stomach rolled and dropped. She didn't mind most animals, but rats not in a cage bothered her. "Let's go down."

Julian pulled out a flashlight and flicked it on to illuminate a set of steep wooden stairs. Turning, Cassie placed her pizza on a shelf, more curious about what was beneath than her food. She used the thin wooden rail to guide herself, and prayed the stairs would hold their weight as she followed Chris down.

The basement floor was hard packed dirt, and the scent of mildew was stronger down here. Cassie covered her nose against the harsh smell as her stomach turned over. Julian played the flashlight around the room. The beam bounced off the old rock walls, a beaten down oil heater, and pallets loaded with more feed. Sitting on top of the bags of feed were half a dozen rats, they paused only briefly in their eating to stare at them. Their noses twitched as their tails thumped against the bags of grain. They squeaked their displeasure and a few of them disappeared into the dark, but the braver ones refused to give up their meal.

Cassie took an involuntary step back from them. "Guess that's dinner," Julian said as he turned the beam away from them. Cassie groaned and her stomach twisted even more at the thought. Julian's eyes were vivid in the glow of the beam. "Sorry Princess, but it's true."

Cassie shot him a look; he merely grinned annoying back at her. Devon took hold of her hand and squeezed it reassuringly as he pulled her a step closer to him. "There's nothing we can use down here," Chris said.

"And it's creeping me out," Melissa muttered.

Melissa hurried back up the steps and nearly bolted through

the open door. Cassie was just as eager to follow her. She stepped back into the store and eagerly inhaled the fresh air. Luther glanced over from his position by the window, his glasses sparkled when they caught the small bit of sunlight filtering through the drawn curtains.

"Anything?" he inquired.

Cassie shook her head as she snagged her pizza. The rats had grossed her out, but they hadn't diminished her appetite. The others eventually filed back out and filtered throughout the store. Though she sensed their exhaustion, she knew their curiosity about what had been done to them was far stronger. She licked the pizza sauce from her fingers as she tried to stall for more time. She wasn't ready to get into the details of the nightmare she and Julian had endured. It was inevitable though, they deserved answers, and she would rather get it done sooner rather than later. Turning to face them, she braced herself for the onslaught of their questions.

Devon's shoulder brushed against hers as he stood rigidly by her side. Chris had taken up position on the other side of the door. Though he stared out at the street, Cassie knew his attention was focused on her. Liam arms were wrapped around Annabelle's waist as he held her against his chest. Melissa and Luther watched her questioningly; Melissa's onyx eyes were sad and caring. Dani was sitting with her back against the counter, her head bent, and her red streaked hair falling forward. She looked even more uncomfortable than Cassie felt.

"Are you ready to tell us what happened?" Devon inquired.

They all stared at her inquisitively, except for Julian, who was scowling at the floor with his arms folded over his chest. Julian lifted his head and met her gaze briefly before giving her a small nod of encouragement. Taking strength in his steady, calming presence she decided to just plunge in. She quickly filled them in on her capture and imprisonment. She didn't talk about the torture she'd experienced and kept everything simple and short. Her eyes remained focused on the ground until she finished. She hated the anticipatory hush filling the room when she was done.

"What did they do to you in there Cassie?" Chris's gaze was keen and inquisitive as he studied her.

She shook her head, she couldn't look at Chris again for fear she would start crying and never stop. She didn't want him, or anyone else to know of her suffering. She planned to keep them sheltered and protected from it.

She ignored Chris's question as she focused on Dani. "Why did you turn on us?" she asked, unable to keep the hurt from her voice. She had brought Dani into her home, thought of her like a sister, and in return she had betrayed them all.

Dani's gold flecked eyes were red and swollen from lack of sleep. The hostility within the room notched up a level as everyone focused their attention on her. "I didn't plan to, but..." her voice trailed off as a sob broke from her.

"My brother went to The Commission after he left town, he told them about you, all of you." Her gaze lingered briefly on Devon before turning toward Julian. Julian glowered back at her as his hands fisted. Dani turned quickly away from the malevolence in Julian's gaze. "He was my brother; I had to help him when The Commission sent him back."

They all stared at her expectantly, but she didn't continue. "There's more to *that* story!" Julian spat.

Dani winced as she bit on her bottom lip. "Easy Julian," Devon cautioned.

Julian glared at him before turning his attention back to Dani. "Either tell the truth, or I will get it from you. All I have to do is touch you, sort through the memories, and pick out the ones I want. For the most part it can be painless, and the person doesn't even have to know I was there. But what I will do to *you*, will be *anything* but painless."

Dani gaped at him as her eyes flew around the room. Cassie had not pity for her, she couldn't summon the strength for forgiveness and mercy, not for Dani. "I'll destroy you if I get into your mind," Julian promised. "I'll make what they did to us in that place look like it was a day in the park!"

"Julian." Annabelle grabbed his arm in an attempt to calm him.

Julian shook her off and took another step toward Dani. "This *bitch* put us in there, and one way or another she *is* going to tell us why!"

"Julian," Cassie said. He had shaken Annabelle off, but he didn't shrug off her grasp as she seized hold of his arm. His reddened eyes turned back to their electrifying blue as his gaze met hers. "It's ok."

He stepped back, but his body still hummed with annoyance. Devon's eyes were questioning as he studied her. He would like to know what had been done to them, and just how close her bond with Julian was. She just wasn't ready to give them to him right now.

"Why did The Commission send your brother, and you, after us?" Cassie inquired.

The tips of Dani's lashes were wet with unshed tears. Cassie was frightened Dani wouldn't speak, and they would require Julian to drag the answers from her, but she finally did. "Because of you."

Cassie blinked at Dani's words. Her gaze flew toward Devon as a low growl emanated from deep within his chest. The hair on the back of her neck stood on end as the resentment in the room notched up to a whole new level. Cassie glanced between him and Julian, whose eyes were a brilliant red again. Between the two of them she may not be able to keep Dani alive.

"What do you mean?" she asked.

Dani glanced warily at the hostile group surrounding her. Using the counter, she rose to her feet. She looked braced for an attack. Cassie's heart trip hammered with the knowledge she wouldn't like what Dani had to say. "Before our Guardian was killed in The Slaughter, he told Joey about this town, and to come here if something ever happened to him. The Commission took us in, kept us with them after The Slaughter, and helped us to survive until we were ready to go out on our own. They also taught us about our heritage."

A growing feeling of unease moved through Cassie's body. Dani had lied to them from the beginning; she and Joey had led them all to believe they'd been completely on their own after The Slaughter as they struggled to survive on the streets. Cassie didn't know why Dani had kept this a secret, but she was certain she wasn't going to like the reasons behind it.

"Why did you lie to us about your childhood?" Melissa asked.

Dani shifted nervously as her gaze settled on the door. "When The Commission eventually sent us out in search of other Hunters and Guardians they told us not to let them know about this town until they knew if we could trust them. There was no way of knowing how The Slaughter had affected people, and how they now felt about The Commission. They never suspected anything like what we discovered with you and Devon; no one *ever* thought a Hunter and a vampire would fall in love. It was unthinkable. Unheard of."

"I never thought it was wrong," Dani breathed. "I thought your relationship was special, different; good."

Her eyes flitted over the two of them, before turning briefly to Julian. His lip curled, his eyes darkened as he glowered at her. Cassie was irritated by the confusion and doubt she sensed from Dani, but then again Dani had witnessed Julian kissing her. "It is," Cassie told her.

Dani shot her a questioning look. Cassie met her gaze head on, refusing to be judged by the girl who had nearly gotten her killed, and *had* gotten her tortured. "The Commission also wanted us to make sure that any of The Hunters we met were not The Hunters who have nothing," Dani continued.

Cassie was mystified by her strange words. "The ones who have nothing?" Luther inquired with a sharp edge to his voice.

Dani nodded as she swallowed heavily. "The evil ones amongst us. The Hunters who turn."

Cassie took an involuntary step back as Dani's gaze settled on her. Devon stopped her backward momentum by resting his hand in the hollow of her back. Cassie turned into him as she sought his comfort. His arms wrapped around her as she rested her head against his chest and took solace in his solid presence.

Luther released the curtain he had been holding aside. "The *evil* ones? Are you mad?"

Dani shook her head ardently. "There are evil ones amongst us, and Cassie is one of them! Or that's what I believed anyway. It's what I was told from the time I was a child! They said the ones with no power would eventually turn into mindless monsters that sought to destroy everything in their path! When I first met Cassie, I didn't believe what they'd said; I thought they'd lied to me, or they'd been wrong. I thought there was no way she could turn against someone, no way she'd hurt some-one, and then…"

"And then you saw me kill Isla," Cassie filled in when Dani trailed off. Her mind flashed back to that night, and the over-whelming hatred that had consumed her. She'd been a monster, and if it hadn't been for Devon she could have been lost to the rage trying to overtake her. "And you were scared."

Dani's lower lip began to tremble, and despite her best intentions not to have it happen, Cassie felt her heart softening toward the girl. "Yes, and I thought they'd been right. I was so frightened that one day you would hurt one of us."

"And you called your brother?" Luther inquired.

"Yes. When Joey left me behind, he came back here to the people who raised us."

Horror curdled through Cassie as the true depth of Dani's betrayal set in. "He didn't leave you behind because you actually *wanted* to stay. He left you behind to spy on us."

Her mouth opened and closed as her eyes rolled in her head. She looked like a crazed horse that had been trapped and cornered. The only difference was Cassie would have sympathy for the horse; she had none for this girl.

"Well?" Chris's shout caused Dani to jump.

"Yes," she admitted in a strangled voice.

Chris sneered as his eyes raked her. Melissa remained unmoving, but Luther cursed loudly as he slammed his fist into the windowsill. "We trusted you!" he exploded.

Cassie was more rattled by Luther's lack of composure than Dani's admission. "Luther," Melissa admonished.

Luther scowled at her as he turned on his heel and began to pace in frustration. "What happened when you called your brother?" Cassie was surprised by how composed her voice still was.

She was surrounded by people who hated her, but Dani had regained her composure. "The Commission has grown stronger over the years; some lost members have even been relocated. They have been working here for years doing new research."

Dani's hands were turning red from twisting them back and

forth. "They were trying to create more Hunter's!" Chris deduced.

Cassie buried her face in Devon's chest as she tried to retain her unraveling composure. "Yes," Dani confirmed. "Our race has to be rebuilt before it is completely extinguished. Otherwise there will be no protection for the human race against the vampires."

"We aren't all monster's you know," Liam grated.

Dani's hands were turning red as she continued to twist them. "I know that, but for the most part, you *are*."

Liam glared at Dani as he pulled Annabelle closer to him. "In order to create new Hunters you must have vampires. That's why I was captured," Julian deduced.

Cassie lifted her head as Julian began to restlessly pace back and forth like a caged tiger ready to pounce. As much as she had grown to despise Dani, she couldn't allow Julian to kill her while in a fit of temper. Cassie truly believed he was trying to better himself, and killing Dani was not the way to do that.

"Yes," Dani admitted. "And they also needed your power. They tried using younger vamps, but it didn't work well. The Commission felt an Elder's blood might be the key to what they were missing to get the combination of human and vampire blood right." Julian shot her a nasty glare as his eyes briefly flickered red. "They couldn't take Devon because they couldn't be sure they would be able to keep his ability for mind control locked down. They didn't think they could keep him under control, especially with Cassie around. So they took Julian."

Devon's attention was focused on Julian, who looked about ready to rip the store apart with his bare hands. Cassie clung to Devon as she fought back the shudder threatening to shake her physically. Devon rested his cheek against her hair. "Breathe love, just breathe."

She hadn't even realized she had stopped breathing until then. Air exploded out of her before she inhaled deeply. They never would have been able to control Devon in there. He would have lost complete control, if he had seen what they had put her through. They probably would have destroyed him as a result. The thought left her hollow and barely able to breathe as she held him against her.

"But they couldn't figure it out," Dani continued in a shaky voice. "Everyone knew The Hunters had been created from vampires, but no one knew how, and no matter how hard they tried they couldn't get the combination right."

Devon's hands rubbed over her as he tried to put some heat back into her suddenly chilled body. "So they ended up creating monsters," Cassie whispered. "They created the monsters running loose in this town right now."

"Yes, but they didn't mean to. They were trying to do right; they were trying to protect people."

"How did I not know anything about this?" Luther demanded. "Why had I never heard about the other Hunter's like Cassie, but *you* were told about them?"

"It was only The Commission who knew about the ones with no powers, and what they could become. They kept it hidden from the other Guardians," Dani informed him.

"Why would they do that?" Melissa asked.

"To limit the liability," Luther's voice was full of revulsion at the realization. "The Commission could take out The Hunter without having to deal with a fight from their Guardian's. If The Guardians weren't informed about the threat the lack of abilities might hold, The Commission could make the death of The Hunter look accidental or they could blame it on vampires. Their Guardian's never had to know what had really happened to them."

Melissa looked like she was going to cry as her shimmering onyx eyes met Cassie's. No one spoke; Cassie didn't think any of them could find the words after Luther's observation.

"That's why some of the people in this town are simply gone, and others have been viciously murdered," Annabelle whispered. "The ones who were taken, and experimented on, have come back to hunt the innocents. And the other people in this town were members of The Commission, Guardian's, or Hunter's and they were down there with you."

Dani bit on her trembling bottom lip. "There were a few escapes before tonight," she admitted.

"And tonight all hell broke loose," Julian muttered.

"Yes."

"How many escaped?"

Dani shook her head. "I don't know how many were down there to begin with, or how many were able to break free."

"What happened there tonight?" Luther inquired.

Dani shook her head. "I don't know for sure; they had been having problems with the security. Those things weren't as easily drugged as the two of you." Devon's hands twitched on Cassie as he glanced down at her. "They were too crazed and unstable to be suppressed so easily. But I thought they were getting it under control."

"Why didn't they just destroy them? Why were they keeping them alive?" Luther demanded.

Dani's mouth opened and closed before she shook her head helplessly. "They were trying to gain control of them somehow."

Cassie shuddered as Chris swore vehemently. Luther and Melissa simply stared at Dani. Liam and Annabelle remained as still as stone as they held each other. "And you call *us* monsters!" Julian spat. "In all of my years I have never leveled an entire town!"

Dani was shaking as tears streamed down her face. "I didn't know what was going on there, what they were trying to do! I trusted them; they helped to raise me. They kept me safe and alive during a time when Joey and I had no one. I thought I was doing good!"

"Why was that place built in the bottom of a school?" Cassie asked.

"It's under a school?" Chris demanded.

Cassie shot him a censuring look as she shook her head. There was enough animosity in this room right now without adding to it. "Yes," Cassie informed him. "Dani?"

"It was originally a bomb shelter built in the late forties. They had decided it would be a good place to turn into a laboratory, to keep all of their records, and to hide just in case something should happen. It is where they hid during The Slaughter. After The Slaughter they began to gather as many Hunter's and members of The Commission here as they could. The school was built on top of it in the sixties because they felt it was a good cover for what was hidden beneath the foundation."

Cassie knew The Commission had come to the U.S. during World War Two, when they'd fled England. They had taken up residence in the U.S. but no one, outside of The Commission, had known the exact location of where they had escaped to. Now they had all stumbled across that location by incredible misfortune.

"How long have they been doing experiments down there?" Cassie managed in a choked voice.

"Since the beginning," Dani whispered. "But they became more frequent after The Slaughter."

There was a collective inhalation of breaths. "So it was only a matter of time before it all fell apart. I was always proud of what I was..." Luther broke off as he shook his head. "Now it makes me sick."

Cassie's heart ached for him, but there were no words to help him feel better. "So this town was built around The Commission and these people were mainly here for The Commissions purposes?" Devon asked.

Dani nodded. "Yes."

Cassie choked as bile rose up her throat rapidly. Devon pressed her firmly against his chest, his hands entwined in her hair as he kissed her forcefully. "Did the people know?" Melissa inquired.

"I don't think so," Dani whispered. "Very few were ever taken into the laboratory, until recently, and I'm sure The Commission went for people outside of this town too."

"I'd like to kill you myself," Chris muttered in revulsion.

Cassie didn't disagree with him. "How involved in this were you?"

Dani shook her head. "This is the town where we stayed after our parents were killed; I even went to the local middle school until eighth grade. That was when The Commission decided to send Joey out in search of other Hunters and Guardians, but I didn't know about the laboratory until recently."

Cassie was starting to have a difficult time breathing. Dani's betrayal had almost cost Cassie and Julian their lives. It had almost cost her Devon and her friends. If she allowed her anger to grow, Cassie thought she may kill Dani herself.

"Where do I come into all of this?" Cassie didn't want to hear the answer, but she had to ask the question.

"I thought you would hurt one of us," she whispered. "So I told The Commission about you. I didn't know what else to do."

"Talk to one of *us*. Tell us your doubts!" Devon exploded.

Cassie grabbed him as he took a step toward Dani. He stopped moving, but his eyes were an inhuman shade of red. "You could have come to us. We saved your worthless life. It would have been far better if I had just let Julian rip your throat out when he'd had the chance!"

"I second that," Julian muttered.

"Devon stop. Julian, don't egg him on," Cassie warned.

"I thought I was doing a good thing!" Dani wailed. "I helped them capture Julian because he was our *enemy*! I was helping to rid the world of him. And they… and they told me they could help Cassie," she said brokenly. "They promised me they wouldn't hurt her, and they could make her better. They promised me she would be returned afterward. I didn't know what they were going to do to you Cassie, I really didn't. I never would have done it if I had known!"

Tears streamed down Dani's face as she looked at the hostile faces surrounding her. Devon's body was as taut as a bowstring, if he hadn't been holding her, he would have gone after Dani, and he would have killed her.

"I am sorry," Dani whimpered.

"Ok fine," Cassie said. "Let's say you really did mean to help me, and you didn't know what they were going to do. Why didn't they just kill me?"

"Because you were somehow able to survive, you were somehow able to control the darkness inside you after you killed Isla. You were able to come back from it when that darkness tried to claim you."

"But only because Devon helped me back," Cassie told her.

"They didn't know that for sure though. They had to take a chance you might be able to come back on your own," Dani said.

Cassie closed her eyes as she fought against the frustration and confusion threatening to pull her under. "But they kept me drugged in there; they never let me lose control. They never gave me a chance to try and come back on my own."

"No, you were too valuable to them. If you lost control, you might be able to break free of the drug induced stupor like the others had. But if they could keep the human in you calm, they could try to discover the secret of what made you work. What makes you only rarely volatile? Could they make you stronger, but still allow you to control it?"

A strange new sensation began to creep through Cassie's stomach. There was an awful ringing in her ears as she recalled the vast amount of blood they had taken from her, and the stuff they had injected her with. What had they been trying to do to her?

"What did they give me in there? What were they trying to prove with those injections?" she asked aloud.

Dani glanced nervously around the room. Devon turned toward Cassie, his eyebrows furrowed as he studied her. His eyes slid over her body as they turned a fiery red. His nostrils flared; she could almost feel him inhaling her scent. Ice ran through Cassie's veins in the face of Dani's petrified expression and the strange shaking taking hold of Devon. Dani glanced at Julian before focusing her attention on Cassie and Devon once more.

"They were trying to see how much blood you could handle," Dani whispered. "How much *vampire* blood you could take. Julian's blood."

"That explains it," Chris breathed.

Chris stared at her with a dawning, horrified comprehension that made her heart plummet. Cassie opened her mouth to question him, but before she could say anything all hell broke loose.

CHAPTER FOUR

"SON OF A *BITCH*!" Devon roared.

Cassie tried to grasp hold of him again, but he had already moved out of her reach. Grabbing hold of the glass countertop, he lifted it as if it weighed no more than a feather, and flipped it off the back wall. Metal twisted and glass exploded outward when it shattered against the wall. Cassie jumped back as glass scattered around her feet, and bounced off of the mountain boots she'd found. Knives, jewelry, and other assorted miscellaneous clattered loudly on the floor.

Dani let out a frightened cry, her face turned white as she scrambled to get out of his way. Liam and Chris intercepted Devon's murderous rampage, and managed to knock Devon back a few feet when he grabbed for her. Dani let out a terrified scream and ducked low as she ran behind Luther and Melissa.

"Devon calm down! Devon!" Liam shouted.

Devon seized hold of a rack of winter hats and gloves. Melissa cried out and scurried to the side as the rack sailed at her head. Annabelle rushed to help Liam. Cassie found she couldn't move. Dani's words were just beginning to fully sink in. They had given her *Julian's* blood! They had pumped her full of *vampire* blood! Maybe that was the reason she felt so connected to Julian now, but although the idea sounded reasonable, it didn't feel right. She felt a bond with Julian because they had *formed* a strong bond while being held captive together. It had nothing to do with his blood, and everything to do with the man she had come to know.

Liam grabbed hold of Devon's arm to try and hold him back. Devon swung him forward and slammed him into the wall with a resounding thud that shook the store as he seized hold of Liam's throat. A picture near the window fell and shattered on the floor. Windows rattled in their frames as Liam's feet kicked against the wall.

Chris launched himself at Devon's back, but Devon flung him away like an annoying gnat. Chris skidded across the floor and smashed into a rack of magazines, knocking it over. He shoved it off of him and tossed it aside. Melissa rushed to help him to his feet as Devon slammed Liam off the wall again.

"Devon, no!" Annabelle screamed and tried to pull Devon off of Liam. "No, stop! Cassie! Cassie *help* me!"

It was the utter panic in Annabelle's voice that finally freed Cassie from her shocked stupor. Dismay filled her when she realized the extent of Devon's rampage. He *would* kill everyone in this room if he wasn't stopped. Liam being his first victim, and if he killed Liam, Annabelle was as good as gone too.

Cassie raced forward and grabbed hold of Devon's arm and tried to pull him away. "Devon stop! Devon please!"

Tears streamed down Annabelle's face as she continued to pull uselessly at Devon's arm. She had no idea how she was going to get Devon off of Liam, and although Liam didn't require air, his eyes were beginning to bulge from his head. "Devon!" she screamed, but he didn't seem to hear her through the bloodlust consuming him.

And then it hit her, bloodlust. He was in the throes of it, and what he wanted most was blood, and the blood he craved more than anything was *her* blood.

Cassie ran back toward the ruined counter in search of one of the knives. She fell to her knees as she scrambled through the mess. She ignored the small nicks the jagged glass left on her hands and knees. Seizing hold of the first knife she found, a wicked looking one with a six inch curved blade, she jumped back to her feet. Chris was coming forward again, and Julian appeared to have decided to help as he began to move in, but they would only be two more useless fighters in the already overcrowded ring.

"Stay back!" she thrust the knife at them as she rushed past.

"Cassie!" Julian shouted when he realized her objective. "Cassie *no*!"

He tried to intercept her, but she dodged him. She thrust herself in between Devon and Liam. Liam's feet kicked against the back of her calves, and she could smell the tangy scent of his blood in the room. "You don't want him Devon," she whispered. "It's my blood you want, take it instead."

Tossing her hair back, she took the knife and made a small slit at the base of her throat. For a minute nothing happened, Devon didn't even look at her. Then the scent of her blood penetrated the thick fog of his fury. His red eyes fastened upon the blood dripping down her neck.

Cassie trusted in the strength of Devon's love to get them both through this. He would take her blood, and she wouldn't deny him. She only hoped he didn't kill her in the process. "It's ok," she whispered. "Devon take it, take my blood."

He shoved Liam back and thrust him away. Liam fell to his knees as he pressed a hand to his bruised throat. Annabelle wrapped her arm around his back; they both hurried to get out of the way. Julian's eyes gleamed at the sight of her blood, he took a step toward her. Cassie shook her head at him; she knew if Julian tried to interfere it would only result in a bloodbath.

Devon's lips pulled back to reveal his fully extended fangs. Cassie's heartbeat picked up, but it wasn't fear that set her blood pumping. It had been so long since he'd taken her blood and they'd been bonded in such a way. She needed this reconnection, needed to feel him inside of her again, enjoying her, and loving her.

His hand entangled in her hair as he pulled her forward and tilted her head to the side. His eyes flashed their brilliant emerald green, and she knew the man was present once again. Not present enough to stop him from taking her blood. It was too late for that, he wouldn't be stopped, but he was there enough so that she could see the person she loved so dearly. He pulled her forward much more tenderly than she'd expected.

She remained immobile in his arms, her eyes closed as anticipation thrummed through her body. "It's ok," she whispered again. "It's ok love."

He struck suddenly and with the speed of a rattlesnake. Cassie's body jerked as his teeth sank deep. Though the sting was piercing, it was also fleeting and swiftly replaced by the euphoria this experience always brought her. She clung to him as he bit deeper, and drank deeper than he ever had before.

His confusion and undying love engulfed her. She could feel his mind mingling with hers, feel it touching upon hers as they started to blend together. For a frantic moment Cassie almost pulled away. She didn't want him to see what they'd done to her in there. Didn't want him to see her weakness and pain, and there had been far too much of it.

She didn't want him to see her conflicting feelings about Julian either.

She knew she couldn't keep it hidden from him. If she tried to do so, it would only cause him more distress and doubt over her feelings for Julian. She could sense he already felt shut out, threatened and confused by her relationship with Julian, and it was making him even more unpredictable. She couldn't continue to let that happen; it would only result in more devastation, and next time she might not be able to stop him.

Slumping against him, Cassie gave herself over to his questing mind. All of her barriers slid away as she allowed him in to see it all. She knew she risked his temper again, but she couldn't hurt him anymore. She loved him far too much to keep anything from him. He embraced her as her memories enveloped them both. She could feel his distress and sorrow as he sought to comfort her. His love enveloped her and eased the torment of her soul as only he could do.

She could also feel his torment, the constant strain he'd been going through since she'd been taken and the battle he'd waged to keep himself under control enough to find her again. She could feel the agony her loss had caused him; the torment that had plagued him endlessly and his concern over her relationship with Julian, but it was eased by the taking of her vein.

His head dropped into the hollow of her neck as he withdrew from her. His lips were warm against her neck; his body trembled as he held her close to him. He licked the marks closed with the healing agent in his saliva. She shuddered at the delicious touch of his tongue over her skin.

"I've warned you repeatedly not to put yourself in my way," he whispered as he nuzzled her ear with his nose and lips.

Her fingers curled into his back when her knees began to tremble. "I'll always be here for you."

His lips brushed tender kisses across her face, her nose, her lips and then back again. "My Cassie," he breathed in her ear. "It's not your fault what they did to you in there, you did *not* deserve it. And you aren't in love with him. You were confused and you were brutalized both physically and psychologically. You care for him. He kept you alive and sane, and you love him, but you are not *in* love with him."

She burst into tears; her knees gave out as she fell against him. She hadn't realized until then that she required his forgiveness and understanding or just how much she'd feared her strange feelings for Julian. But Devon had seen it all, had understood it all, and because of his unconditional love she now understood it better too.

She also hadn't realized just how much she blamed herself for what had happened in there. She had gone against her own kind by loving Devon, and she was abnormal. She was an abomination, lacking and dangerous in ways none of the rest of them were. His forgiveness helped to ease the torment and self-hatred that had been eating her alive.

He bent down and swept her into his arms. She burrowed her face into the hollow of his neck, unable to face the others right now. "I'm sorry," he said briskly to Liam. "We're going out back. Will you be ok for a little while?"

She assumed this question was directed at Luther as he was the one who answered yes in a somewhat strangled voice.

Devon's strides were purposeful as he carried her past the racks of merchandise and toward the area where the feed was kept. She watched him as he placed her down on a feed bag. He drew the curtains shut but fragments of light still filtered through the edges. Lamps and flashlights had already been gathered and set out in the room. The small beam of one of the lamps cast shadows about the room. Grabbing two of the sleeping bags they had stashed here, he unrolled one and laid it down on the floor. He used the other sleeping bag as a pillow for the two of them.

He held his hand out for her. Cassie rose and clasped hold of it as he pulled the zipper back to let her in. Cassie's entire body was aching and tired as she lay down. Her mind was numb as tears continued to roll down her cheeks. Devon crawled in beside her and wrapped his arms around her as he pulled her against him.

He rested his cheek against hers and wiped the tears from her face. "I missed this so much," he whispered.

She squeezed his hands and pressed them against her chest. "And I missed you." She brushed a kiss against his full mouth. "Devon, about Julian…"

"Let's not talk about it right now Cassie. I know what happened to you." His voice trailed off as his eyes became distant. "I know what they did to you and they will pay for it, and we will talk about it soon. But for tonight, I would just like to hold you and know you're with me again and safe."

She smiled at him. "Yes, I would like that very, *very* much."

His grin was the most beloved, cherished thing she had ever seen. She had missed his smile even more than her own freedom. His eyes sparkled when he smiled, the angles of his face eased to make him appear younger and more approachable, even with the rough stubble lining his jaw.

"You're exhausted."

"Yes." She burrowed closer to him and savored his deliciously masculine scent. It was familiar and comforting and welcoming. His love enveloped her, wrapping her within a secure cocoon that lulled her into a dreamless sleep.

CHAPTER FIVE

CASSIE BLINKED against the sleep adhering to her when she awoke sometime later. Devon's arm was wrapped loosely around her waist as he slept peacefully. A small snort behind her caught her attention. A smile quirked her mouth as she spotted Chris a few feet away, snoring quietly. She had spent many, many nights of her life listening to his incessant snoring.

She relished the warmth of Devon and the blessed noise of Chris's snores. The pressure in her bladder was what eventually got her moving. Wiggling the zipper on the sleeping bag down, she untangled Devon's arm from around her waist and slid from the bag. She zipped him back into it and rose to her feet. She winced as she stepped onto her bruised and battered feet. She hobbled over to the lit lantern and lifted it from the bags of feed.

Everyone except for Liam and Julian was asleep in the room. She made her way gingerly into the main store and headed for the bathroom they had discovered behind the coolers. She washed her face and hands, and used a small towel to sponge down the rest of her. Though she would have killed for a shower, the simple act of washing herself felt amazing. Picking up the small hairbrush someone had left by the sink, she patiently began to unravel the knots matting her hair. She bit into her bottom lip as she diligently worked through the tangles. Finally the brush flowed freely through her hair once more. Dark circles still shadowed her eyes, but some of her color had finally returned.

Feeling a little better, she made her way out of the bathroom and toward the front of the store. "Turn it down Princess," Julian whispered to her.

She jumped a little; she hadn't seen him amongst the shadows. Her hand fumbled with the switch that turned the small electric flame down and left it a mere flicker within its plastic casing. "Where are you?"

"Front window."

Cassie shuffled forward until he came into view. He leaned against the wall as he watched her from beneath lowered lids. Though he had gotten no sleep, he didn't appear on the verge of exhaustion. "What time is it?" she inquired.

"About nine."

"Don't you think you should get some sleep?"

He shrugged negligently as his customary lazy smile slipped into place. She couldn't help but return it. "I've become accustomed to someone talking my ear off till I fall asleep from boredom."

Cassie couldn't stop herself from chuckling. "Where is Liam?"

He nodded across the way. Cassie turned to find Liam sitting in a chair. He was leaning against the wall, his eyes closed, and his head tipped back as he slept soundly. "He's a good guard."

"I think he's mainly supposed to be guarding me."

"They don't trust you yet."

"No, they don't. It's understandable though." He crossed his legs as he peered out the window again.

"They'll learn to," she told him as she placed the lantern on one of the shelves and hobbled closer.

"If you say so Princess."

"I do. Has there been anything out there?"

The white blue band encircling his irises seemed to glow. The darker blue of them shone as he watched her move toward him. "A few of those things skittered across the road about an hour ago, but I haven't seen anything since."

Cassie joined him by the windows. "There might be others who survived whatever happened down there."

"There probably are, but if I find them they won't be alive for long."

"Julian…"

"I'll stay here with these people, and I won't hurt them because of you. I may even stop killing when we get out of this town, if it will make you happy. But if I come across those bastards who put us in there I *will* kill them. They don't deserve to live."

Cassie's lips parted at his words. It wasn't that he planned to destroy the people who had tortured them that staggered her, but that he would stop killing for her. "You would really stop killing?"

Confusion and hurt flickered briefly through his eyes. "I would do anything for you, Cassie."

She inhaled sharply, a deep ache for his unhappiness bloomed in her chest. "Julian…"

He held a hand up and shook his head. "I know. I've always known you would choose him. It doesn't mean my feelings for you will change though."

Cassie managed a small nod as she focused on the covered window. "I never meant to hurt you."

That familiar amusement played over his features again. "Don't get ahead of yourself there, Princess."

"Don't call me Princess," she responded automatically.

His perfect teeth flashed at her. "Your wish is my command."

"That's even more annoying."

His laugh vibrated through his chest and warmed her to the tips of her toes. She was immensely relieved he was still speaking with her, that he could stay her friend. "Thank you, Julian."

"For what?" he demanded gruffly.

She smiled over his discomfit, taking some pleasure in aggravating him as much as he liked to aggravate her. "For keeping me sane, for being there for me, for being my friend." He scowled at her before turning his attention back to the window. "And for not ripping my throat out the first chance you had."

He laughed again. "The night is still young."

Cassie grinned at him as she leaned against the wall on the other side of the window. She moved the curtain aside to peer out at the dark street. Nothing moved but the street lights, apparently on a timer, had come on. They cast shadows across the road and spilled into the darkly lit woods.

"Thank you also, Cassie."

She poked her head back out from behind the curtain to look at him. "For what?"

He grinned at her and wiggled his eyebrows comically. "For keeping me sane, for being my friend, and for making Dani come back for me."

She looked at him surprise. "How did you know about that?"

He shook his head as he rolled his eyes. "Blondes," he muttered, though he smiled kindly at her. "You and Dani did have to touch me to help get me out of there."

"Oh," she said dully as a small flush stained her cheeks. "Then you already knew everything that Dani told us about what was going on in there. Why would you threaten to get that knowledge out of her forcefully?"

"I didn't already know what she knew. I can't read two people at once, it's too overwhelming. And since I can't stand that *bitch*, I concentrated on you instead. You also kept hold of me for a lot longer than she did."

Cassie nodded while she digested this information. "I see."

He was quiet as he seemed to debate his next words. "I'm not sure I can promise anything when it comes to her."

"She got us out of there," she reminded him.

"She helped to put us *in* there," he retorted.

Cassie was torn between her desire to get even with Dani for her actions, and her desire not to see her hurt. At one time she'd thought of Dani as a little sister, she had cared for her, trusted her, then that trust had been betrayed. "No Julian, Dani will get hers in the end, but we won't be the ones to give it to her. Besides, we may need her still."

He grunted and folded his arms over his chest. "Are we staying here all night?" she asked.

"That's the plan."

"If you would like to get some sleep, I'll keep watch for awhile."

"I'm fine."

Cassie rested her head against the wall as she studied the street. Though they'd spent every night in their cells talking endlessly, they remained silent as the moon moved across the sky. Cassie pulled on the edges of her over large sweatshirt.

"Did you know they were giving me your blood?" she asked after a while.

Julian tore his attention away from the window. "I suspected," he admitted.

"Why didn't you tell me?"

His platinum hair fell across his forehead as he shook his head. "You had enough to worry about in there without me adding to it, especially when I wasn't certain."

"How did you know?"

"The discoloration in your arm, it's what happens when vampire blood is introduced into the human system."

"I'm not human."

"You're more human than not."

"I couldn't have said it better myself." Cassie jumped and spun around as Devon emerged from the darkness. The shadows hugged his powerful frame as he strode forward purposefully. Her mouth went dry as her heart began to thump enthusiastically. He was the most magnificent thing she'd ever seen, and he was hers. She glanced away as she tried to get her body under control. Julian may understand where she belonged, but she wasn't going to rub her relationship with Devon in his face.

Devon's arms encircled her waist as he pulled her against his chest. He stared at Julian before bending to drop a kiss on top of her head. Apparently he didn't care what Julian thought, or how it affected him. "You should be asleep."

"I slept all day," she reminded him.

"Hmm. Has there been anything out there?"

"Not in a while," Julian answered.

She could feel the tension humming through Devon as he watched Julian. Devon was still uncertain what to make of him, uncertain how to handle this change in events, or if he should trust him. They'd once been good friends; she hoped they could get that friendship back.

Minus the murder, destruction, and women that had once bonded them together, of course.

Cassie shifted as she became acutely aware she was now surrounded by two of the most powerful men on the planet. Men that could destroy each other if she wasn't careful. Sensing her distress, Devon rubbed her back as he tried to soothe her.

"You can get some sleep if you want," he said to Julian.

Julian shook his head. "I'm good."

Cassie pulled the curtain aside again. Devon leaned over top of her with his chin resting on her head. "How long are we going to stay here?" she inquired.

"We'll gather things tomorrow, then leave tomorrow night," Devon answered.

Cassie hated the idea of being cooped up in here for that much time. "Why so long?"

"Everyone needs a rest, including you." She chose to ignore the censure in his words, and Julian's soft chuckle. She hoped they would be friends again, but she didn't like them ganging up on her. "Plus, we have to formulate a plan, and exhausted people don't think well."

"The same with vampires," she retorted.

She felt his smile as he rested his cheek against her hair. "Yes, and vampires."

Cassie leaned into him as she savored his strength. "You can't send me away again," she told him. "Even if it is for my own good."

His body tensed against hers. "I won't," he promised.

"Ever."

"Ever."

She turned to search his intense emerald eyes. She saw the

sincerity in his gaze and read the determination in the lines of his face. "Good."

He smiled wanly at her and kissed the tip of her nose. Her gaze darted to Julian as a wave of guilt crashed over her. Whenever she was around Devon she forgot all sense of reason and everything around her. Although Julian's face remained impassive, she could sense the strain in him. Guilt ate at her as turned back to the window.

Devon leaned around her to pull the curtain back further. "Where are they all?" he murmured.

"Somewhere up to no good," Julian answered.

The moon moved over the horizon as an hour slipped past. Cassie's feet began to throb; her back grew sore from standing. She leaned more against Devon as she tried to ease some of the pressure on her already injured feet. "Would you like me to get you a chair?"

She shook her head; she wasn't ready to move out of his arms. She was opening her mouth to speak when Devon stiffened against her and Julian's head whipped to the right. Cassie leaned forward to pull the curtain back further. Devon seized hold of her hand, stopping it in mid air.

"Don't move," he commanded.

Her heart thumped loudly as her breath froze in her lungs. Devon released the curtain and pulled it into place with barely any movement. He pulled her back a step as his arms tightened around her.

Then she heard it. All three of their heads tilted back as a scurrying noise rattled across the roof from the back to the front. It paused halfway across the roof. Adrenaline coursed through her as she waited to see what the thing was up to and what it was going to do.

A loud crash from above reverberated through the room.

Liam jolted awake; his eyes bulged as he searched the darkness. The lantern she had set on the shelf vibrated toward the edge and tilted precariously. Julian moved with deadly speed to catch hold of it before it clattered to the floor. Another crash resonated through the building and shook the windows. Devon pulled her back another small step as the scurrying sound resumed toward the front of the building.

He glanced at Julian and nodded toward the back. Julian moved as soundlessly as a wraith toward the back of the store. Liam's hands were fisted as his gaze remained focused on the roof. Another loud bang echoed from the back of the store.

"Move slowly," Devon's voice was barely audible, even to her.

The three of them crept toward the back as something scurried over the roof again. A series of loud grunts and shouts could now be heard coming from somewhere outside. Though they had once been human, Cassie couldn't help but see the creatures as anything more than apelike monsters now. She hated herself for it, but she knew she had to keep that attitude if she was going to be of any use against them.

Everyone was awake and on their feet when they made it to the back room. They stared at the ceiling as another thumping crash shook the building. "Do they know we're here Chris?" Cassie whispered.

His eyes were dark and troubled, and his face was pinched in concentration. "There's no reason to them," he answered. "There's nothing but confusion and mayhem. I can't tell what they do and don't know, or what drives them, other than blood."

A shiver worked through her at his words. She had the urge to bolt out of there, yet she remained frozen; her legs unwilling to move. Julian emerged from the shadows with four crossbows tucked under his arm. Cassie reluctantly pulled away from

Devon as he handed each of them one and tossed the other to Liam.

"Do not hesitate," Julian told her.

She frowned back at him severely. "I won't." His eyes were pointed and harsh as he continued to stare relentlessly at her. "I won't."

He nodded briskly before turning away and moving to stand by the doorway to the main room. Devon squeezed her arm before taking a stance opposite Julian. Another loud thud rattled the building as one of the things began to jump up and down on the roof. Its loud squeals echoed throughout the building. Cassie winced against the harsh sound, but the crossbow stopped her from covering her ears.

Another loud thump rattled the windows. There were four of them on the roof now, and they had no way of knowing how many more might join them. Straightening her shoulders, Cassie held the crossbow with both hands as she moved toward the back windows. She heard Devon's faint sound of displeasure, but she didn't stop.

Pausing at one of the windows, she carefully pulled back the curtain. She could see nothing in the backyard amongst the mangled corpses of animals. A shadow suddenly jumped from overhead and another bang echoed throughout. Though it had startled her, Cassie didn't even flinch. To do so might have meant the death of all of them.

She cautiously dropped the curtain and backed away from the window. She crept to the middle of the room. "They're coming from the roof of the bank," she whispered as she pointed toward the building next to theirs.

Devon and Julian turned to stare at the wall as if they could magically see through it to the bank. They stood in tense antici- pation as they waited to see what would happen. The noises and thumps continued, the grunts and squeals grew louder and more frantic before dying down.

After about an hour the shouts died down, and the noises drifted away. Cassie began to relax, her shoulders eased, but the muscles in them remained stiff and aching. She unfolded her hands from their death grip on the crossbow and stretched them out in an attempt to get the cramps out of them.

She gave Chris a grateful smile as he took the bow from her. Devon propped his crossbow against the wall; his attention was still focused on the ceiling. "Where did they go?" Melissa asked.

"They're hunting," Julian answered as he propped his crossbow against his shoulder. "The food supply is getting scarce though, so they're going back through the areas where they have found food before."

"Why didn't they come in here?" Cassie inquired.

"Because they've never come in here; the place is in too good of shape for that to have happened. Next time they come back, they'll come in. They'll start to tear this town apart before they spread out of it," Devon told her.

Cassie bit on her bottom lip, Chris's hand slid into hers and squeezed. Relief washed through her as she held him. Chris had been distant ever since they'd found her, but for the first time she actually felt as if she had her friend back. Julian was watching them with an odd expression on his face.

His shoulders were braced as if he were prepared for battle as he turned toward Devon. But if he was expecting one from Devon, he wouldn't get it. Not when it came to Chris anyway. Devon understood their close bond and had actually become close to Chris before Cassie had been taken. She didn't know what their friendship was like now, but she suspected it hadn't changed much. Julian looked confused as his attention focused on her again. She offered him a wan smile. This was all stuff he would have to figure out on his own, but he'd eventually remember what it was like to be human again.

"Why haven't they spread out yet, if their food supply is low?" Chris inquired.

"Because even though they may not remember what they had here, or maybe they do, this place is still safe and reassuring to them on some level," Devon answered.

She fought back the pity for the creatures trying to enter her mind; she couldn't afford to feel pity for these creatures. They would attack her, and if she hesitated because she sympathized with them, they would kill her. "We can't let them out of this town," Luther said sternly.

"We have to get out of here," Melissa whispered.

"And go where? We can't leave this town until all of those things are dead. If they get out of this town they'll destroy anything they come in contact with. We'll formulate a plan to draw them out, but we need more weapons," Devon told her.

"We also have to fortify this place," Julian said. "Get some boards on these windows. I don't think those things have enough reason left in them to realize the windows will be boarded up when they come back. And we need blood." He looked pointedly at Devon before glancing at Cassie. "Unless you plan to keep draining her."

Devon's hands fisted, a muscle jumped in his cheek as he grit his teeth together. "Watch it."

Julian's face remained impassive as he leaned against the doorway. "Ok, so we have to figure out how to get those necessities," Cassie inserted quickly.

"Yeah, because that's an easy list to fulfill," Chris retorted.

"Not helping," she told him.

His shaggy blond hair fell into one of his clear sapphire eyes as he shot her a rueful look. "I know where we can find weapons and blood," Dani offered hesitatingly.

"Where?" Luther demanded.

Dani nervously began to wring her hands again. "In the compound. There is plenty of blood and a room full of weapons. "

Cassie felt as if she had just been kicked in the gut. Julian cursed loudly, spun on his heel, and disappeared into the dark store. Cassie knew exactly how he felt as she stared after him. The last thing either one of them wanted was to go back into that place, but it seemed they weren't going to have a choice in the matter. Chris squeezed her hand as her skin began to crawl.

CHAPTER SIX

"YOU DON'T HAVE to do this."

Cassie didn't respond to Chris as she stared at the ominous school. Her stomach cramped at the mere thought of entering the school again. She tossed the crossbow higher up on her shoulder. "I'm not letting you guys go in there alone," she told him.

"We're not alone."

She glanced over at where Devon and Julian's heads were bent together. At least they were being cooperative with each other about going in there. Devon had done everything short of tying her up to keep her from coming with them, but there was no way she was staying behind. Dani stood off to the side, her arms wrapped around her as she tried to ward off the chill. Though this had been Dani's idea, she hadn't planned on going back into the school. However, she was the only one who knew where the weapons and blood were stored and the only one who knew her way around the compound.

"Cassie," Chris said quietly.

She glanced up at him and shook her head firmly. "It's too late anyway; I'm already here, and I'm not going back alone."

"One of us can take you back."

"No, I'm going in there with you."

He sighed loudly in resignation. "Fine."

Devon and Julian stopped conferring; their attention came back to the rest of them. "Ok, Julian is going to take the lead with Dani behind him, then Chris, Cassie, and me."

Devon's eyes were tumultuous as they met hers. She hated the tension in him, and that it was because of her, but she couldn't let them do this alone. She was one of the strongest fighters, and if something happened to any of them, she would never forgive herself if she hadn't been there to help.

"Come on," Julian said coldly. He hadn't wanted her here either, but in the end it hadn't been his decision to make.

Cassie bit on her bottom lip as she tried to calm her trepidation at the thought of being trapped within those awful bowels once more. Devon's jaw was clenched as he held her back. "You are to stay close to me," he ordered gruffly.

"I will," she promised.

"You should have stayed with the others."

She squeezed his hand reassuringly. It had been decided it was better if they separated. If something happened to them down there, Liam, Annabelle, Luther, and Melissa would have to stop the evil seeping out from this town, starting with the school.

"I'll be fine, but I couldn't stay with them Devon, and you know that."

His hand caressed hers before he released her. Cassie fell into line behind Chris. She fought to keep herself steady as they moved toward the school. She knew Devon would have no problem with taking her back if he felt she was too distressed to go on. Julian's hair was a beacon in the moonlight spilling across them as he kept his crossbow at the ready. The moon's beam lit a path over the snow straight to the double doors of the school. It should have looked pretty, it was gloomy and threatening to her.

Behind Julian, Dani kept her head bowed and her shoulders hunched in her jacket. She carried no weapons. Chris was carrying another crossbow at the ready as he rapidly searched the open landscape of the school grounds. There was nowhere to hide once they stepped out of the woods.

Devon's chest brushed against her back as they moved forward. She caught a glimpse of the gun he held. They had found the gun amidst the scattered remains of the shattered countertop. It must have been hidden in the shelves, or perhaps even in the register. Though it may not kill the monsters, it would slow them down.

Julian reached the doors and cautiously pulled them open. Dani took a small step back as Julian clicked on his flashlight and directed the beam inside. "Move," Chris ordered gruffly as he pushed Dani forward.

They slipped into the darkness of the school. Though she fought against it, Cassie couldn't stop the shudder of dread tearing through her. Devon rested his hand on her shoulder to comfort her, but there was no comfort in this place. Julian's beam bounced off of the concrete walls as he searched the interior for any hint of danger.

Cassie pressed closer to Devon as the beam revealed large streaks of blood running down the walls. Julian's shoulders became rigid as he tore his attention away from the blood soaked walls. "Julian," she said anxiously.

He held up a hand and shook his head. "I'm fine," he

muttered as he focused the beam on the blood free walls. "Where to?"

Dani inhaled shakily and pointed ahead of Julian. "Straight ahead." They moved cautiously down the hall; the only sound the occasional squeak of someone's shoe on the linoleum. Dani led them down another hallway and turned to the right. "Here."

Cassie recognized the doors they had escaped through. A sign on them read, 'Basement, Authorized Personal Only.' The right door had been ripped from two of its hinges; it hung at an awkward angle, the bottom hinge the only thing keeping it attached to the wall.

Julian stepped over the ruined remains. Cassie remained rigid as she fought off the rush of memories threatening to consume her. "You don't have to go," Devon murmured in her ear.

She was extremely tempted by the prospect of not having to return to those dark depths of torment. But she had to face it. "Yes, I do."

Chris glanced back at her as he moved through the double doors. Cassie kept her gaze focused upon Chris's back, refusing to look around and take in her surroundings. She was greatly afraid she would run the other way screaming, if she allowed herself to think about it too much.

She didn't bother to count the floors as they steadily wound lower. The next set of double doors were both firmly intact, but Julian pulled them open easily. Cassie clearly recalled Dani locking those doors behind them. How had they gotten unlocked, and why were these doors still intact, while the ones above had been ruined? It didn't matter why the doors were the way they were, she realized, all that mattered was more of the creatures had escaped after them.

Cassie took a deep breath and swung the crossbow off her

shoulder and grasped it firmly in preparation for an attack. "Get us to those rooms as quickly as you can," Julian grumbled at Dani.

She nodded as they moved through the doors and swept into the hallway. The smell caused her stomach to flip and an involuntary gag to escape her. Dani's hand flew to her mouth; Chris took a quick step back as he turned three shades of green.

"What is that?" Cassie instantly regretted opening her mouth because now she could also *taste* the foul odor.

"Death," Julian answered.

Cassie's stomach rolled again. It took every ounce of willpower she had not to vomit. Dani retched forcefully; her vomit splattered across the floor. Cassie pulled her shirt over her nose before she threw up everywhere too. Though it blocked the smell a little, it didn't help much. Devon placed his hand smoothly over her nose to cover it with his jacket. She gratefully inhaled the wonderful smell of him, it helped to block out the stench of the halls.

She smiled at him thankfully. His gaze searched her as he pulled her against him while keeping his hand firmly in place. He and Julian seemed not to be affected by the scent, but then again they had probably smelled it many times before. They had probably *caused* it many times before. She shuddered at the thought and tried to shove it aside.

She turned her attention back to the dimly lit hallway. The emergency beacons had still been flashing when they'd fled, but now there were only sickly yellow lights lining the lengthy hall. "Why are the lights on?" Julian demanded.

Dani wiped her mouth with the sleeve of her coat as she studied them. "I don't know. It must be a safety thing."

"You don't *know*?"

Dani shook her head. "I don't think I can take this smell."

Julian glared at her as his eyes blazed red. "Too bad. You helped create it, now you have to deal with it," Cassie frowned over his harsh words, but didn't protest them. "Now, where do we go?"

Dani trembled as sweat continued to pour down her face. Finally, she lifted a shaking arm to point straight down the hall. Julian turned and strode rapidly away. They hurried to keep up as Dani pointed him down another hall.

Cassie kept expecting to come across the source of the smell, but the halls remained clear of any blood, or human remains. But then again, they had been clear during their escape also. She knew they wouldn't remain that way though, the horrible stench told her that much. They made another right. Cassie became excruciatingly aware of where they were within the compound.

Her step faltered, her hand clenched upon Devon's over her nose as she stared into the room she'd been held captive in. Across the way she could see the window she and Julian had spoken through, the window that had helped to keep her alive.

She hated the helpless feeling swamping her once more as she looked to Julian. His eyes were callous as he stared into the room, his jaw locked forcefully. The force of his gaze burned into her as he turned toward her. Devon leaned over her to look into the room. He stepped partially into the doorway before turning his attention back to her. She was unable to meet his gaze as unreasonable shame flooded her. Pulling her against him, Devon cradled her head against his chest. Cassie managed to keep a firm hold on herself as she stared into the tiny cell that had been her prison.

Devon kissed her forehead roughly as a shudder ran through him. Cassie could sense the unraveling control and anger suffusing him. "You will *never* know anything like this again," he vowed in a harsh whisper.

She nodded as she took a deep breath. They had to get out of here before she unraveled completely, or before any remaining creature's lurking within this place discovered their presence. Devon placed his hand over her mouth again and held her firmly as they moved further down the hall.

CHAPTER SEVEN

D‌EVON'S SENSES were on high alert as they continued to rapidly make their way forward. He wouldn't allow anything bad to happen to Cassie again while they were down here. He wouldn't allow anything bad to happen to her *ever* again; he would die first. Anger coursed through him as he recalled the sterile little cell she'd been held captive in, imprisoned in, *tortured* in. He hated to think about the misery these people had caused her. That *Dani* had caused her.

He had to fight the urge to rip her traitorous throat out as they turned another corner. He knew it wasn't entirely Dani that had his killer instincts so aroused, or what had been done to Cassie, but also the harsh scent of death in the air. It was both enticing and repulsive. The demon in him was thrilled by the mayhem and destruction that had gone on here. The man was completely repulsed by it.

He pulled Cassie closer and drew on the strength she always brought to him as he tried to suppress the thrumming bloodlust inside him. He could still smell something off in her blood, and knew now it was more than just the drugs they had pumped into her, but also Julian's blood inside of her. Devon searched past the strange scent inside her to find her own deliciously sweet smell flowing just beneath the surface. Her body was already beginning to filter out the remnants within her.

Julian stopped suddenly, his hands fisted as he glared into another room. Devon was certain they had come across Julian's cell, but when Cassie began to tremble too he knew it was something more. The color drained from Chris's face as he turned toward Cassie, sympathy was etched onto his youthful features.

Devon tried to block Cassie's view of the room as he stepped forward to peer into the darkness. He noticed the table first with the straps hanging off the bottom, side, and top of it. Straps that were extremely thick and painful looking, and had been used to keep Julian and Cassie pinned to *that* table.

Then he noticed the thing hanging from the ceiling like some twisted electronic snake with electrodes dangling from a thick metal rod. Devon had never seen anything like it before, but it looked to be some sort of an electrical conductor designed to send a vast amount of electricity into a person, or vampire. Designed to send a vast amount of electricity into *Cassie*.

When he'd fed from her, he had glimpsed part of what she'd gone through in here, seen some of her suffering. He had understood the depth and purity of her feelings for Julian, understood her trust and love of him, even though she hadn't. He had seen so many things, but he had never truly seen the full amount of torture they had put her through. Never fully glimpsed the torment she had suffered at the hands of these monsters.

He would kill them for it. He would destroy *every* one of the people who had harmed her in here. His rage escalated higher as he glared at Dani. Seeming to sense his murderous thoughts,

Cassie touched his arm. She had lost all color in her face, and she was shaking like a leaf, but she was still seeking to comfort *him*. Her eyes were haunted, her lips nearly as pale as her skin as she pulled his hand away from her mouth. He moved to block the smell from her again, but she shook her head at him. He could sense her composure slipping, if he touched her he would be her undoing. He dropped his arm back to his side as Cassie's gaze clashed with Dani's.

"Keep going Julian," Devon ordered. Julian's gaze was also focused on Dani, his eyes a deadly shade of red. His lips pulled back from his fangs. "Go Julian."

Devon stared at him relentlessly as he willed him to continue. There was a good possibility Dani wouldn't make it out alive, or that Devon and Julian would end up fighting in order to purge some of the emotions running through them. "Don't Julian," Cassie whispered shakily.

Devon moved closer to her as Julian's gaze spun in her direction. Devon was prepared to destroy Julian if he attacked Cassie, though he was no longer certain he wanted Julian dead. They had once been best friends; brutal killers yes, but also friends.

Yet Julian had somehow managed to move on from that monster, as Devon himself had. Julian had learned to care about Cassie enough to keep her sane and hopeful in a world of desolation and torture. Julian had come to care about someone more than he cared about *himself*, something Devon never would have thought Julian capable of. Though Devon hated that Julian fancied himself in love with Cassie, he was also grateful to Julian for everything he had done for her.

Julian closed his eyes and nodded briskly to Cassie before spinning on his heel and heading back down the hallway. Cassie kept her gaze focused on Chris as they followed noiselessly behind. Dani took a stumbling step into Chris as they turned another corner. Devon knew they had finally come upon some of the carnage they had smelled. Cassie straightened her shoulders as Chris pushed Dani roughly forward again.

Cassie seized hold of his hand as they turned the corner. Devon steadied himself as exhilaration and revulsion tore through him in equal waves. Blood splattered the walls; mutilated bodies littered the floor. Though he had committed some awful atrocities in his life, he'd never seen the destruction of the human body quite like this before.

Cassie's hand trembled in his as her lower lip began to quiver. She needed his protection and comfort right now; she could never know about the excitement tingling through him. She would be repulsed by him if she did, and he never wanted that to happen. "Don't look."

She closed her eyes as he helped to guide her through the mutilated bodies. The metallic scent of the blood was enticing as it aroused his thirst. Though Cassie helped him to keep control of himself, Julian was on his own. Julian had only had a few small rats today, and he didn't have Cassie in his arms to help keep him grounded.

Devon began to worry Julian might not make it back out of this. There was only so much a vampire could take, and Julian had only recently stopped killing. Julian may even go back to killing when all of this was over, and Cassie was at Devon's side. Devon couldn't blame Julian if he did; Devon knew he would instantly return to killing if he ever lost her completely.

Devon wouldn't blame Julian for returning to that lifestyle; he couldn't take the chance of him cracking in here. He would hurt people if he did, he could hurt *Cassie* if he did. Devon moved to place Cassie a little behind him. He hadn't liked the idea of her in the back, but she couldn't be close to Julian right now, and he intended to get Chris out of the way if it became necessary. Dani was on her own.

They moved into another hall, this one just as littered with bodies but housing even more destruction. Devon assumed it was the hall where the uprising had started. Doors littered the floor, shattered glass cracked and splintered beneath their feet. They picked their way carefully through the debris to avoid the deadly shards of wood and metal crowding the floor.

"How much further?" Julian demanded.

"Not much," Dani answered shakily.

They came across more destruction in another hall before slipping into a hall strangely empty of all debris. "Here," Dani said.

She pulled a set of keys from her pocket. Her hands trembled as she tried to slide the key into the hole. Dani nervously jumped back as the keys slipped from her fingers and clattered upon the floor. She glanced at the group before bending and scooping them back up. She grappled to find the right one and get it in the hole again.

Julian cursed violently and snatched the keys from her hand when his patience finally ran out. He shoved himself in front of her and slipped the key into the hole. "Wait!" Chris shouted as his face lost all color and he lurched for Julian.

It was too late though, Julian had already thrust the door open. Devon seized hold of Cassie and shoved her behind him as a booming shot echoed down the hall. Julian fell back; shock and pain twisted his features as blood bloomed where the bullet had torn across his shoulder. Devon grabbed Julian and shoved him to the floor as another shot rang out. It bounced down the hallway in a zinging rush that shattered concrete and deafened him.

"Crap!" Chris yelled as he ducked out of the way of another shot.

He released Julian as Julian rolled away from the door. Devon rushed back to where Chris and Cassie lay upon the floor, their hands over their heads in a vain attempt to protect themselves. Crawling on top of Cassie, he used his body to keep her blocked from anymore ricocheting shots. Pulling her head beneath him, he held her against his chest when another shot fired. Chris ducked lower as it ripped past his head and shattered the wall inches from his ear.

Cassie cried out and burrowed closer against him. The urge to destroy whoever was in that room surged through him. Another shot was fired, he grunted loudly as it sliced across his calf in a fiery blaze. Cassie's breath was warm against his neck, her fingers clawed at him. "Are you ok?" she demanded harshly. "Devon are you ok? Julian was shot, is he ok?"

"Fine, I'm fine. Julian will be fine." He ignored the sting in his leg as he tried to push Cassie out of the way of fire. "Move!" he hissed to Chris. Chris stayed low as he crab crawled toward one of the open doors and disappeared through it. "Cassie, follow Chris."

"I can't leave you."

"You have to! Now *go*!"

He withdrew from the top of her and kept his body up to protect her as she scrambled after Chris. The minute she entered the room, her head poked back out and her violet blue eyes latched onto him. "Get back!" he commanded as another shot rang out.

Cassie ducked away as it shattered off of the wall. Fury boiled through him as he crossed the hall and scrambled back toward the door. Julian was sitting against the wall on the other side of the door. His lips were twisted into a scowl; his fangs fully elongated as his eyes blazed red fire.

Devon knew exactly how he felt, if he got his hands on whoever was in that room he would kill them, and he wouldn't have a problem doing it. Devon pushed Dani out of his way as he made it back to the door. She curled up against the wall, her knees hugged to her chest as her eyes rolled. Another shot rang through the hallway and sizzled around the corner.

"Stop!" Dani screamed hysterically and threw her hands over her ears. "Stop!"

Silence followed her shrill cry. "Dani?"

Devon spun on her. She wasn't looking at him though; she was staring at the door with her mouth parted and tears in her eyes. "Joey?" she choked out.

Devon turned as the young man stepped out of the room. Julian sprang up and seized hold of Joey's neck. He slammed Joey against the wall with a loud bang that shook the door in its frame. Joey's eyes bulged out of his head as Julian squeezed on his throat. "I'll rip you to shreds," Julian promised.

"No!" Dani screamed at the same time another shot boomed out of the room.

"Son of a bitch!" Devon snarled, tired of being shot at.

He dashed past the door to join Julian on the other side. Another shot resounded through the hall. "Devon!" Cassie screamed.

"Stay in there!" he shouted at her.

Julian glanced at him as he choked the air from Joey with no remorse. "How are we getting that bastard out?"

Though the shots wouldn't kill them, not unless they had their heads blown off, they could incapacitate them enough for someone to kill them, and the bullets still hurt like the devil. Devon nodded toward Joey. "We can use him as bait."

"No!" Joey cried as Julian's smile widened.

"Wait! No! You can't!" Dani protested.

Cassie's head popped back out of the room, and Chris's appeared above hers. He felt no remorse about killing any of the people who had kept her here, especially if it would keep her safe in the end. He just couldn't do it in front of her though.

"Get back!" he shouted. She lingered in the doorway as she watched them. "Get her *back* Chris!"

Chris nodded before grasping hold of Cassie's shoulders and pulling her away. Devon waited to make sure she didn't come out again before he turned to Julian. Excitement rushed through Devon as memories of the way he'd once been, of the things he and Julian had done together, pounded through him. Bloodlust and the demon surged forth, eager to break free of the cage Devon had locked it away in for over a hundred years.

A sardonic smile curved Julian's mouth. "Welcome back."

Devon would love to destroy every human around him, and savor the slaughter, but he couldn't allow the beast out. He wasn't sure he could control it without getting Cassie involved, and he couldn't do that again. No matter how much he yearned to, he could not kill Joey with her here. "Give me his shirt," he ordered.

Julian stared at him before his gaze slid toward Cassie. Disappointment was evident in the slump of his shoulders. Julian smashed Joey against the wall and released him to rip the shirt off of him. He tossed the shirt to Devon, who snagged hold of it. "If anything happens to me…"

"I'll make sure she gets out of here," Julian promised. Devon studied him curiously, unable to understand this person beside him. Julian had been brutal and almost as bad as he himself had once been. But now Julian was completely different, and Devon knew it was because of Cassie.

"Julian," he said gruffly.

"She doesn't desire me Devon," he said. "But I'll keep her safe."

Devon glanced down the hall, not at all surprised to find Chris and Cassie peering into the hall again. "Stay there," he ordered briskly. She opened her mouth to protest. "I mean it."

Devon turned away and wadded up Joey's shirt and threw it in front of the door. Bracing himself, he bolted through the doorway a split second after the shot rang out. The older man holding the gun took a startled step back as Devon rushed him. He took another step back and raised the gun as he attempted to fire it again. He didn't have time to squeeze the trigger before Devon seized hold of the gun and ripped it out of the man's hands. The man cried out as two of his fingers snapped.

Throwing the gun aside, Devon thrust his elbow into his windpipe. He carried the man into the wall, and slammed him against it. The man made a gurgling noise as he kicked against him. "Devon!" Cassie screamed. "Devon!"

He caught a flurry of motion as she came skidding around the corner. She barely caught her balance when her feet slipped out from under her, but she quickly righted herself. Anger spurted through him as he shook his head; he should have known she wouldn't stay where she was told. "I'm ok," he assured her.

She nodded briefly before turning her attention to the man he held. She stood perfectly still for a minute, and then everything changed. Her mouth closed, her eyes blazed a ferocious shade of red as her beautiful features hardened like stone. "You!" she accused.

The hairs on the back of his neck stood on end as he turned toward the man he held. The man's blue eyes rolled as his face became a florid shade of red. Devon dug his arm in more harshly. Judging by Cassie's reaction to him, this was the man who had hurt her the most.

And Devon hated him for it.

A venomous curse shot Devon's head around. Julian's hand was still wrapped around Joey's throat, but his eyes were focused upon the man Devon held. A sneer twisted his mouth, his fangs cut into his lower lip. He brutally shoved Joey away from him and bounced the young man off of the wall. Devon was certain Julian was going to charge at them, but he remained where he was.

Chris held onto Dani's arm as he pulled her into the room. "You could have killed me!" Dani yelled at the man.

The stranger scuffled within Devon's grasp as the air began to whistle in and out of him. Though Devon would have preferred to crush his windpipe, he eased his grip on him. He was sure they would need him for some answers. The man choked and sputtered as Devon stepped away. He took hold of Cassie's hand and pulled her behind him as the stranger stumbled forward.

Cassie stepped away from his back. "Who are you?" she demanded.

The man held his bruised throat as he labored for air. He glanced around the room as he searched for an escape route that didn't exist. "You had better start talking," Devon snarled.

"You should close the door," he said in a hoarse whisper. "There are still a few of them running around out there."

Chris closed the door and slid the lock into place. "Who are you?" Cassie demanded again.

The man's eyes lit upon her and hatred bloomed in them. Devon growled low in his throat and moved to block her from the man's loathsome stare. "I haven't killed in over a century, but

I won't hesitate to rip out your throat if you look at her like that again!" he spat. "Now, who are you?"

"Derek," he answered. "My name is Derek."

Cassie inhaled sharply as her hand clenched around his. He could hear the quickening beat of her heart as she pressed closer to him. Her breath came rapidly in and out, her chest rose and fell against him as the stranger pinned her with his hate filled gaze.

"Her father."

CHAPTER EIGHT

DEVON GRABBED Cassie before she hit the floor. The constriction in her chest made it almost impossible for her to breathe. He grabbed hold of her face and held it within his grasp. "Breathe," he told her. "Just breathe."

Air seared into her lungs and burned all the way down to the hollow pit of her stomach. Her breath shuddered out of her, but Devon kept her somewhat grounded. She gulped down another harsh breath and let it out in a hitching sob that threatened to shatter her.

Her father! This man, this cruel *bastard* who had so easily tortured her, was her *father*! It couldn't be; her father was *dead*. Her father had been a good man! At least she had convinced herself he was a decent man when she'd daydreamed about what he'd been like over the years. Her grandmother had always told her he was a good man, that he had loved her mother, and Cassie, dearly.

But apparently she had been wrong. Her *father* had brought

 aTI

INFERNO 87

her here. Her *father* had been the one in charge as they had tortured and drugged her. Her father *hated* her!

Her fingers curled around Devon's wrists as she tried to gain strength from him. Devon loved her, her friends loved her, and that was all that mattered she tried to remind herself. She had never known her father, and although this man claimed to be him, he was not. This man was a stranger, a monster. This man may have helped to create her, but he hadn't made her the person she was. He was nothing to her. Yet she still felt as if someone had slammed her in the chest with a baseball bat.

Devon pulled her close to kiss her. "Are you ok?"

Cassie managed a nod as she tried to steady the shaking in her body. He held her against him as he turned back to her father. There was absolute hatred etched into the man's features, his blue eyes were unremorseful. Cassie couldn't bring herself to look at him anymore. Turning away, she focused her attention on Chris who was watching her with confusion and sympathy evident in his sapphire gaze.

Releasing Dani, Chris came over and pulled her from Devon's arms. Devon reluctantly released her to Chris before focusing on her father again. Julian remained unmoving, his hands fisted, and his entire body ramrod straight as fire burned in his eyes. Dani's eyes flitted between Cassie and the stranger who was her father. Even Joey looked astounded by the revelation.

"I didn't know," Dani blurted. "I swear I didn't know Cassie."

Julian scowled maliciously at her father as he stormed past him and shoved into a door at the back of the room. The door crashed open and swung wildly back and forth on its hinges. "Here!" he shouted back to them.

Cassie hugged Chris against her. Devon grabbed her father

by the arm and roughly hauled him into the other room. The man stumbled as he tried to keep up with Devon's furious strides. Joey remained unmoving on the floor as he stared up at them.

"I really didn't know," Dani whispered again.

Cassie reluctantly pulled away from Chris and moved woodenly to the door they had disappeared through. She pushed it open and did a double take as she took in the wooden boxes piled from floor to ceiling against two walls. Devon and Julian weren't in the room but there was another door across from her.

Cold air hit her as soon as she pushed it open. She pulled her hands into the sleeves of her baggy coat as she shivered. Devon and Julian glanced up from where they stood by a set of cooler doors. Inside the coolers were bags of blood lined up in rows from floor to ceiling. Both Devon and Julian's eyes were like molten lava as they gleamed in the dim illumination of the room.

Though she could feel her father's gaze upon her, she didn't turn to him. "I'll get one of the boxes," Devon said as he hurried toward her.

"Is it drugged?" Devon's forehead furrowed as he stared at her questioningly. "The blood. The food they fed us in here was drugged before. Is it drugged now?"

Devon's jaw clenched as his nostrils flared. Julian cursed loudly; the door of the cooler slammed against the other one as he flung it open. He snatched a bag out roughly. Glowering at her father, he ripped the top easily off of it. He inhaled deeply before nodding briskly to Devon. "It's good," he muttered. "They must have drugged it right before they brought it to us."

They all turned toward Cassie's father, but he remained immobile, his face as cold as stone. "Drugs are probably stronger that way," Cassie muttered.

Julian shrugged and downed the contents of the bag before tossing it aside. Devon slipped his arm through hers and led her into the other room. Squeezing her arm, he released her to grab hold of one of the stacked boxes. Cassie watched in amazement as he ripped off the top, which had been nailed on, as if it were nothing. He dropped it to the floor, turned the box over and dumped its contents on the ground. Cassie took a small step back as stakes clattered across the floor and skittered about her feet.

Chris, drawn by the noise, poked his head into the room. His nose wrinkled as he studied the stakes. "Hope they have better weapons than those," he muttered before ducking out again.

Cassie agreed as she stared at the wooden weapons. She was hoping to find something that wouldn't require them to get so close to the Halflings roaming the town. Devon opened the door to the room with all the blood and threw in the box and lid. His body hummed with tension as he turned back to her. "Let's see what we have in here, hopefully it *is* better than stakes."

Cassie glanced at the hundred or so boxes piled within the room. They were of all shapes and sizes, but she was a little nervous they might all contain the same thing. Grasping hold of one of the boxes, she tugged at the top but was unable to pull it off. Devon reached around her, the muscles in his forearms bulged as he ripped the lid off with apparent ease.

Her mouth parted, her heart hammered with excitement as she glanced up at him. Even in this god awful situation, he still managed to entice her. His gaze returned to hers, his eyes once again became the vivid emerald color she cherished. His finger stroked over her jawbone as he bent to kiss her. Cassie lost herself to the touch and feel of him as he held her within his warm embrace.

A disgusted sound tore her away from the bliss his kiss

brought to her. Cassie turned to find her father standing in the doorway with his hands fisted at his sides. Loathing and revulsion blazed from him and pounded against her. Devon turned her away from the man's glare.

Julian appeared in the doorway with a box propped under his arm. He remorselessly shoved her father forward as he glared at the smaller man. "Move," he ordered gruffly. He propped the door open with the box so they could keep an eye on the three of them, and Chris. "Let's get what we can out of these boxes and get out of here."

Cassie reluctantly pulled out of Devon's arms as she turned her attention back to the boxes.

CASSIE HEFTED the box of weapons onto her hip. Aside from stakes, the room had held more crossbows, a long bow, more guns, and a nifty little thing that appeared to be a flame thrower when assembled. She braced herself as Julian pulled the door open. He peered into the hallway and searched it quickly before nodding briskly. He stepped into the hall and was followed closely by Dani, Joey, and her father. Devon's hand encircled hers as he stepped into the hall next.

Covering her mouth and nose with her shirt, Cassie followed them out the door. She closed her eyes before they returned to the hallway with all of the carnage. Devon led her through the mutilated bodies. They turned another corner, but Cassie kept her eyes shut against seeing her cell and the room where they had electrocuted her again.

She shuddered at the reminder it was her own father who had ordered such a thing done. "Almost there," Devon assured her.

The hair on Cassie's neck stood up and her whole body erupted in a tingling chill. She stopped so suddenly, she jerked Devon back and caused Chris to slam into her. Her eyes flew open as she rapidly searched the deserted hallway. "Cassie?" Devon inquired.

She held her hand up to quiet him as she strained to hear whatever it was that was watching them, and there was something watching them. She could feel it out there, creeping steadily closer, hunting them from the shadows of the compound.

She glanced at Chris. "There is something here," Cassie said.

"There is," Chris agreed.

Devon stepped closer to her. "Where is it?"

Chris shook his head. "I don't know."

Devon used his body to move her toward the others. "Move carefully."

Cassie was braced for the imminent attack as they continued down the hall. Her body hummed with adrenaline, her fingers trembled on the box she was prepared to drop at a moment's notice. Her edginess grew as they turned another corner; she knew the closer they got to freedom, the more likely the attack would be.

A loud clatter overhead caused her to jump. The box slipped from her grasp as Devon pinned her against the wall with his body. Everyone braced themselves for the battle, but the hall remained eerily still. "We have to get out of here," Julian said.

"They're stalking us," Devon muttered.

"They?" Cassie asked in a choked whisper.

His black hair fell across his forehead; his emerald eyes were relentless as he scanned the ceiling and hallway. "Yes."

A shiver ran down Cassie's back. "Devon we have to move," Cassie whispered.

He bent to retrieve her box and moved away from her cautiously. Cassie took her box back from him as he bent to retrieve his own. "Let's go," Julian ordered gruffly.

Cassie pulled her crossbow from her back and grasped it with one hand as she juggled the box under her arm. "You should give us some weapons," Joey said in a choked whisper.

"Forget it," Julian grumbled.

"You're going to need our help against them. We have a right to protect ourselves in here."

"You have no rights as far as I'm concerned!" Julian barked.

Joey stared at him in startled disbelief; Dani steadily moved forward, her head bowed in resignation. "Monsters," her father muttered.

"I think *you're* the monster," Cassie retorted. "You're the one who created this mess. You're the reason we're being stalked right now. You're why we're all here."

She was shaking by the time she was done talking and tears burned her eyes. Her father stared coldly back at her, hatred evident in his twisted features. She had so often dreamed about what her father had been like, and that he had miraculously survived The Slaughter, but this man was nothing like what she had pictured. This man was an atrocity who had been twisted by hate and violence, a cruel stranger she wished had never come back into her life.

"You might want to stop looking at her like that," Devon cautioned. "You're not getting a weapon, and if it wasn't for your DNA, you wouldn't have made it out of that room."

Her father turned abruptly away from them. "Devon," Cassie said.

He shook his head to silence her protest. She knew he was

telling the truth; it was simply that Derek was her father that had allowed him to make it this far. Devon wouldn't hesitate to kill him though, especially if he felt it would help keep her safe. Cassie thought she should be more upset by the notion, but right now she couldn't bring herself to care. Even if he was her father, she didn't know the man, and a very big part of her hated him right now.

Devon nudged her in front of him again to shield her from anything that might attack from the back. Cassie wanted to protest, she didn't want him in peril, but arguing would be futile. He wouldn't back down when her safety was involved. "I meant what I said. Stay close to me Cassie, they'll attack soon."

Though she couldn't hear the creatures, she knew they were shuffling through the shadows as they relentlessly stalked their progress. "Almost there." The hope was evident in Dani's voice.

Cassie was desperate to inhale air that didn't reek of the dead, to see something outside of this horrid place, and be free of the monsters hunting them. She held her breath as Julian pulled one of the double doors cautiously open. He poked his head out and inspected the stairwell before beckoning them forward. He disappeared through the door and held it open for everyone else to follow. Cassie was almost through when she saw it coming. It leapt easily down the hall in graceful strides that rapidly ate up the distance between them. Cassie threw her box through the door and grabbing hold of Chris she spun him off of Devon as she shoved him out of the hallway. Devon and Chris tripped over each other as they fell through the doorway.

She barely had time to register it was the most ungraceful fall she'd ever seen Devon take. She only had a split second to swing up her crossbow, and no time to aim before pulling the trigger. The arrow slammed into the things shoulder, jerking him back, but barely slowing its rapid pace, and most certainly *not* stopping it. She didn't have time to grab another arrow and reload the weapon before the thing was upon her. Grasping the crossbow in two hands, she slammed it into the creature's chin and knocked its head back as it seized hold of her.

Devon bellowed her name and shoved past Chris as he scrambled to get to her. Cassie lifted the crossbow again and smashed it against the monsters face. Its/his cheekbone caved beneath the blow to leave a brutal wound that would have left a human helpless and would have staggered a vampire, but did nothing to ward off this monster.

Its hands dug into her skin, leaving bruises across her arms as it tried to get closer. Its teeth snapped eagerly as it attempted to mutilate and destroy her. She could smell its fetid breath and the lingering stench of death engulfed her. Panic swamped Cassie, this thing was crazed, irrational, and driven only by its goal of seeing her dead. She jerked the crossbow down and shoved it into its chest in an attempt to further block its attack.

Teeth snapped inches from her cheek; she turned her head to avoid it as she tried to hold it away from her face. A loud roar enveloped her. Devon grabbed hold of the thing by the back of the neck and flung it off of her with one mighty heave. Cassie staggered forward and nearly fell as the weight quickly disappeared.

The monster screamed as Devon grasped hold of her and shoved her toward the double doors. "Go!"

Chris grabbed for her, but she shook him off. She was unwilling to leave Devon alone with the creature. She turned as another creature came barreling out of the darkness. It leapt over its downed friend and crashed into Devon. Cassie gasped as the woman slashed her tapered fingernails down his side. Blood flowed forth as his shirt and flesh was ravaged.

Cassie raced toward him as he grabbed hold of the woman's

throat. He pulled her off of him and held her at arm's length. The woman spit as she swung at Devon. Cassie's heart leapt into her throat; her fingers trembled as she fought to pull another arrow free.

She loaded it into the crossbow and took aim at the man who had regained his feet and was coming back at them. Pulling the trigger, Cassie took satisfaction as the bolt slammed into his chest and knocked him ass over tea kettle down the hall. It writhed upon the ground, clawing at its chest as its breath heaved in and out in a rattling whistle.

She raced toward Devon as Julian burst back into the hall and overtook her in his rush to get to Devon's side. Devon seized hold of the woman's head and twisted it violently around with a sickening crack that made Cassie's stomach lurch. He shoved the disfigured creature away from him and slammed his fist into the back of its twisted head. The woman, no, the *thing* staggered forward a few steps before falling to her knees. Cassie felt as if she was watching a grotesque movie as the woman's head lulled around on her broken neck, but she didn't die.

Cassie took a staggering step backward and stumbled into the door. "Get out of here!" Devon bellowed at her.

Disgust twisted Julian's features as he watched the creature blindly crawl around. Chris grabbed hold of her arm to pull her free of the hallway. Chris's eyes bulged from his head as he gawked at the creature. Julian and Devon remained unmoving for a moment, before bursting into action again.

Julian spun toward Cassie and shoved her through the double doors so roughly she fell over Chris and both of them staggered into the stairs. Cassie's palms and knees screamed in protest as she landed roughly on the concrete steps. Dani was still in the hallway, but Cassie's father and Joey had taken the distraction as an opportunity to flee.

Cassie spotted them two flights above. Cursing loudly, Cassie untangled herself from Chris as Devon and Julian burst into the stairwell. "Give me the keys!" Julian demanded of Dani.

Her hands shook as she tossed him the keys that fell a few feet short. They clattered to the floor as the woman slammed into the door, and then something else slammed into it. Dani screamed as Devon threw himself against the door to hold it closed as the creatures screamed and howled on the other side. "We have to stop them!" Cassie cried as she bounced back to her feet.

Cassie leapt onto the stairs as Devon and Julian strained to keep the doors closed against the monsters inside. Dani grabbed the keys and rushed over to help them get the doors locked again. Forgoing the weapons and supplies they had gathered, Cassie raced up the stairs. She took them two at a time as she sprinted to catch up with her father and Joey.

She couldn't let the two of them get free to reign down more terror on some other unsuspecting town and its inhabitants. They couldn't get away without some type of punishment, and they had to explain what they had done to these creatures, and how many there really were.

"Cassie!" Devon bellowed after her.

She ignored him as she pushed herself faster up the stairs. She had to stop them before they got to the top; they could easily disappear into the darkened hallways, and then out into the night if she didn't. Joey's head appeared over the side of the banister; his eyes widened when he spotted her just a flight beneath them now.

"Hurry!" Joey cried.

She poured on the speed as she gathered her vast reserves of power. Her father was at the mangled door when she hit the top of the stairs. "No!" she cried and fury propelled her across the landing as if she had wings. She pulled him backward and pushed him into Joey and the wall. She fell against the one good door as she tried to catch her breath. Her father's furious eyes blazed into hers. He grabbed hold of her and tried to pull her away, but she shoved him off refusing to let him near the door again. "You will *not* get away that easy."

"You have no right!"

"I have *every* right!" She smacked his hand away when he grabbed for her again. "You have no right to be free! Look at what you have done here, the atrocity you've created. This world is far better without you roaming it!"

"You have no right to judge me you traitorous *bitch*!" he spat. "You've turned against your own kind. You're an abomination, a monstrosity, a *nothing*!"

Before she could say anything more, he slapped her with the full force of his might. Cassie's hand flew to her cheek as her head was knocked to the side. Tears flooded her eyes, but she rapidly blinked them back as she gazed hatefully at the stranger across from her.

Cassie straightened away from the door. "Think what you will about me, I don't care because you are *nothing* to me also. But you will not leave here, and you will not be set free in this world again. This *nothing* will make damn sure of that!"

Devon leapt out of the stairwell and skidded to a halt at the top of the stairs. His eyes were the color of fire as he raked Joey and her father with a scathing glare. "Are you ok?" he demanded.

Cassie nodded; she knew the red mark on her cheek could easily be explained by the attack below. She had no doubt Devon would kill her father if he learned the man had just slapped her. "Are they locked in?" she asked.

"Yes, but I don't know for how long. We have to get out of

here." His eyes latched onto her reddened cheek. "What happened?" he demanded.

Julian, Dani, and Chris arrived on the landing with their arms laden full of boxes. "That thing down there," she muttered, unable to look at him as she uttered the lie. "Let's help them."

Devon tried to stop her, but she dodged his grasp as she hurried forward to take two boxes from Dani. She could feel Devon's gaze burrowing into her back, but she didn't look at him again. "Cowards," Dani hissed at Joey and Derek.

"Most definitely," Cassie agreed.

CHAPTER NINE

CASSIE SAT by the window with her legs drawn up against her chest and her chin resting upon her knees as she stared at the hushed street. The sun had come up a few hours ago, but she had yet to speak since they'd arrived back here. There was so much to ask, so much to know, but she didn't want to know any of it. She was tired of being blindsided by fate, and she was very tired of being betrayed by those who were supposed to care for her.

She turned her head to stare across the room at the man who claimed to be her father. She had never known him, but she had once loved the idea of him. This man was none of the things she'd dreamed him to be.

He stared back at her; his eyes were narrowed and ringed with bags from lack of sleep. His arms and legs had been tied to the chair; there would be no escaping for him, and she would make sure of that. She turned away from him and tightened her grip on her legs. In the far back she could hear murmured words, and from down below she could hear the whispers of Devon and Julian's conversation. Joey had been placed downstairs as it had been decided it was best to keep the two of them separated.

Everyone had moved away from her after the first few hours. Her father hadn't said a word either, despite Luther's incessant and furious questions. Cassie had the odd feeling he would speak to her, if she asked, but she wasn't willing to ask. Not right now anyway.

Shadows played off of the street as skeletal branches clicked against the sky. There was no sign of life, not even a bird chirped in the distance. "My grandmother used to talk about you and my mother once in a while," she finally said. "Apparently she didn't know *you* very well."

His head tilted to the side as he studied her. "Where is Lily?" he inquired.

A twinge tugged at her heart, guilt and loss swamped her. "Dead."

He grunted quietly. "And I'm sure it was one of *these* monsters."

They stared at each other. "No, it was another monster."

"And where is that one?"

Cassie swallowed heavily as her hands fisted against her legs. "I killed her. Something I'm sure Dani has already informed you of."

"You have your mother's spirit. Though I'm sure she is better off dead than seeing what you have become."

Unwilling for him to see her distress over his words, she turned her attention back to the deserted street. "My grandmother was very proud of me, for everything I did. She accepted Devon, she welcomed him into her home, and she welcomed him into our lives. She loved me, and she was the best person I have ever known. She would not be proud of *you,* however. She loved you like you were her own son, and she would despise everything you are now. I am not ashamed of myself, of what I am, or who I love, but *you* should be."

Cassie knew she should leave, but she was unable to bring herself to move. "How did you survive The Slaughter?" she inquired.

His feet shuffled briefly against the wooden floor. "We were all taught how to fight, how to use our abilities, and how to be a survivor."

"And you're a survivor?"

"Yes."

"And my mother?"

"Was not."

Cassie was unable to stop herself from shooting him a fierce look. "Did you even love her or me?"

His dark blue eyes were hostile in the small amount of light penetrating the room. "That is why I have made it my quest to make sure these monsters are eradicated forever."

"By creating even worse monsters?"

"We were trying to help."

"And you created things far worse than anything we could have ever imagined. You made these things, and *you* destroyed this town. You destroyed hundreds of people only to have your own creations turn against you. Good job, Dr. Frankenstein."

He stared back at her unblinkingly. "And you've crawled into bed with a monster. I made a mistake; you made a choice."

Cassie wasn't going to bother to deny his accusation or defend herself. Not to him. She realized he wasn't entirely sane. There would be no changing his mind, and she didn't particularly care to try. Whatever had happened to him over the years had completely changed him from the man her grandmother had loved and admired greatly.

"What is your ability?'

He grinned at her as he shook his head. "That's my secret."

Cassie glared at him but decided to let it go for now. They would find it out one way or another. Cassie folded her hands before her as she rested her elbows on her legs. "The ones down there aren't the same as the other ones I encountered. They're stronger, faster, and they seem even more blood thirsty. How and *why* did you make them?"

"We were doing some different experimentation, to see what would go right, and give us the best results. Give us the best *fighters*. There were some failures along the way."

Cassie winced at the word failures. They had been humans, people with families and loved ones. People that had lived, loved and laughed, until these lunatics had gotten a hold of them. Now they were monsters with no rational thought other than to mangle and destroy. "Why would you keep them alive?" she managed to ask.

He finally turned his attention back to her. "To study them of course, to see if they could be controlled and to see how they thought and reacted to things."

Cassie swallowed back her loathing as she fought the urge to flee the room and this monster. Her father. "I thought they didn't think."

"They do. They react to external stimulation, to blood, to movement. And they think about death and violence, and blood. They *do* react, and they *do* think."

"Where are the children? Did you do this to them also?" His silence made her heart pump louder; her skin chilled as if an icy hand had grabbed hold of the back of her neck. "Did you?"

"Some of them."

It took all Cassie had not to throw up or fly across the room and attack him. She remained immobile, for to move would only instigate one of those two reactions. She took a deep breath as she strived to keep herself under control. She couldn't stand the thought of coming across children who were like the other monsters in this town. She couldn't stand the thought of having to *kill* one of those innocent beings.

"The children were even more unstable than the adults. We don't know the reason why, but they were not viable as further candidates in our experiments."

Bile rushed up her throat, but she was able to shove it back down. Her legs quivered as she climbed to her feet, but she couldn't sit anymore. She couldn't look at him anymore; she knew she would kill him if she did. She couldn't be the person who killed her own father, no matter how much she thought he deserved it.

"How many children are out there, running free now?" she choked out.

"The children were all destroyed, as I said they were even more volatile and uncontrollable than the adults. They couldn't be allowed to survive. The havoc they would have wreaked would have been unstoppable."

Cassie was disgusted by the relief filling her. She couldn't have destroyed a child; no matter what kind of monster it was, she couldn't have killed it. She hated herself for feeling grateful none of them would have to do so. She hated her father even more for putting her in this horrendous situation.

Tears shimmered in her eyes but she wiped them quickly away. "And the other children?" she asked. "The ones you didn't put down?"

She knew he was waiting for her to look at him again. Straightening her shoulders, Cassie turned toward him and managed to keep her face as impassive as possible. She instinctively knew he wouldn't approve of weakness, and would shut her out because of it. "They were shipped off," he finally answered.

"Where?"

His mouth quirked into a sneer as he studied her impassively. "Like I would tell you. I don't want you anywhere *near* those children."

Cassie snorted as she shook her head. "You don't have to tell me anything," she retorted. "I can just have Julian forcefully drag the memories from your mind. I'm sure you know what he is capable of. I'm also certain the experience can be extremely uncomfortable, if he wants it to be."

Her father paled visibly. "I am aware of what Julian is capable of, but I will not tell you."

That was fine; she didn't particularly care how they got the information, only that they got it. She wasn't going to leave those children lost and adrift in the world, possibly being tortured like their unlucky friends had been. She would find them, and she would make sure they were safe afterwards. She *would* make sure they didn't suffer anymore than they already had, if it was the last thing she did.

"How did you make these creatures so strong?" She was interested in hearing what he had to say for himself, before Julian got his hands on him.

His glance once more returned to the window. "You know if they break in here, I'm vulnerable to an attack while tied to this chair."

If she released him he would tell her, but there was no way she was releasing him. She didn't trust him enough to even give him a leg back. "I'll just have to make sure they don't get near you, if I'm motivated enough," she added coldly, hoping he got her point too.

"I suppose you will." They stared at each other before he finally nodded. "Vampire blood alone wasn't working; we couldn't figure out the combination. So we decided to add a new blood with the vampire blood."

Cassie had lost the capacity to be horrified or dumbfounded. "So you added mine."

"Yes."

"Why did you give me Julian's blood?"

He shrugged to the best of his ability. "To see what it would do. To see if it would make you stronger, or if eventually you would become one of them. Either way it would have been interesting to see the effects his blood would have on you."

"You must feel like a real hero, running all of those experiments, testing them on your own daughter."

"You're not my daughter."

She was unable to understand why his words were still like a stab to her heart. "You're right, I'm not." She turned away from him, meaning to leave, meaning to get as far away from this monster as possible. But call her a masochist there was one more thing she had to ask. "Why didn't you come for Chris and I, when we were younger?"

A muscle in his cheek twitched. "I was injured in the battle, by the time I recovered enough to come after you, your grandmother had already fled the state. I didn't know where you were, or anything about you, until Luther started poking into the history of The Hunters, and Joey arrived here. I'm glad I didn't find you."

Cassie couldn't stop the tears burning her eyes as she nodded. If he had found her, he would have destroyed her the moment he realized she didn't have any abilities. Or she would have been locked away and experimented on until she went insane, or her body finally gave out on her. "So am I."

She rigidly moved away from him, unable to listen to anymore. She turned the corner to find Devon and Julian standing by the cold cases. They were large and powerful as their eyes glistened in the illumination from the coolers. Cassie could feel the animosity radiating off of them in waves. Luther stood behind them, the lenses of his glasses shone like cat eyes, and anger had made the lines in his face harsher. Chris was leaning against one of the glass doors, his arms folded over his chest as he stared into the darkened room behind her.

Melissa stood beside Chris, her onyx eyes glistened with unshed tears. The blue highlights in her black hair glistened in the light from the cooler. Dani was immobile, her mouth parted as she stared behind Cassie. Annabelle and Liam stood close together with their hands entwined. Annabelle's sea green eyes gleamed while Liam's oddly silver eyes were narrowed in concern.

"You ok?" Devon asked.

"Yes."

She moved into him and encircled his waist; she rested her head on his chest as she savored in the strength he radiated. No matter what happened, no matter how awful things were, as long as he was here she could get through anything. "How much did you hear?" she inquired.

"Most of it," Devon informed her.

"I'll go watch him, you should rest." Julian turned away and hurried into the store.

"Julian." There was an odd gleam in his crystalline blue eyes when he turned back to her. "We will have to learn what he knows."

Julian flashed a feral grin at her. "Oh, it will be my pleasure," he purred.

Cassie thought she should feel bad about what Julian might do to him, but she was unable to find the energy to conjure up those feelings. She was too tired to feel compassion for someone who had never shown her, or Julian, any. But she couldn't allow Julian to be cruel to him.

"Not tonight Julian and not cruelly. We can't sink to his level, no matter how much we would both like to."

"It doesn't matter." Luther pulled his glasses off and cleaned them as they all stared questioningly back at him.

"Of course it matters! The children!" Cassie retorted when Luther didn't continue.

Luther shook his head as he slid his glasses back on. "Yes, yes, of course the children matter," he said quickly. "That's not how I meant it to sound. We must find the children, but Julian will be unable to help us do so."

"Like hell I will be unable to," Julian snarled. "If you have a problem with me hurting him…"

"I don't," Luther stated flatly.

Cassie started in surprise, Chris's eyebrows shot into his hairline, and Melissa openly gaped at Luther. None of them had ever heard Luther sound so uncaring. "Luther," Cassie breathed.

His gray eyes were unyielding as they met hers. "My main mission in life is to see you all stay safe. That man out there is a threat to you and many others. It is essential we know what he knows, no matter how it has to be done, even if he is your father."

Cassie didn't know how to react to that. She burrowed closer to Devon as she tried to keep control of her swaying emotions. "Then why won't you let me to do my thing?" Julian demanded.

"Because Derek had, *has*, psychokinesis too."

Luther's tone was bitter, irritation simmered in his eyes as they met Cassie's. Though Luther had never met her father, Cassie knew he'd respected and admired him. They had believed Derek had given his life in order to help keep Chris and her alive. There were only three things Luther cared about, and they were Melissa, Chris, and her. To Luther, the fact Derek was still alive, and a threat to the three people he cared about most was an ultimate sense of betrayal. To Luther, Derek was already dead.

Julian cursed loudly, his lip curled into a sneer as his hands fisted. He swore again and slammed his hand onto a shelf. Cassie, Chris, and Luther jumped a little as cans fell off and rattled across the floor. Devon swung down and scooped one of the cans up. He shot Julian a censuring look as he tossed the can to him. "Keep the noise down."

Julian's eyes flashed a sadistic shade of red. Cassie was frightened that being denied his revenge would shove Julian right over the edge. Devon grabbed hold of Cassie's arm and pulled her behind him as he braced for an attack.

CHAPTER TEN

"Don't!" Cassie dodged Devon's questing grasp as she jumped in between them. "Julian stop!" She placed her hand on his chest as she spun toward Devon. His eyes were also now a turbulent red as he sought to get her out of Julian's range again. "Stop Devon, it's fine."

She allowed him to seize her hand in order to try and calm him down. He tried to tug her away but Julian's fingers wrapped nimbly around her hand and pressed it against his chest. Cassie hated the torment she sensed in him as his ice blue eyes met hers. His fingers squeezed around hers before he reluctantly released her.

Cassie stared back at him helplessly as Devon tugged her away and enveloped her in a hug. "Stop doing that!" he whispered low in her ear.

Cassie shivered as she hugged him briefly. "I'm fine," she assured him.

He rested his lips against her neck as he struggled to regain complete control. Finally, he pressed a smooth kiss against her skin before pulling away. Cassie turned toward Julian, but his attention was now focused on Luther. "Are you certain of this Luther?" Julian's voice was raspy but calmer.

Though he tried not to, Cassie felt his eyes settle on her. She smiled at him feebly. She truly did love him, but she wasn't the person who could give him that happiness. Maybe, when they got out of this and Julian knew what he was going to do, he would find himself an amazing woman who made him feel the same way she felt for Devon. Hurt lingered in Julian's eyes, but then they sparked with their usual amusement, and he winked at her. Cassie grinned back at him, relieved to see her friend again.

"Yes, I'm sure. Every Guardian knew what the other Hunters were capable of. It was recorded into the books, and the Guardians were informed of them in case they ever required certain abilities from a Hunter. Especially Hunters with an ability like Derek's, which is powerful and very handy, as you know."

Julian's cocky grin was back in place as he crossed his arms over his chest. "Yes, I do, except for now."

"Can *you* make him tell us?" Cassie asked as she craned her neck to look up at Devon.

Julian's eyes gleamed as his fangs flashed. Cassie tensed as she glanced questioningly between the two of them. "He will fight it Cassie," Devon finally replied.

"So?"

"If he fights it, it will be painful. *Very* painful."

"Ok, that's not good, but…"

"If he fights it, and I still burrow in, he could go mad."

Cassie's heart flipped over in her chest. Go mad? Devon could actually drive him insane? Cassie shuddered at the thought and the sheer strength of his power. "But will you still be able to find out what we need to know?" Chris asked.

"Chris!" Cassie said in disapproval.

"It has to be done," Liam stated flatly.

Cassie searched for someone who would agree with her. Unfortunately, she seemed to be the only one finding something wrong with this scenario. "Devon…"

His jaw was set as he met her gaze. "We have to know, Cassie. Everything. I can make him tell us all of it."

"Even if it drives him crazy?" Annabelle inquired. Cassie was grateful for someone with a little reasoning. "Can you live with that Devon?"

"Yes."

Annabelle's strawberry curls bounced around her shoulders as she nodded. "Ok then."

"Devon…" Cassie started.

"We'll give him the choice to tell us, or not, but either way he will reveal what he knows. It will be his choice, if he survives it, or not."

"Survives it?" Cassie croaked.

"It won't kill him, but it won't leave him the same."

She hated the man for everything he had done to her, and to her friends, but she couldn't do this to him. "No, we are *not* these people! We are better than this. We are better than *him*!"

"The children Cassie," Melissa said softly. "We *have* to find those children before any more harm can come to them. Think of all they have lost so far; we *must* save their lives."

Pulling away from Devon, she straightened her shoulders and stormed back into the room where her father was tied. His head was bowed, but he lifted it as he heard her approach. She studied him carefully, trying to find something she could relate to in him, some spark of humanity, but she found none.

Why on *earth* did she feel bad about hurting him when he had no compunction over hurting her?

"We must know what you know," she told him crisply. He simply stared at her, his face emotionless, his eyes flat. "I know Julian is useless against you." His cruel mouth quirked in amusement. "But Devon's not."

The smile slipped from his face, and his eyes flitted behind her as the others filtered into the room. "I will fight it."

"He will destroy you if you do. You will either tell us, or you won't be the same afterward. Those are your only choices. You have until tomorrow to decide."

She turned away from him, suddenly needing to get as far from this monster as possible. Her skin itched, her heart beat rapidly in her chest as her impulse to escape became almost frantic. Devon came toward her. "Come on."

Taking hold of her hand he led her into the small side room. A ladder door had been pulled down into the middle of the room. She frowned at it; her gaze shot up the ladder to the dark space beyond. "What is that?"

"The attic. Luther found it while we were gone."

He stayed behind her as she climbed the rickety stairs. She stepped into the small attic space and took in the wooden beams running across the ceiling, and the old curtains covering the tiny windows. She wrapped her arms around herself in an attempt to fight off the chill.

Devon appeared behind her and crouched down to avoid the beams. Cautiously moving forward, he was bent nearly double as he tugged a group of sleeping bags from behind a few old boxes. "I put these up here earlier. I thought you would like some time alone."

Tears of gratitude burned her eyes as he laid the sleeping bags out. She admired the play of shadows across his magnificent face and the glow in his emerald eyes. Her heart swelled with love and pride. He was hers and there was nothing she wouldn't do for him, nothing she wouldn't give him.

"They have already given me vampire blood, and I am no different than I was before."

He was taken aback by her words, but she could sense the spark of hunger that shot through him. "Cassie…"

"I want this Devon," she whispered.

"As do I," he groaned in a hoarse voice. "But there is no way of knowing what would happen if you were changed."

She hated he was right and she couldn't be with him completely right now. It had taken her a while to even decide she would join him. It seemed from the minute she had, everything had aligned against them ever being together completely. She refused to think it was some sort of omen, but it was difficult not to sometimes. She had to remind herself fate hadn't aligned against them, but horrid men like the ones tied up below.

Taking a deep breath, Cassie decided to try another route, one that would give them both what they longed for. "Then don't change me, not yet anyway. Not until all of this is over, and I won't be needed for the battle as much…"

"Cassie!" he interrupted harshly. "This has nothing to do with the battle, and everything to do with my fear over what could happen to you."

"I know that, Devon," she assured him, hoping to ease some of the tension radiating from him. "But I would like to be with you forever, and once this is over I want you to change me, consequences be damned."

"Cassie…"

"But until then, I would just like to know what it is like to taste you, to have *your* blood inside of me."

His hands fisted so forcefully the corded muscles of his arms stood out starkly. She thought he would deny her again, that he would argue with her. Instead, he pulled the sleeping bag back and held his hand out as he beckoned welcomingly to her. Cassie's heart leapt into her throat; she didn't hesitate as she slipped her hand into his.

He helped her between the blankets before sliding in next to her and wrapping it snuggly around them. Cassie savored the strength of his body as he enveloped her. She could feel the excited hum of tension radiating from him as she rested her cheek on his chest.

He ran his hand over her hair and face as he caressed her. Their fingers slid over each others as they lay together, simply touching. After a while, she lifted her face to his and kissed him tenderly. She lost herself to the feel of his lips against hers. His hand slid through her hair as he deepened the kiss. Cassie's body hummed with excitement, her heart hammered in her chest as she opened her mouth to his invasion.

His tongue swept into her mouth in deep, penetrating thrusts that left her limp and trembling. Cassie gave herself over to his touch, smell, and taste. There was nothing as magnificent as he was; nothing as all consuming and needed.

He rolled her over and pressed her into the sleeping bag as he continued to touch and stroke her. Unlike the other times when things had become this passionate and intense she felt no panic, no sense of self-consciousness. She didn't think about the many women in his past, but only of him and everything he was to her, everything he would always be.

"Cassie," he breathed in her ear.

Her fingers curled into his back as tears of pure joy burned her eyes. His lips pulled back, his fangs brushed over her neck as he scraped them against her skin. Cassie shook in anticipation of what was to come. She gasped as he bit deep. Ecstasy filled her as he took nourishment and pleasure from her. He encompassed her completely as he filled her with the golden warmth of his unadulterated love and joy.

He pulled away from her, but didn't close the marks on her neck as he bit into his wrist. Cassie winced at the pain it must have caused him, but he showed not even a flicker of response. His eyes were ablaze with desperation as he lifted his wrist to her.

Cassie held his gaze as she grasped hold of his wrist and brought it to her mouth. She hesitated, it was blood after all, but the longing in his eyes drove her forward. He groaned when she bit down; his eyes closed in ecstasy as he pulled her against his chest. The blood was strange, metallic tasting and warm, but it wasn't unpleasant, and was surprisingly sweet. Cassie drifted on the contentment flowing through her as he filled her. She could stay like this forever, never changing a thing, never leaving the secure embrace of his arms.

CHAPTER ELEVEN

DEVON WATCHED Cassie as she slept soundly, curled up on her side with her hands tucked beneath her head. She was unbelievably beautiful and serene. It was the first time he had seen her at peace in long time. Even yesterday she hadn't slept soundly, but had tossed and turned and moaned. Not today though, today she was an angel with no cares, and that's the way he planned to keep it for at least a little while.

He was unable to believe she was his; unable to believe she gave her love and blood to him so freely, especially after everything he'd done in his miserable life. Though he could taste the remnants of Julian's blood in her, he didn't smell it upon her anymore as it faded from her system.

It was *his* blood he smelled upon her now, his blood pulsing through her system to mark her as his. Even though he coveted her by his side forever, for now he was more than content to hold her, taste her, and love her. He glanced around the cramped room, grateful for its distance from the others.

When they were out of this mess, he would think about taking her completely. He might consider making her his forever, but not here, not in this place, and not with the horror haunting them outside of this building. Not with the uncertainty of what that change might do to her hanging over their heads. She deserved something special, and she deserved the peace she hadn't experienced in years. He definitely didn't want her monster of a father anywhere near them when it happened.

She stirred and her sweeping lashes fluttered open. Her violet blue eyes were groggy with sleep, but she beautifully smiled up at him. He bent to kiss her; he could taste his blood upon her lips as he relished in her. His body tensed as he fought the urge to lose himself in her completely. But he couldn't do it, not right now anyway.

Pulling away, he traced the silken curve of her cheek. "How are you feeling?"

"Wonderful," she purred as she curled up against him. "Simply wonderful."

He couldn't stop the satisfied grin spreading over his face. "Good. Are you hungry?"

"Not hungry enough to leave here right now." He chuckled as he pulled her against him and rolled onto his back. Her hair spilled across the both of them as she lay on his chest. "When will you change me Devon?"

He stiffened beneath her as his hands clenched on her back. "Because you can handle vampire blood doesn't mean the change wouldn't have dire consequences for you."

She yawned before shaking her head forcefully. "It doesn't matter."

He slid his hand through her silken hair. "And the fact that you can never be in the sun again?"

Her eyes darkened as delicate frown lines marred her forehead. "It's a small price to pay."

"Cassie..."

She propped her chin on her hands to stare down at him. "I want this more than I have ever wanted anything. I want nothing more than to know I will spend eternity with you."

He groaned as he closed his eyes and fought against his baser urges. "And if things go wrong?"

"We will deal with them then."

He cupped her cheek with his hand. "What if I lose you?"

"You'll lose me anyway if I stay mortal. I think my body can handle this Devon, I'm almost positive it can. You won't lose me, I won't allow it."

He couldn't help but smile at the conviction in her voice, the intensity in her face and eyes. "I'm sure you will do whatever you can, but..."

She shook her head; her eyes twinkled as she grinned down at him. "No buts, we'll get through it, look at how much we've already gotten through. This is a small hurdle compared to the others."

He smiled at her as he tugged lightly on her hair and twisted it around his finger. "Is that so?"

"Very much so." His grin faded as he stared at her beautiful features and hopeful eyes. "Besides, since I *am* your mate everything has to be completed right?"

His hand stilled on her. "That is the way it's supposed to be, but this is a special case Cassie. We may never be able to."

"We will," she said forcefully.

"Are you willing to give up children? A family?"

She snorted as she shook her head. "I gave up hopes of children years ago Devon, when I found out what I was. My family is here, with us. Just because we don't share blood doesn't mean they aren't my family. The one I do share blood with is the one I don't consider family."

Pain and resentment resonated in her voice, but there was also a steel rod of strength hardening her jaw and resonating from her eyes. "But you *could* have children; you don't have to give up that dream."

Her jaw clenched, her nostrils flared, as she eyed him. She was one of the most stubborn people he'd ever run across, and right now that little character trait was on fire. There would be no talking her out of this right now; he knew that, just as he knew he didn't really want to. He only had her best interests at heart, but he also loved her more than he'd ever loved anyone.

"No," she whispered. "I would rather have you."

He managed a sad smile for her. She deserved to have children and a normal life, but a normal life had never been her destiny. Even before he had walked into it, her life had been chaotic and uncertain. But if she was human she could have children, and she would make an amazing mother. "You share my blood," he said as he tried to distract himself from his turbulent thoughts.

He recognized the passion blazing through her and reacted to it instantly. "Yes," she murmured.

He tugged on her hair to pull her down to him and claimed her mouth savagely. Taking her blood on a regular basis helped to keep the beast within him under control, but he wondered if it would always stay that way.

A loud crash from downstairs tore him away from her. Wood splintered as glass shattered. Devon tossed the blankets from them and leapt to his feet as a startled cry echoed up the stairs. "Stay here!" he ordered briskly.

He didn't have time to make sure she obeyed his command as he hurried forward. He ignored the stairs as he jumped down and landed gracefully upon the floor. The front of the store was still secure; Cassie's father was still tied to the chair. Another crash sounded from the back as Devon bounded forward, oblivious that he wasn't wearing shoes or a shirt.

~

CASSIE LEAPT down the stairs behind Devon and landed soundlessly upon the hardwood floor. Her father's eyes bulged out of his head as he gawked at her. "Let me out of here!" he cried.

"Stay quiet!" she commanded.

Her blood pumped fiercely as a strange thrill of power pulsed through her. She was primed for this fight and determined to win. A loud crash shook the floor beneath her feet, but she barely felt it as she honed in on her prey. Passing by the racks of hunting equipment, she grabbed one of the knives they had placed there earlier. It was a wicked looking foot long Bowie knife with a honed blade.

She felt oddly tranquil and focused as she strode toward the chaos she could hear radiating from the back room. Her mind and instincts rapidly took in the scene as she stepped into the fray. Five of the creatures had burst through two of the back windows. Glass lay scattered across the floor amongst the broken bits of wood that had been used to try and blockade the windows.

Annabelle and Liam were fighting off one, and Julian was engaged with another. Devon had one, and Chris and Melissa were methodically beating on the fourth, while Luther and Dani were battling the fifth. Cassie aimed for the one Chris and Melissa were struggling with. Another one leapt through the window and squealed as it spotted her. Cassie braced herself for its attack; she was eager to take out some of her frustrations on something.

Cassie ducked away from its initial rush and thrust the blade upward as she drove it into the creature's chest. It howled and fell back as it clawed at the blow she had just delivered. Cassie felt no sympathy, held no remorse as she pulled the blade free and drew it deftly across the monsters throat.

Her mind seemed to turn off as she moved rapidly away from the mutilated monster toward her next victim. She barely heard Devon calling her name through the red haze of death encompassing her. Her world wasn't filled with thoughts of the living, and the people she loved; it was consumed with death and destruction.

She flowed through the motions of the scuffle as she drew on her abilities to help push her through. She blocked out everything else as thousands of years of intuition and breeding took hold.

DEVON SHOVED ASIDE the creature he had been fighting with as he fought to get to Cassie. She moved with the easy grace of a ballerina as she slit the monster's throat. He was mesmerized by her grace, and the speed and confidence with which she struck.

But it was only for a moment, because then he realized it wasn't natural. She was almost as fast as he and Julian, and she seemed to be twice as deadly right now. Devon broke out of his daze as one of the creatures grabbed hold of her arm. He barely had time to move before she slammed her elbow into its jaw and snapped its head back. With the thing's throat exposed, Cassie drew the blade swiftly across its neck before plunging it deep into the creature's chest.

She flinched and recoiled as blood splattered all over her. Devon's chest clenched, terror suffused him as she reached up with trembling fingers to wipe some of the blood from her cheek. The room was eerily hushed after the noise of the fight. Cassie held her hand in front of her as she stared at the blood on her fingers. She rubbed it back and forth between her thumb and index finger. Melissa winced at the piercing sound of Cassie's knife clattering onto the floor.

Cassie spun suddenly, her blood splattered hair flailed around her as she stormed out of the backroom. Devon burst into motion as he bolted after her, greatly afraid of what she might do. She didn't flee outside like he had half expected, but instead turned the corner toward her father. Devon cursed loudly and shoved a shelf out of his way to get to her faster. He didn't care about the noise as it bounced off the ground, and its contents crashed and rolled across the floor.

Devon caught up to her as she stopped before her father. Her eyes were a vivid red; her fingers trembled as she lifted the blood coated tips toward him. "*What* did you do to me?" she whispered in a desperate voice that broke his heart and caused tentacles of ice to encase him.

The man simply stared at the hand she held before him. A single drop fell from her tips; the muted splat on the wood sounded loud in the hush filling the room.

"*What did you do to me?*" Cassie screamed causing everyone to jump in response.

Her father's eyes gleamed as his lip curled. "What had to be done."

Devon felt the blast of fury blazing from her. It thundered through the room and filled it with her pulsating power. Her hands fisted, for a moment Devon thought she was going to hit him. Then, like a sucking vortex, it seemed to go back into her as the trembling of her body eased and her hands unclenched.

"You're not worth it," she breathed. "You're not worth anything."

A malicious smile curved his mouth. "It seems you may be one experiment that succeeded."

"Son of a bitch!" Julian spat.

Cassie held up her hand to keep him away. "Maybe I am," she agreed.

Her red eyes landed upon Devon as she turned away. There was a bleak hopelessness in them that tore at his soul.

"If you won't do it, *I* will." Melissa stormed out of the shadows. Before Cassie could stop her, Melissa slapped her father. The slap resonated throughout the building as Derek's head was knocked aside. "You deserve worse, but it's a start."

Shock filled Devon as Melissa glared at the man in the chair. Derek's head came back around; a trickle of blood had formed in the corner of his mouth. Then the smell of that blood hit him. Cassie's burst of rage was nothing compared to the one instantly engulfing him and ripping free of Julian.

CHAPTER TWELVE

DEVON'S EYES turned the color of rubies; his fangs lengthened instantly. Hatred blazed out of him as he took a step forward. Cassie had no idea what was going on, or what had caused such a passionate reaction in him. Julian had the same stunned look on his face Devon had held. Then that look also faded into one of murderous rampage.

Julian picked up a shelf and heaved it out of his way as he stalked forward. Derek began to bounce up and down on the chair; strangled sounds escaped him as he tried to get away from Julian's onward charge. Cassie didn't know what had caused this strange reaction, but Julian was going to kill him. She lurched forward, but Devon reacted faster than she did. He jumped in front of her when she attempted to block Julian from killing her father.

Julian tried to push Devon aside, but Devon grabbed hold of his arm. "Get out of my way!" Julian spat.

Cassie's heart flipped over, her stomach felt as if it plummeted straight to the ground. She had no idea what was going on here, no idea what had set them off, but she was fairly certain they were going to end up fighting. "Wait! Stop!" she cried.

She took a step toward them, but Devon held up his hand. "Stay there!" he barked.

Cassie started in surprise; he never talked to her like that, he never even raised his voice to her. Her shock was short lived though as exasperation and frustration rose up inside her. She refused to be intimidated by either of them, even though they both looked about ready to rip her father to shreds. Luther grabbed hold of her arm and tried to pull her back.

"Luther!" she protested.

"Stay out of this one," Luther instructed.

Devon blocked Julian from his attempt to get at her father again. A startled cry escaped Cassie; she jerked free of Luther, but she had no idea what to do now. Julian rammed into Devon and knocked him back a few feet, but Devon managed to keep her father protected from Julian's rampage.

Julian shoved his shoulder into Devon's ribs. The loud cracking of bone echoed through the air. Julian shoved Devon into the wall with enough force to rattle things off the shelves near them. Cassie lunged forward, determined to get to them, to stop them before they really hurt each other.

Liam stepped in front of her. Cassie glared at him, but he continued to block her. A loud shout drew her attention back to the fight. Devon had somehow managed to rotate their positions, and now had Julian pinned against the wall; his hand around his throat as he lifted him off the ground.

Cassie squeaked, Liam continued to block her as she tried to step around him. "Liam!" she cried.

"Stay back," he warned.

Julian released an uppercut that caught Devon beneath his

chin. Devon staggered back a step, but he didn't lose his grip on Julian. Devon lifted him as if Julian weighed no more than a feather and slammed him into the wall again. Julian's eyes rolled, but he quickly regained control of himself. Cassie dimly realized they weren't actually trying to kill each other. If that was the case this fight would be a lot more brutal. However, they were hurting each other.

"Calm down," Devon commanded as he placed his hand against Julian's chest.

"He's mine!" Julian spat.

Cassie's limbs went numb as Devon's gaze found her. She could see the hesitation in his face, the ferocious battle he waged with himself between making her happy, and satisfying the monster within. A lump formed in her throat. There was something in his gaze, something so lost and yet so loving and protective it left her breathless.

Devon focused on Julian once more. "Yes, he's yours, but you can't kill him until we know what he knows."

"Fine," Julian relented.

"Wait!" Cassie took a step toward them, but Liam moved to block her again. "Get out of my way!"

Liam hesitated before finally relenting and stepping aside. Devon released Julian and let him slide back to the floor. Though his reddened neck had to be killing him, Julian didn't raise a hand to it. He took a step toward her father, but Cassie instantly thrust herself in between them. "No!" she shouted as she threw her arms out to block him.

Derek was still making strange noises as his chair pounded up and down on the floor. Though it was strangely out of place in the pulsing tension of the room, the sudden thought of Chunk tied to his chair trying to get away from Sloth in *The Goonies* popped into her mind. She shook it away; her father's life was at stake here. She had to keep her mind focused on the present.

"Cassie…"

"No," she interrupted Devon brusquely. "This is *not* going to happen. I know you both hate him, but I will not let you kill him in cold blood. I know what a monster he is, but he is still my *father*!"

The chair stopped clattering across the floor as Derek came up against a shelf. Merchandise rattled, but nothing fell to the floor. A strange whimper escaped the man. Cassie disliked his fright, even if he did deserve it. Devon and Julian took a step toward her. They would never hurt her, but they were larger, and far more powerful than she was. No matter how much of a fight she put up, they could forcefully move her out of the way if they chose to do so. Though she didn't think Devon would do that to her, Julian seemed determined to get at Derek.

Narrowing her eyes, Cassie braced herself for the battle. She glanced back at the sounds of shuffling behind her. Dani and Luther had taken up residence in front of her father. Chris glanced rapidly between Cassie and Derek before reluctantly moving to stand behind her. Melissa eventually moved to stand beside Chris, but Liam and Annabelle hung back, looking more than a little confused.

Devon took another step closer. He was going to force her to move, and if he did, things would never be the same again between them. She could never forgive him for standing back and allowing her father to be viciously murdered. Her heart lumbered in her chest as sweat began to bead her brow.

"Cassie." Her arms trembled; she braced herself for him to grab hold of her and move her, but he didn't. "Cassie, that man is not your father."

The breath whooshed out of her in an explosive exhale. Her

chest constricted as disbelief and confusion swirled through her. "What?" She shook her head in denial. "That can't be… What?"

Devon's emerald eyes were caring and so unbelievably loving. "He's not your father Cassie."

Her arms fell limply to her sides as astonishment stuttered through her. "How could you possibly know that?" she whispered.

"His blood."

Cassie frowned in confusion. "Like knows like, blood knows blood," Julian explained. "That blood is nothing like yours. It smells nothing like yours, and it certainly isn't Hunter blood. He is *not* your father."

Cassie couldn't breathe; she couldn't think. She tried to process this information, but it wouldn't slip into place when her world was tilting so precariously. "He lied," Devon said gently.

She thought she should be angry, but it completely escaped her. There was only a sad acceptance, and a joyful relief that left her shaken and weak. "He's not my father?" she breathed.

"No."

Cassie inhaled shakily as she turned around. "Ok, ok good."

The man, this stranger she didn't know, was watching her with the eyes of a trapped animal. The others had moved out of the way, apparently having decided he was now fair game for Julian and Devon. A strangled cry escaped him as he fought desperately against the bonds holding him to the chair. She knew he wasn't her father, but she still couldn't stop the rush of sympathy she felt for him. Because of this man she knew what it was like to feel trapped and at the absolute mercy of other people. But where he had shown her no compassion, she would show him some.

"Why did you lie?"

His eyes rapidly looked around the room, apparently

searching for something he wouldn't find. Feral, stuttering noises escaped him, but he formed no coherent words. Devon grasped hold of her arm as she took a step toward the strange man. "Cassie."

She touched his hand; she needed him to understand this, even if *she* didn't. "It's ok."

Devon gave her arm a brief squeeze before releasing her. "Devon!" Julian hissed.

Devon held up his hand to hold Julian back when he came forward. "Wait," he ordered gruffly.

"Are you out of your *freaking* mind?" At Devon's head shake, Julian continued. "Is *she*?"

Cassie knelt before the stranger. He cowered away from her, but she made no move toward him. "Who are you?" The man simply stared at her.

Cassie rested her hand on his leg; he instantly jerked away. For the first time, something other than terror shone from him as his lip curled in revulsion. Cassie sighed as she leaned back. It didn't matter what she offered him now; he was still repulsed by her. She found it didn't bother her as much anymore.

"Fine, you hate me, I don't care. But we must know what you know." She glanced toward where Julian and Devon stood side by side. She was briefly amused that they probably didn't realize they had identical stances. They both had their arms folded over their chests and their legs braced as they watched her with nearly identical expressions of disbelief. They may not know exactly how they felt about each other right now, but they were still very in tune with one another. "If you don't talk to me, then Julian will be the one to find the information out."

Julian's full lips curled into a small smile as he gave her an approving nod. The man sputtered more disbelieving noises that drew Cassie's attention back to him. "He won't hurt you…"

"Like hell!" Julian snapped as his pleasure vanished instantly. Devon placed his hand firmly against Julian's chest to hold him back. Julian's eyes flashed red; his temper heated at the thought of being denied his revenge.

Cassie ignored him as she continued on. "But this *is* going to happen."

DEVON WATCHED as Cassie leaned forward again, instinctively going to comfort the monster before she thought twice about it. Her hands fell helplessly back to her thighs again. She'd always been a bit of a puzzle to him, but right now she was a downright enigma. The deep sadness in her eyes was almost more than he could bear. Devon remained where he was as he waited for her to come to him. Whatever was going on inside her, she had to sort it out for herself.

Finally, she turned and hurried toward him. Reaching out and pulling her close to him, he buried his face in her hair to savor the delicious scent of her. He would never understand her completely, and she would never cease to amaze him, but he loved her more than he had ever thought possible.

Pushing her thick hair aside, he kissed her silken skin. She shivered as she pressed closer to him. He pressed his forehead against hers and traced her face with his fingers. "You should go out back with everyone while I talk to Julian." She opened her mouth to protest, but he quickly cut her off. "It will just be for a minute, and there is something we must discuss. We have to get those windows boarded back up."

She frowned before nodding. "Ok." Devon didn't like the idea of her out of his sight for even a minute, especially with those *things* running around, but this had to be done. She stepped out of his arms and gave Julian a determined look. "Don't hurt him," she ordered briskly.

Disbelief and something akin to amazement flitted across Julian's features. "If he fights it, it will hurt."

Cassie focused on the man watching them attentively. "Try your best not to."

Julian's mouth dropped as he shot Devon a look that clearly asked if she was out of her mind. Devon shook his head at him, trying to quiet him before he could say anymore. Julian's mouth closed and his arms folded over his chest as he studied Cassie. It was obvious he was trying to figure her out, but Devon knew that was impossible.

Chris wrapped his arm around her shoulders and pulled her against his side as his head dropped against hers. Melissa and Luther enveloped her in an effort to comfort her. Annabelle and Liam held back for a moment before turning and disappearing into the back of the store with Dani.

"Is she serious?" There was a bewildered expression on Julian's face.

"Yes."

Julian blinked before turning toward the stranger in the chair. "After what they, what *he* did to us in there?"

Julian thrust an accusatory finger at the man in the chair. Devon couldn't bring himself to look at the man again. If he did, he was certain he might kill the bastard himself. He knew Cassie's wishes; he didn't understand them, but he also knew what *should* be done to the man. He was going to do whatever it took to make sure this man never hurt her again, even if she didn't like it. He wasn't going to lose her again, and this man was the biggest threat to that happening.

"You heard what she said."

Julian's jaw clenched and unclenched as he ground his teeth

and murder radiated out of him. Devon's own murderous urges simmered just beneath the surface. "I don't understand."

Devon closed his eyes and took a minute to steady himself. "Neither do I," he admitted. "But Cassie is different than us; she's everything good and right in the world. It's why I love her; it's why we *both* love her."

It killed him to say those words, but they were true. Julian did love her; even if he didn't understand her. Julian would keep her safe, and he would do anything he could to make her happy. But they both knew this couldn't be one of those times. Julian's eyes were hooded and thoughtful as he studied him. Devon's hands clenched as he fought the urge to punch Julian. He didn't blame him for loving Cassie, it was impossible not to, but she was his.

"Is *that* why we love her?" Julian inquired. "Or is it because of the darkness inside of her? Is it because we both know something else resides in her, and we both respond to it?"

Devon's eyes narrowed. "What do you mean?"

"You know what I mean Devon. Yes, she is exceedingly giving and caring and loving, but there *is* darkness in her. That darkness was there, even before those bastards took us. I recognized it from the beginning, and if you really think about it, you did too. So was it her goodness, or her darkness that pulled us both in?"

Devon opened his mouth to protest Julian's statement, but he snapped it closed. He knew what Cassie was, he knew better than anyone what she was capable of, but he had never truly acknowledged what was inside of her. He thought back to when he'd first seen her and been drawn to her like a moth to a flame. Her inner aura had shone brilliantly against the dark night surrounding her. He hadn't known what she was, but he had been unable to resist her; unable to leave her side from the instant he'd seen her.

He'd believed it had been her *light* that had pulled him in, but had it also been the darkness inside of her? Had he also been drawn in by the power that had taken control of her and enabled her to kill Isla even before she had been experimented on, tortured endlessly, and injected with Julian's blood? Had the darkness and the monster inside of him recognized its likeness in her?

Devon despised the thought, but it was one he had to face. Cassie had enabled him to keep the beast locked away as best he could, but she also had one inside of her waiting to break free. Waiting to destroy whatever enemy it had to destroy. He believed she was everything good, but he also knew there was a shadow living inside of her; there always had been.

"It doesn't matter what pulled us in," Devon answered, though he chose to believe it was only the good for both of them. "We're both here now, and the good in her far outweighs the evil."

"Does it?"

Devon spun on him. "Yes, it does. I *know* what pulled me in! It may not be the same for you, and I don't care, but we will *not* kill him."

Julian leaned back on his heels. "I don't know what pulled me in either," he admitted. "Even before I began to have suspicions about her abilities, I found myself oddly obsessed with her. At first I told myself it was just for revenge against you, and a challenge, but if I truly think about it I believe it was *more*. I desired her from the beginning..."

"Julian!" Devon was unwilling to listen to him talk about his desire for Cassie.

Amusement finally flickered over Julian's features. "Ok," he said with a chuckle. "I get it, don't poke the bear."

"Screw you," Devon spat at him. "You're an ass."

"Yes," he agreed. "But, I'm an ass with a point. You and I both know that to change her is risky, to *all* of us."

"That's why I don't plan to change her, not unless we know she'll be safe."

Julian rolled his eyes. "Come on Devon sell that line to someone who will buy it. They may believe you, *Cassie* may even believe you, but I've known you for years, and you're teetering on the edge my friend. I'm amazed you've held out this long, but it is only a matter of time before you take what you want. And she *is* what you want."

"I can control it…"

"For now," Julian interrupted. "But you have to realize the state you are in, and the position you have put us all in."

Devon's jaw clenched, his gaze darted to the man in the chair. He was watching them carefully, listening to every word of their conversation. Devon itched to sate his overwhelming thirst on the bastard. The man leaned as far away from them as possible as he recognized the murderous intent in Devon's eyes.

"I have not tasted her, and though I *do* love her, it's not the same." Julian's voice was oddly thoughtful for Julian. The guy had never been thoughtful about anything. "I've touched you both, so I know your feelings run deeper and stronger than anything I've ever felt. It's why I've stayed away from her, and why I've let you have her. You *are* who she loves. But I also know she means more to me than anyone I've ever known, and I would like only the best for her. I cannot give her what you can; I'm not ready for that yet." Devon stared at him in disbelief. Julian was actually being self-less? "I'm just not sure if you're what *is* best for her right now."

"Excuse me?" Devon growled.

"I don't want her hurt, and changing her could hurt her. And you will do it eventually, no matter what you think."

"Do you have premonitions now too?" Devon demanded.

Julian flashed a frustratingly maddening grin that Devon wanted to punch right off his face. "Nope, I just know you. I also know when it comes to you, she has no thought of herself or her own safety."

Devon's hands fisted and un-fisted as he glared at the man in the chair. There was too much frustration inside of him, too much anguish and hunger. He had to take his irritation out somewhere; there just wasn't anywhere to do it now. Not without risking all of their safety.

"If I didn't know it would destroy her, I would take her away," Julian continued.

Devon's head felt as if it was going to explode. "You even *think* about taking her from me, and I will hunt you down and rend you limb from limb!"

Julian held his hands up as he took a step back from Devon's angry advance. "I just said it would destroy her if she lost you, I wouldn't do that to her. But I worry about her safety around you, and I fear for your sanity."

His gums throbbed; he could feel the familiar tingle of his fangs. "Do what must be done here. Find out what they did to her, and why. Find out who he is, find out how many of those things they created, and where the children are. Do it quickly Julian. I would like to get her out of this town and away from this ass."

"But don't hurt him," Julian muttered, disappointment evident in his voice.

Devon would like to uphold Cassie's wishes, but he knew

there were times when being kind wasn't an option. "*Whatever* it takes."

Julian's eyes gleamed as his eyebrow crooked. "That's the Devon I know."

Devon's lip curled into a scowl. He had to get out of this store, he needed to hunt and kill. Even if he normally tried not to kill the animals he fed from, tonight that was *all* he wanted to do. He was beginning to think he may be turning into an even bigger threat to all of them than the creatures outside the building.

Devon turned away from Julian, leaving him to his own devices. He wouldn't interfere with what Julian decided. Julian may hurt him, but he wouldn't kill him, not if Cassie had said no. His eyes instantly latched onto her as he strode into the backroom. She was standing by one of the back windows, helping to heap bags of feed before the shattered glass and wood. The other three windows had already been blocked off, and the bodies had been stashed against the back wall. They would have to be removed before they started to smell. But then, he had no intention of staying here for that long.

Cassie turned toward him, and her spectacular eyes widened. Though he hoped to keep the worst part of himself from her, he knew it was impossible. She saw everything when it came to him.

Her shoulders slumped as realization and acceptance settled over her. He yearned for her to come to him, but she didn't move. He didn't like the look in her eyes, but it was time to start doing things he didn't like to do. It was time to start taking control, even if it meant letting the monster rule part of him.

CHAPTER THIRTEEN

CASSIE TURNED AWAY from Devon as Julian entered the room. Her heart hammered; her hands shook with the uncertainty pounding through her. She had never seen that look in Devon's eyes before, but she knew what it was. Detachment enveloped him, determination clenched his jaw. He wasn't the man she knew, and he was terrifying her right now.

Would the man she knew and loved come back to her when this was over? Had she lost him for good?

Her heart raced even faster at the thought; blood hammered in her ears. Tremors shook her, her hands fisted at her sides. Julian's eyes were hooded, his head bent slightly as he studied the floor. Then, ever so slowly, he lifted his head to look at her. She had always known they were powerful, deadly; that they were two of the cruelest vampires to ever walk this planet, she realized now she had never truly *believed* it.

She had been mistaken in her thinking. They may be more civil than most vampires, but they were not tamed. They were wild, and right now they were both on edge and deadly. Devon remained unmoving, his eyes as tough as steel. She wanted her Devon back; she wanted the loving man she knew.

But he wasn't there.

A lump clogged her throat as tears burned her eyes. "Done?" Devon asked.

Julian shrugged. "For now."

"Is he alive?" Luther inquired.

"As much as I would like to, I wouldn't kill a man tied to a chair. I would give him a fair chance at escaping first. Well, as fair as it could be anyway."

"I see," Luther said, but there was a hint of disappointment in his voice. "What did you learn?"

Julian's ice colored eyes met hers; the sympathy in them caused her to take a step back. No matter what had happened between them, *to* them, he had never pitied her. He had never looked at her like *that*. Whatever he had learned had been awful, and she knew instantly she wasn't going to like it. She took another step back and bumped into the wall of feed they had placed before the broken window.

Melissa placed a hand on her shoulder, steadying her as her breathing became shallower. "It will be ok," Melissa whispered.

Cassie nodded her agreement, but she didn't agree. She had seen that awful look in Julian's eyes; she had felt his uncertainty, his hesitance. No, it was definitely *not* going to be ok, and there was nothing she could do to stop it. "What were they trying to do to me?" she asked.

Devon's lean body moved with exceptional ease as he skirted the bags of feed and made his way toward her. His eyes thawed as he stopped before her, but she saw the hesitance in them. She knew he needed her understanding; she was lost and confused by what was happening with him, but she could never deny him anything he needed.

Her hand slid into his; the soothing balm of his skin against hers caused a sigh of relief to escape. She could sense a cool aloofness about him still, but he pulled her closer. "Julian?" Cassie breathed.

"You were their project," Julian told her. "Their *pet* project."

His gaze moved to Dani, who had backed herself into the shadows. "They were trying to turn you into a living vampire."

Disgust curdled through her. "What do you mean?" Chris asked.

Julian's gaze remained locked on her, sympathy radiated from him, but he wouldn't take it easy on her. "They were trying to see what would happen, how much blood it would take, and if they could turn Cassie into a vampire while still keeping her human."

"Is that even possible?" Melissa demanded. "And why?"

Julian turned toward her. "I don't know if it's possible. It's never been tried before, I've never heard of anything like it or known anyone who would even try to attempt it. Every vampire has had to die in order to be reborn. They were trying to keep Cassie human and have her turn without her actually dying first. They were trying to see what she might be capable of and hoped they would be able to control her. If it worked, they were going to see if it would be possible to do it to others while keeping them under the thumb of The Commission."

Cassie swallowed heavily, though she was wearing heavy clothes, she was suddenly freezing cold. "It's why they devised all of those tortures, why they gave you my blood. They were trying to see if one of them would push you into making the change into a human vampire. What they wanted from you Cassie was to see how much time it would take before you changed, or before you died, and either way they planned on you becoming a vampire."

An intense shaking racked through her. "Ok, all right," she whispered. "So that is why I feel different now, why I'm stronger."

"It is why you are stronger, but not why you feel different. You feel different because you *are* different. The vampire blood, *my* blood has changed your basic DNA. As has Devon's." Everyone glanced at them questioningly but Cassie chose to ignore them. "Our blood may eventually leave your system, but not without changing you on some basic level first. That is how the Hunters were eventually made after all, and in you, it is still making those changes."

Cassie was finding it increasingly difficult to breathe. "So what am I now?"

Julian shook his head. "I don't know Cassie, neither does he."

Sheets of ice crept down her back as her thoughts turned to the man in the other room. "Who is he?" she whispered.

Julian slipped his hands into his pockets. "His name is Patrick Woodard. He became the head of The Commission after The Slaughter. He was scared, and rightly so, that we would kill him when we discovered him. He lied and claimed to be your father in the hope we would keep him alive."

"I've heard of him," Luther said. "He was higher up in The Commission even before everything happened. I didn't know he had survived."

"Unfortunately," Chris muttered.

"The children?" Cassie whispered.

"Are at another facility in Canada, I can find them when the time comes," Julian answered.

"What are they doing to them?"

Julian shook his head. "From what he knows, nothing. They are just being held. Some of them are actually future Guardians. There are a couple of Hunters amongst them, and the rest are human. There are ten of them still alive."

Relief filled her, her shoulders slumped. As soon as they were free of here, they would rescue the children. "How many of those monsters are here?"

Julian shook his head. "They have been moving people steadily out of this town for the past year. They've been buying up land and pushing the people out in preparation of the experiments they planned to perform. Including the children, there were only sixty people left in this town by the time they were done. The ones at the motel who weren't killed outright were brought in. Some of the others have already been killed off, but he believes there are still at least twenty-five to thirty left."

"What?" Melissa croaked.

Julian glanced around the room. "We have killed off six of them."

"How are we going to kill twenty or so more though?" Chris demanded.

"We'll figure that out," Luther replied. "For now it's more important we keep them trapped in this town."

"How?" Melissa asked.

"Bait," Cassie whispered.

Devon's hand clenched on hers as his body thrummed with tension. "Absolutely not."

Cassie ignored his growled warning. "It's the only way to draw them out, especially since their food supply is running low. We have to have bait. They will come to us then."

"And I know who we can use," Julian murmured.

Cassie's head shot toward him. "That is not going to happen. *I* will go out there."

"Like hell!" Devon exploded.

"Devon…"

"You are *not* going out there."

"If you would just listen."

His eyes flashed red, his jaw clenched. "For *once* you are going to listen to *me*!" he snarled. "You are not going out there. If you would like to use bait, I will personally carry that man and Joey outside, but you will *not* be the bait."

Dani let out a strangled cry as she lurched from the shadows. Liam grabbed hold of her arm and pulled her back a step. Cassie was unsure how to respond or react. She had seen him furious; she had seen him on the brink of losing all control, but she had never seen him like this. He'd never ordered her about so aggressively before, and she'd never thought he would so willingly offer up someone for death.

"Devon," she breathed.

His eyes briefly flickered green again. "Your safety is first."

"I know, but…"

"No buts, you will not be the bait."

She swallowed the heavy lump lodged in her throat. What was wrong with him? What was going on here? She looked at Julian questioningly; he stared back at her, his icy eyes unwavering. He gave a subtle nod of his head that left her trembling.

"I'll do it," Chris volunteered.

"No!" Cassie protested. "No, Chris, I'm faster than you, and stronger."

He folded his arms over his chest and glowered as he took affront to her statement. "It won't be either of you," Luther said flatly, his gaze was focused on Devon. "Will it?"

"No," Devon answered in response to his question. "It will be Julian and I."

Cassie glared up at him. "Oh, so it's ok if something happens to you?" she demanded. "You and Julian are the strongest and the *most* essential to stop them from leaving this town!"

Devon's eyes dripped with blood as he bent closer as her. "And if something happens to *you*, I will be an even bigger threat to everyone in this room than those things out there. Do you understand me?"

"Devon I'm still going to be in on the fight. Once they come, you will need our help, we're going to be out there no matter what."

Cassie had to fight the urge to take a step back as he leaned even closer to her. Her heart flipped crazily as their noses almost touched. For the first time, she was actually a little frightened of him and the intensity blazing from him. She had never seen him like this; she didn't know what had brought it about, but she didn't like it. She hated to be intimidated, but she was, and she had never thought Devon would be the one doing the intimidating.

"Not you." Cassie's mouth dropped, strange sputtering noises escaped her. "*None* of you will be out there," Devon continued.

"What? Are you kidding me! Of course we will!" everyone exploded at the same time.

"No," Devon replied crisply. "Julian and I will take care of this."

"Devon, you can't handle them *all*. That's a suicide mission, why would you choose to do that?" Cassie demanded.

He subtly moved away from her, allowing her to breathe a little easier. "They won't all come at once; we can handle the ones who do."

Tears burned her eyes, her hands clenched and unclenched in frustration. Devon grasped her chin and tilted her head so she had to meet his gaze. "We will be fine."

A single tear slid down her face. He wiped it away before bending to press a tender kiss to her trembling lips. When he pulled away his eyes were emerald again, but they were dark with uncertainty and concern. "You *will* stay inside."

Cassie couldn't bring herself to speak, she wouldn't lie to him, and she couldn't make that promise. Cassie watched as he stiffly moved toward Julian. She was suddenly hit with the realization she didn't know exactly what he was capable of when it came to her.

Liam and Annabelle walked over to join Devon and Julian where they conferred in whispers by the doorway. Chris and Melissa silently stared back at her. They were her best friends, the two people she had relied on the most, until Devon walked into her life. They looked just as confused and frightened as she felt.

CHAPTER FOURTEEN

CASSIE WAS immobile with dread as she stood by the window. The timed streetlights spilled across the street, creating shadows on the pavement; the skeletal trees moved and swayed with the breeze. Cassie shuddered, foreboding filtered through her as Devon stepped into the middle of the road.

She was barely able to take her gaze away from Devon to look at Julian. He stood by the door, his hand resting upon the handle, his powerful body unmoving as he waited for the attack to come. "You know I won't stay in here once you go out," she told him.

His eyes skimmed over her. "I know you will *try* to go out there."

Liam and Annabelle were standing by Julian, their arms folded over their chests as they stared at her. They would also try and stop her, she knew that, but when it came to Devon she knew she could be capable of doing anything.

"Cassie." Her attention was drawn back to Julian. "I will tie you down if I have to, but you are *not* going out there."

Indignation flashed through her. "I am one of the strongest fighters you have!"

Julian's hand clenched around the handle. "And Devon *is* the strongest fighter we have, and if you keep pushing him, he *is* going to break."

Cassie shook her head forcefully. "No..."

"Yes!" Julian interrupted harshly. "Open your *eyes* Cassie! He's unraveling right before you. He will change you, whether it's for the best or not, he *will* do it, and he'll hate himself for it. Is that what you want?" Cassie could only manage a small shake of her head in response to his heartfelt words. "And if something were to happen to you, there will be no stopping him. *Ever.* Do you understand that?"

Cassie opened and closed her mouth, but no words would come out. "He'll kill us all Cassie, so for once, please just do as he asks."

Cassie buried her frustration and heartache as she turned to focus her attention on Devon again. Her heart was heavy as it labored to push blood through her veins. She was beginning to understand the distance encasing Devon now. "He can't fight it anymore."

"Not as well as he could, and not for much longer," Julian said flatly. "If it wasn't for his concern about what would happen to you, it would have happened by now." Cassie hastily wiped away the tears slipping down her face. Her hand clenched around the curtain she had pulled partially back. "You will stay inside, because there is no way of knowing how he will react if you don't."

Though she hated it and rebelled against it, she would do

anything for Devon, even if it meant leaving him out there alone. "They're coming," Chris stated.

He walked over to stand beside Cassie and rested his hand on her shoulder. He squeezed her before bending forward to stare out the window. "Where?" Julian demanded.

"I don't know yet, but I can feel the confusion and thirst that usually precedes their arrival." They all remained unmoving; barely breathing as they waited for the creatures to emerge.

"How many?" Cassie inquired.

"I don't know," Chris breathed. "It's impossible to differentiate one from another; they're too far gone for that."

They were too far gone to tell anything about them, and they were heading straight for Devon. Panic slammed into her like a locomotive as she was overtaken by a sense of complete helplessness. She had to fight the urge to bolt out the door, tear across the street, and join Devon. She would rather die with him than live without him.

"Stay!" Julian commanded.

She pressed her fist to her mouth and bit down to stop the scream threatening to rip from her lungs. Devon turned; his shoulders were stiff, and his eyes blood red. He knew they were coming, he was ready for them. Please, she prayed ardently, please let him be ok.

The creatures burst out of the woods behind Devon. She grasped hold of the curtain, pulling herself closer as the three monsters hurtled across the street at him. "No," she breathed.

Devon braced himself as the first one launched itself a good ten feet off the ground at him. Its fangs extended as its face twisted into an animalistic sneer. Devon seized it by its throat and flung it over his head as another one came at him. He grabbed the second one, but the third slammed into him and clawed at his back. Chris slammed his hand over her mouth as a scream escaped her.

"Stay quiet!" he breathed in her ear.

Cassie managed a small nod as tears streamed down her face. She didn't realize Julian had left until he pounded across the concrete in a blur that would have been nearly indiscernible to the human eye. He grabbed the first one Devon had tossed aside and smashed it into the concrete. The creature's skull caved as it bounced off the ground, but its arms and legs still flailed about.

Nausea twisted Cassie's stomach, she couldn't move, she could hardly remain standing. Chris held most of her weight as he removed his hand from her mouth.

Liam suddenly emerged from the alleyway and raced forward as he moved to join the fight. Annabelle remained by the door. Annabelle wanted in the fight as badly as Cassie, but she would stay in order to ensure Cassie didn't escape. Cassie briefly contemplated trying to get past her anyway, but she wouldn't do that to Annabelle, not unless it became completely necessary.

She turned her attention back to the fight as two more monsters emerged from the woods. One of them went straight for Liam, while the other streaked toward Devon. Five on three. She could get away from Chris; she could make it out this window if she had to. She didn't give a rat's ass what the glass or wood would do to her, not if it got her free.

Devon flipped one over his back and spun as he drove an elbow into the nose of another one. The creature's face twisted as it was knocked back a few feet. Blood exploded over its tattered and filthy shirt, but it didn't stop, didn't hesitate as it launched forward. Julian grasped hold of another's head and twisted it completely around. Its arms and legs continued to flail, but their movements were slower.

Deciding the creature was momentarily not a threat, Julian leapt back to his feet as Devon tossed his monster over his head and grasped hold of the throat of the one behind it. He jerked its head to the side as the thing howled. Its scream echoed throughout the night and rattled the windows.

"Awful," Melissa took a step away from the window where she stood by Luther and Dani.

Melissa didn't turn away from the fight before her though, and neither did Cassie though her stomach rolled with nausea. A gag escaped her as Devon grasped hold of its head and turned it with enough force to rip it off. Dani gagged as she spun away from the window and raced toward the bathroom. Cassie's hand tightened on Chris's as she tried to assimilate the vicious killer out there with the man she loved so completely.

Liam shoved his creature aside and leapt forward to help with the two still trying to battle Devon and Julian. It was obvious it was going to be a losing battle for the hybrid monsters.

Deadly. That was the only thing Cassie could think and see now. Devon and Julian were deadly, cold, blood thirsty, and so very good at destroying life. Liam was out there with them, but he didn't have the murderous zeal radiating from Devon and Julian. He didn't relish in the kill the way the two of them did, nor was he as good at it.

From her little hole, she watched as Julian and Devon took the next one down. Julian pressed his foot into the creature's throat as it squealed and squirmed uncontrollably. She couldn't watch anymore, yet she couldn't look away until she knew Devon was safe. Not until she knew the man she loved would come back to her, but she was beginning to think that would never happen. She was beginning to worry that man was gone.

The monster Liam had been battling scurried back to its feet, but it didn't return to the fray. Cassie's forehead furrowed as it scurried into the shadows. An uneasy feeling filled her. She'd never seen a Halfling back down from a fight, even when they were losing. They didn't have enough reason left to realize they were going to be killed. Or did they?

A shiver raced down Cassie's spine; a chill filled her veins. Maybe these things had more reason and sense than they had attributed to them? If that was the case, then things could become a lot more difficult, and a lot more deadly, than they had anticipated.

She turned back to the window as Julian and Devon easily removed the head of their victim. She took a step back from the window as the three of them turned toward the remaining creature. It was still squirming and squealing, trying to crawl away from the spot where Julian had left it.

She couldn't watch anymore. Bowing her head, she fought to withhold the tears and nausea boiling through her. The hair on her neck and arms suddenly stood up; a chill swept through her. She glanced toward the front door. Annabelle was standing on a chair in order to peer out through the small glass window in it. The other windows had been boarded, or blocked, under the assumption these creatures would be too far gone to notice the difference.

Devon, Julian, and Liam had exited the building through one of the small windows in the basement so they wouldn't be seen. The window led to the small alley between this building and the bank. They had never bothered with those small windows as the basement was under the trap door they had barricaded. But after the three of them had gone outside, the barricades hadn't been put back in place. They had been left open so Devon, Liam, and Julian could make a rapid retreat if it became necessary.

No one had thought the creatures would be smart enough to figure it all out. They were crazed and incapable of thought. But what if they retained more reason and intelligence than they had thought? What if the monsters had known they were inside this building, blockading themselves, preparing for a fight? What if they had expected this kind of a trap, and had laid one of their own?

The thoughts ran through her mind rapidly, but she was dismayed to realize she already knew the answers to them. The monsters were not mindless; they were cunning and deceiving. She had to turn around, she had to see what was behind them, but her feet felt like concrete blocks.

Gathering her courage, she turned her head to search the dark room. Joey had been brought up, and Devon had reinserted his command on Joey not to use his telekinesis. Behind where Joey and Patrick were tied to their chairs, behind the shelves with all of their goods, she could discern hulking shapes with reddened eyes. There were eight of them, but there could be even more in the back, or still down below. A pulsating hunger radiated from them, but she was the only one who had noticed them so far.

Afraid that any movement would immediately draw their attack, Cassie remained frozen, barely breathing. They had weapons gathered by the windows, but she didn't think she would have enough time to get her crossbow, let alone fire it, before the creatures were upon them. She wasn't even certain she would have enough time to alert the others first.

Taking a steadying breath, she finally managed to whisper to Annabelle. "How are they doing?"

Annabelle didn't look at her. "Another one has arrived, but they're ok."

The creatures would probably keep sending one or two in at a time in order to keep three of the stronger fighters occupied. She knew now these monsters had enough sense to realize it was probably a suicide mission, but they would do what the larger group wanted. They would sacrifice themselves in order for the others, more than likely the leaders, to feed and murder. Cassie shuddered at the organization, the brutality of it, and the thought process that had led them here.

Patrick had said they reacted, but only when murder, mayhem, and feeding were involved. Apparently even *he* had underestimated these creatures. She didn't know why they were waiting; they knew she could see them, but they remained immobile.

What were they doing? She wondered as she tried to get into their thought processes, tried to understand what was going on. But that was impossible.

"Ok good," she breathed. "Annabelle, get away from the door."

Annabelle shot her a look, and then froze. Her hand rested against the door as she moved on the chair. Her strawberry curls fell around her shoulders, her rosebud mouth parted, but she didn't move. Beside her, Chris's hand fisted around the curtain to the point Cassie thought he was going to rip it from the window. Luther stiffened but didn't move. Melissa's onyx eyes widened; she took a small step back.

Though they were all aware of the monsters now within the room, the creatures still didn't move. Patrick and Joey had turned in their chairs; their jaws were on the verge of unhinging. Where was Dani? Cassie's gaze flitted past the creatures. She couldn't see the bathroom Dani had bolted into. Cassie didn't know if she was still in there, or if these monsters had gotten to her first. Though Cassie still didn't trust the girl, her power would come in handy right now.

Very handy.

"What are they doing?" Melissa whispered.

Cassie had no answer for that. She found it more terrifying they hadn't already attacked, and then two more emerged from the dark. Ten on seven. The seven of them were strong fighters, if Dani was still alive, but these odds were far worse than any she had ever faced.

Yet they still didn't move.

"There's more," she breathed. "They're waiting for them."

Chris cursed vehemently; he finally released the curtain as he spun toward them. Patrick and Joey began to make horrified sounds as they bounced their chairs back. Cassie spun; they couldn't wait for them to attack, their numbers would only swell if they did. Hefting the crossbow, she slid a bolt expertly in as a sudden explosion of movement sounded behind her. They were coming, and they were coming fast. She spun back around and took aim at the first one coming at her. The bolt was off target as it hit the creature's shoulder and barely knocked him off of his onward rush.

Annabelle leapt off her chair and used it like a lion tamer as she battled back one of the creatures rushing at her. It fell back a few feet before lunging forward again. Cassie managed to get another bolt into place and found satisfaction as the bolt hit home. The creature made no sound as it fell back and began to wither upon the ground.

Cassie froze; her mouth dropped as the creature continued its soundless death throes. "Jesus," Melissa whispered.

They were being silent, even in death, they were being *silent* to keep this attack as uninterrupted as possible. The thought process that went with that was staggering. No one moved as they tried to blend this new information in with what they thought they'd known. Even Joey and Patrick had frozen to stare at the creature now lying still upon the floor.

What *were* these things? Cassie wondered, trying not to completely unravel. Were they more human than they had all originally thought? Or were they even more demon? If they were more human, should they even be killing them, or should they be trying to save them?

She didn't have time to weigh those questions out. Fear for her own life far outweighed the guilt, and doubt, that flickered through her as the rest of the creatures raced toward them. Shocked into immobility by the creature's bizarre death, Cassie hadn't thought to reload her crossbow. Lifting it high, she braced it against one of the monsters' chests as it reached her side. Using the crossbow as a barrier, she held it off of her as she fought to regain control of this awful situation.

She punched another solidly in the cheek as it reached for her. He fell back from the force of the blow, but the one with the crossbow in its chest continued to claw and swipe at her. They may have had the sense to plan this ambush, but when it came to fighting, the bloodlust took complete control of them. Cassie shoved the thing further back as the other one launched at her again.

A shrill cry rent the air, but Cassie couldn't take her eyes off of the creatures attacking her in order to see how badly Melissa had been hurt. Chris shouted, and then another monster went flying by Cassie with its hands clenching at the knife buried deep in its chest.

Continuing to use the crossbow as a shield, she focused her attention on the other one who kept coming back at her. It clawed and flailed at her in unnerving silence. Trying not to let her panic overcome her, she swung another punch at it.

The thing ducked at the same time it grabbed hold of her fist. A strangled cry escaped her, but she couldn't tug her hand free of its grasp. Her hand clenched on the crossbow as she continued to fend the other one off while trying to tug her hand free. The creature's eyes were like lava as it tugged her closer. "Why do you get to be normal still?"

Cassie gaped at the thing; she was frozen into inaction by its words. That it *could* speak! She hadn't associated speech with these half crazed things, but it was speaking to her, and it made sense, even if its voice was the most horrid thing she'd ever heard. It was low and grating as it slithered out of him like a snake crawling out of a hole. The sound of it sent chills down her spine and made her blood run cold.

And its *question*! Why did she get to be normal? How did this creature know what had been done to her? How did it have enough reason to understand any of this?

The world seemed to slow to a crawl as Cassie studied the creature before her. The features of this being were a mangled blur of human and monster. Its red eyes were filled with hate but there was something oddly familiar about it.

Then, she remembered. She had been locked in her cell still, before Dani had rescued her. One of the creatures had peered into the window as it tried to get into her cell. It (no not *it*, this thing before her), had been chased off by Dani's power. It knew she had been in that laboratory too, knew she had emerged, not unscathed, but certainly not the same thing these monsters had become.

"Why?" it demanded.

Cassie had no answer for it, she couldn't think of one. It wasn't fair she had come out almost normal after what had been done to all of them, but that wasn't her fault. She hadn't done this to them, she hadn't done this to *herself*. It shouldn't blame her, but it did.

Cassie opened her mouth, but before she could respond, it yanked her forward. Cassie was thrown off balance by the abrupt tug. She tried to keep hold of her crossbow at the same time she tried to regain her footing. A hand entangled in her hair; her head was ripped roughly back.

She swung her fist up, hoping to connect with something, *anything,* but came up with nothing but air. Using the crossbow, she bashed it into the chest of the one she had been fending off and knocked him back a good five feet. She took the brief reprieve to turn toward the one with its fingers entangled in her hair.

Before she could do anything it struck with the unnerving speed of a cobra. Her terror and confusion were buried as a scream rose in her throat. It was unable to break through the suffering searing her veins as it died in her throat. Devon had said it was painful to have blood drained against a person's will, but this was far worse than anything she ever could have imagined. Her muscles went rigid, her lungs stopped working, and her veins burned as the blood was greedily sucked from her body. She felt as if a million fire ants were crawling over her, tearing at her flesh as they ripped it away from her.

She couldn't get the air into her lungs to breathe. She wanted to cry, but her eyes were on fire, and they burned away the tears forming in them. She wanted to fight back, but her muscles were as unbendable as rocks. She wanted to do many things, but all she could do was stand in shattering agony as she listened to the slurping sounds of her blood being siphoned from her neck.

The one she had shoved back came at her again. Her arm had frozen with the cross bow still pointed up, and her fingers had clenched around the trigger. It knocked the crossbow aside, but she still didn't release it, even when it snatched hold of her arm and sank its teeth in deep.

A groan finally escaped her, or at least she thought it did, she couldn't tell beyond the explosion of agony seeming to shatter her skull. Red and white stars blazed before her eyes. She barely heard the small cry before she felt the small rumble in the earth that indicated power was being sucked from it. She dimly realized Dani had arrived. Cassie felt a small amount of relief, it would be ok now. But before Dani could release her power on a blast that would have rocked the earth, shook the walls, and rattled the glass within the windows, one of the creatures pounced upon her. Dani fell back with a startled cry as the wave of her power was abruptly cut off.

Cassie's vision blurred as darkness threatened to pull her under. She tried to gather enough of her wits to regain some kind of control of herself, but she couldn't push the pain away enough to do so. Her heart thundered as she realized the darkness was going to win, a darkness she would never wake from.

CHAPTER FIFTEEN

DEVON'S HEAD snapped up as he felt the pulsing electricity within the earth. He knew what the familiar rumble in the ground meant. He braced himself for the jolt that inevitably followed it so he didn't get knocked on his ass. But the earth didn't rock, and the jolt never came.

Confusion filled him; his attention fixated on the store as the energy receded from the air. Julian was kneeling beside him; his brow furrowed as he stared at the store in confusion. He rose from the carnage of the creature before him. Liam stepped beside Devon as he searched the quiet storefront.

There was no sound, no movement that Devon could see within the interior, but something was wrong. He had become so focused on the release of his frustration, and his compulsion to feed and appease the demon inside of him, he had shut himself off to Cassie. He hadn't wanted her to have an inkling of the pleasure he had taken from the death of the monsters scattered about him.

"Something's wrong," Julian said.

Devon strained to hear anything, but the night remained completely still. Devon opened his mind to search for Cassie's. He came up against an ominous cloud that left him startled and confused. Then her mind gave way. Pain lashed into his skull and completely encompassed him as it wrapped *into* him.

Devon retreated before he was unable to escape, before he was buried within her torment. The street filtered back into focus as he moved with more speed than he had ever thought possible. Leaping forward, he turned sideways as he threw himself at one of the boarded windows. Glass shattered inward, the board caved against the force of his weight as he plunged into the store. Falling to the floor, he rolled swiftly before leaping back to his feet. Fury encompassed him as his attention was immediately drawn to the two creatures beside Cassie.

At his entrance they had both stopped feeding from her, but her blood still stained their mouths, and the smell of it hung heavy in the air. Her blood, blood that was only supposed to be tasted by *him*, had been taken from her.

She staggered forward as one of the creatures abruptly dropped her arm and spun toward him. A bellow ripped from him as the other one tried to pull her along with him as it attempted to escape. Cassie tripped and her legs collapsed beneath her as weakness engulfed her. He grabbed hold of the other one who had been feeding from her. His hand encompassed the thing's face as he slammed it backwards, pounding its skull off the wall until he heard the reassuring sound of it caving in. Devon tossed him aside as another window shattered inward. Julian landed inside the store with Liam close on his heels.

Devon paid them no attention as he stormed after the one still trying to drag Cassie with it. He was going to tear the creature limb from limb when he got a hold of it. The creature hauled Cassie against its chest, pulling her up by her arm when her legs proved too weak to support her weight.

A small moan escaped her; Devon could sense the life just barely thrumming through her veins. The creature tried to keep hold of her as Devon shoved his arm up under its throat. The creature's red eyes bulged as it realized it was about to be destroyed.

A moan escaped Cassie; she tugged on her arm as the thing continued to cling to her. Devon seized hold of its arm and squeezed down until he felt the bone crack within his grasp. The creature squealed, but it continued to cling to her. Wrath pounded through Devon, his vision blurred as a fiery haze of red exploded in front of him. He had never been so infuriated, never been this far out of control.

Dropping his arm down, he seized hold of the creature's throat. Its eyes bulged; a crazed cry escaped it as his fingers dug into its throat. With one brutal tug, he ripped its throat out. Wild sounds escaped the torn hole of its throat, but Devon ignored it as he shoved the creature aside.

Cassie nearly fell as its grip on her was finally lost. Devon scooped her up and held her against his chest as he turned back to the store. Her hand curled into his shirt as she strained to lift her head. Panic thrummed through him as he met her unfocused eyes. Her mouth was pinched and her jaw clenched.

"Devon," her voice was a bare whisper.

His eyes flew around the destroyed store. Bodies were scattered about the floor, blood was splayed around the room, wood and glass littered the ground. The creatures that hadn't been killed outright had fled the room the minute they arrived. Liam was helping Annabelle back to her feet; her shirt had been torn, and a deep cut marred her delicate face. Though it was deep, it would heal quickly, and wouldn't leave a scar. Luther's glasses hung askew on his face, his hair was standing straight up as he rose to his feet. Blood slid down his arm and dripped off his fingers onto the floor.

Chris was leaning against the wall, panting heavily as he tried to catch his breath. He appeared uninjured. Melissa however, was unmoving. She was slumped against the wall, her breathing shallow, and her skin unnaturally pale. Blood had pooled beneath her; it poured down her side from the jagged gash that had sliced her. Julian knelt before her and turned her head as he checked for a pulse.

"Annabelle get over here," he ordered crisply.

"Hold on." She knelt beside Dani who was also unmoving upon the floor. "Just knocked out." She rose to her feet and hurried to where Melissa lay.

"Melissa?" Cassie whispered as she strained against his hold on her. "Devon?"

He couldn't move as she stared up at him questioningly. The demon in him was in control right now, and it wanted her, badly. It needed her blood, blood that was supposed to be only his, because *she* was his. His fingers trembled as he brushed her hair back. His nostrils flared and his jaw clenched at the sight of the jagged cuts marring her perfect skin.

"Devon?" He could hear the rapid beat of her pulse as she searched his face. He didn't know what she saw on his face, but it was frightening her.

"Cassie." She shook in his arms as he bent over her. He could smell the creature on her neck; smell its fetid breath against her skin. He gritted his teeth against the urge to bite deep in order to renew his mark upon her. Instead, he nuzzled her neck and relished the smell of her delicious scent. Ever so tenderly, he licked the jagged wounds and relished in the blood lingering upon her skin as he closed the marks. He pulled away from her, took hold of her hurt arm and also licked those cuts closed.

He trembled as he fought to control himself. She was still weak from the blood that had been forcefully drawn from her. Without thought, he turned away to shelter her from the view of the others within the store. Though, none of them were paying him much attention as they knelt by Melissa's side, trying to keep her alive.

He didn't feel the bite as he bit into his wrist. Shifting her, he held his wrist out to her to help her recuperate from her ordeal faster. Her eyes latched onto the blood sliding down his wrist. Her small fingers encircled his wrist and drew it to her mouth. A moan escaped him; ecstasy filled him as she bit down. His hand clenched upon her, his body thrummed with the pleasure her drinking from his vein brought to him. If his heart still beat it would be pounding now, if he could still breathe he wouldn't be able to do so.

Her eyes drifted closed as she bit deeper to take more of his blood into her. Her joy thrummed from her body and into his. Devon inhaled her scent as his blood steadily replaced the scent of the monsters that had fed from her. Her desperate desire to join him radiated outward, to be everything he needed her to be. Over it all he sensed her terror that she might never be able to join him. She drank deeper as she tried to take as much of him as she could into her.

"Devon, Devon." He turned further away to shelter Cassie from Julian as he came at them. "Devon stop."

A low growl escaped him as Julian's hand seized hold of his shoulder, and he tried to pull him back. He huddled closer to Cassie as she clung to his wrist; she was unwilling to let go, as was he. Julian jerked Devon back a step. "Stop this. Devon you could *destroy* her!" His voice was low yet frantic with urgency.

Devon wanted to push Julian away, to kill him for the interruption, but he couldn't. There was only one thing he wanted *more* than for Cassie to join him, and that was for her to be safe. She had sustained enough blood loss to make the consumption of too much blood dangerous to her.

"Devon!"

Anguish tore through him as he pulled his wrist from her mouth. Her gorgeous eyes were dazed at the loss of the bond she had been enjoying. His blood marred her full mouth and stained her lips an even deeper shade of red. He was barely in control of himself. The monster inside of him was so very close to the surface. If he was honest with himself, he would admit it was already on the surface, already in control, and it had been for a while now.

Julian was right, he was losing it, and he was going to hurt her if he didn't get control.

Cassie issued a startled cry when he thrust her at Julian. Startled by the sudden movement, Julian just barely managed to catch her. It killed him to hand her over to another man, *especially* Julian, but Julian may be the only one who could keep her safe from him. Or at least he would try to anyway. "Take her," Devon barked.

"Devon?" Cassie scrambled to escape Julian's arms.

She managed to get back onto her feet, but Julian grabbed hold of her waist and pinned her against his chest. His ice eyes were unrelenting as he stared at Devon. Though he would defend Cassie to the death, he was waiting to see if Devon continued to make the right choices on his own. He wanted to finish what he'd started, and end the torment suffusing them both. His hand remained at his side though as the man managed to briefly regain some control over the monster inside. He hastily turned away before he no longer could.

Desperation urged him faster. Grasping hold of the shattered window frame, he heaved himself over the windowsill and into the dark, wintry night. He had to get away, and though he knew he couldn't go far, he also couldn't be near her right now. "Devon!" her terrified scream followed him. The torment in her voice caused his non-beating heart to shatter into a thousand pieces, but he didn't hesitate as he raced further into the night.

CASSIE STOOD IN THE SHADOWS, her arms folded over her chest as she continued to glare at everyone. Julian remained rigid by the door, his hand resting on it and his ice colored eyes focused upon her. The windows had been boarded back up, the bodies tossed into the basement, and the trapdoor blocked by a heap of shelves piled on top of it. No one was sleeping in the backroom tonight; they had all joined her and Julian in the front room.

She knew she'd never sleep as she listened to the low snores filling the room. Chris stood by the other window, his head bowed, and his arms folded over his chest. He looked like he was asleep, Cassie knew he wasn't. Neither was Liam, who was sitting in a chair with his feet propped up on one of the counters.

They were babysitting her, and she resented them for it because the minute they weren't looking she was going after Devon. Come hell or high water, she was going out there, and she was going to find him. Once she did, she would do whatever she could to bring him back here where he would be at least a little safer, and where she knew where he was!

She didn't kid herself, and neither did anyone else, into thinking they were safe here. They simply had nowhere else to go right now. No place could be completely barricaded, and nowhere would have the supplies that the store had. There was no way Cassie was going to leave this store without Devon. She had been separated from him for too long when she had been held prisoner, she was *not* going to take the chance of losing him again.

A small moan drew her attention toward Melissa. Though she continued to sleep, her face scrunched up as she turned onto her side. Melissa healed fast, and Annabelle had used her powers to help mend the gashes in Melissa's side, but they were still sore. Cassie's heart went out to her; she hated to see her friend in such discomfort. Melissa settled down and her mouth went slack as sleep reclaimed her.

Cassie turned back to the window; she wished she could see through the board covering it. Her skin crawled; she itched to jump through the window and run out into the night in search of Devon. Where was he out there? Why had he left her?

A knot formed in her throat; she found it difficult to breathe. She knew *why* he had left her, but she would have liked to have had a chance to talk to him before he decided to just leave. Shuddering, Cassie wrapped her arms around herself as she tried not to completely unravel. She *would* join him. "You're not going out there." Julian issued the command in a gravelly, irritated voice.

"I didn't say I was."

His eerie eyes were oddly aglow in the small amount of rays filtering into the room. "I know you," he grumbled.

Cassie was unable to meet his gaze. He did know her, not only had he touched her, and seen many of the details of her life, but he knew who she was, and what she thought. He knew her strengths, and most of all he knew all of her many weaknesses. He knew she battled with her self-control, not as bad as Julian, and nowhere near as bad as Devon, but there was something lethal inside of her.

"I don't understand why he left," she whispered.

"Yes, you do."

Cassie shuddered as she bit on her bottom lip nervously. Yes, she did, but if he had just given her a chance, she would have agreed to give him everything he wanted. "But he doesn't have to fight it anymore."

Julian shifted; there was a ripple of muscles that reminded her of a sleek panther hunting its prey. She frowned at him; her forehead furrowed as anger spurted through her. She could sense his displeasure, his disapproval. "Yes, he does."

Cassie opened her mouth to protest, but he cut her off. "You may have chosen him over me, Princess, but I'm going to make sure you stay alive. We both know there is no way to know what could happen to you if he were to decide to change you, and I'm not willing to take that chance."

She stared hopelessly back at him, she knew he realized how much this meant to her, but like Devon her safety would always be his priority. "I am," she told him.

"Really?" he demanded. "Are you really? You may not care what happens to you, but I know you care about what happens to Chris, Melissa, Luther, and everyone else in this room."

She recoiled from his words and the vehemence behind them. "Of course I do!" she retorted.

"If something goes wrong you could quite possibly kill them all. If *you* go wrong, then Devon is going to be lost, so there is a good possibility everyone in this room will end up dead. Including me. I love you Princess, and I've lived a lengthy life, but I am not ready to give it up yet. Neither am I willing to lose you."

She swallowed back the lump in her throat. "Julian…"

"He's not going to change you, not right now anyway. None of us can take the chance of losing you."

Tears slipped down her face. "What about Devon?"

She barely caught the small ripple of motion, but he was suddenly before her. Gently clasping her chin, he lifted her face to him. "I swear to you I will do everything I can to help the both of you figure this out. I won't leave you alone in this, but Devon has to have time to himself before he hurts someone."

Her lower lip trembled as he wiped the tears from her cheek with his thumb. The intensity in his eyes burned away to be replaced with a yearning that nearly broke her heart. For a moment Cassie was afraid he would try to kiss her again. She stared back at him with pleading in her eyes, praying he wouldn't try. He cradled her face before kissing her forehead and quickly pulling away.

Cassie remained mute as he stalked across the room, his back as stiff as a board. Unable to meet Chris or Liam's gazes, she turned her attention to the rest of the room and all the people she cared about. Patrick and Joey didn't count, but her gaze landed on them. Joey's head was bowed as he slept in his chair, but Patrick was awake and watching them keenly. The creatures had never gone for them.

A new discomfort began to grow inside of her as she studied them. Why hadn't the creatures gone for them? The one had targeted her because it had seen her, and recognized her. But they would have recognized these two, and no matter how much they may have hated her, their hate for these two would *have* to be worse. There is no way that it couldn't be, not with what these two had done to them.

Taking a step toward them, her head tilted to the side as the wheels in her mind began to spin. She took another step toward them, her heart hammering, and her throat dry. She thought of the creatures that had escaped from here, thought of the ones still lurking within the shadows, and her skin crawled. Icy tentacles crept steadily up her neck and caused her hair to stand on end. How many of them were still out there, hunting, plotting?

"Cassie?" Chris's voice was higher than normal.

She turned toward Julian. "You have to find him Julian," she whispered. "Please, you have to go now. He can't be out there alone, it's too dangerous. They're far smarter than we thought, *far* smarter."

Julian's eyes were hooded and distant as he stared at her. Frustration clawed at her chest as she thrust a finger at Patrick and Joey. "That one recognized me from in there; he came at me because he recognized *me*. You think they didn't recognize *them*. Of course they did, but they didn't go after those two. Why? Because they're tied to the chairs and those creatures *knew* they had to come for us first. They planned everything, they calculated *everything*. We already knew they ambushed us, but we assumed it was the same as wolves hunting a deer. We didn't realize just how much intelligence they do still have. Julian you have to go get him, they're out there, and they're going to come back, or they're going to trap him. He can't be alone Julian, he *can't*!"

Julian turned to the two men tied to the chairs. Anger and hatred flitted over his defined features. "How much ability to reason do they have?"

Patrick's eyes were cold and flat as he met Julian's furious gaze. "Far more than we would have liked. It's why we were destroying them; they were more precarious than we had realized."

Cassie shuddered as antipathy and revulsion filled her. He sounded as if he were simply talking about rabid animals and not human beings with families and lives. She found herself wishing the creatures *had* killed him when they broke in. "They had realized you were going to destroy them all, and they plotted their escape," Cassie deduced.

"Bastard!" Julian hissed.

Patrick showed no signs of remorse as he met Julian's fierce gaze. "Insanity," Luther whispered. "Complete insanity."

Julian shook his head. "I'll find him."

"You can't go out there alone," Cassie told him.

"I'll be fine."

She wanted Devon safe, but she didn't want Julian to be hurt in the process. "Take me with you."

"No."

"Take *someone* with you," she urged.

"I'm not leaving you with even less numbers in here than before. I'll be fine Princess."

Her fingers clenched around his. "Don't call me Princess," she told him.

He grinned at her before releasing her hand. "Anything you say. You are to stay in here, do you understand me?" Cassie nodded. "I mean it Cass, I'm trusting you on this one. I can't save you both."

Chris, having risen from the chair, pulled her back a step. She watched helplessly as Julian slipped out the door.

CHAPTER SIXTEEN

"Cassie." She briefly turned away from the small hole she had found in another window. Annabelle rang her hands as she hovered at her side. "Cassie maybe you should get some sleep, you must be exhausted."

Cassie shook her head as she turned away. She was exhausted, her entire body ached from being so stiff and anxious, but she wouldn't rest until Julian and Devon returned safely. Besides, she couldn't go to sleep when they were still so very vulnerable to attack. It was only a matter of time before the creatures regrouped and came back at them in full force, unless they had decided to spread out from the town in search of easier victims.

Cassie glanced over to where Patrick and Joey remained tied to the chairs. They would be the main reason the monsters came back, but they would have to get through all of them in order to kill those two. Cassie wasn't so sure she would put up much of a fight in order to protect them. "Cass." She disliked the pity and sympathy in Annabelle's sea green eyes. "They'll be fine."

"Yes," she breathed, not at all convinced.

Annabelle squeezed her hand before slipping noiselessly into the shadows. Cassie returned to staring out at the dark night. The moon danced across the snow in sparkling beams of colorful radiance. Stars twinkled in the sky as clouds drifted past them. The skeletal branches of the nearby trees danced and swayed in the breeze as it wafted through them.

A shiver raced down her spine; she rested her fingers against the board on the window. Julian and Devon had to be freezing out there. She hated feeling helpless and alone, but she had promised to stay and she would uphold that promise.

Then she saw it, a darker shadow amongst the night; a figure amidst the woods. Cassie's heart gave a mighty heave that left her breathless. The darkness caressed his firm body and the moon lit his black hair. Though she couldn't discern his features, he was the same size and shape as Devon.

Spinning on her heel, she fled toward the door. Chris jumped toward her, trying to block her before she could get her hand on the knob. But she was faster than he was. Throwing the lock, she tossed the door open. "Cassie!"

She plunged into the night, needing to see and hold Devon again. Her breath blew out in bursts of steam as she raced across the street. She was halfway across the street, when he emerged from the shadows. Relief filled her but was quickly replaced with confusion and surprise. She sprinted forward a few more steps before true realization sank in. Though the man did look oddly like him with his dark hair, and sleek build, it wasn't Devon. His cheekbones were high and well defined like Devon's, his mouth full, but his nose was a little bigger, and his face thinner. He was shorter and stockier, but the differences were so small she hadn't immediately picked up on them. His eyes though, it was his eyes that confused her most. They were not the same dazzling emerald color as Devon's. They were a darker almost forest green, and they were cruel, with an edge of malice that finally slid her to a halt.

She stared at him, her mouth agape; shock hammering her heart against her ribcage. He and Devon were so alike, and yet so different. Who *was* this guy?

She shook her head as she took a step back. She didn't know who he was, but it was more than apparent he wasn't on her side as she could feel the evil radiating from his body. He didn't appear to be one of the creatures though, as his eyes remained clear, and he didn't appear half crazed. Malevolent yes, but half crazed, no. She was tempted to turn and flee, but she instinctively knew she wouldn't get away.

"You must be her," he purred.

Cassie took a step back as she tried to keep her terror under control. She knew what he was, but *who* was he that he thought he knew her?

She took another small step back as she tried not to draw his immediate attack. She could sense his power thrumming from him like a tightly wound guitar string. Taking another step back, she tried to breathe through the lump in her throat and the constriction in her chest.

A small but cruel smile twisted his lips. Confusion continued to churn through her. The similarities were so striking, yet so different. There was no softness in his gaze, no love, no *humanity*.

She took another step back, but knew instinctively it didn't matter what she did, he was going to come after her anyway. "Pretty."

The word was barely a breath, but Cassie heard it as clearly as if he had been standing beside her. She was suddenly certain he *could* be beside her in an instant. Her skin crawled as if he had touched her. The corners of his eyes crinkled as his smile grew. "This is going to be fun."

Cassie's hands clenched as she prepared herself for the attack she knew was imminent. Then she felt the ground begin to rumble, felt the earth shake and tremble as it lifted and shook with mighty waves. A fissure sprouted in the street and zigzagged rapidly toward her as the pavement cracked and heaved. A startled cry escaped her as she jumped out of the way of the rapidly growing hole in the middle of the street.

Her foot came up against the edge of another hole as she took a step back. She spun around, terrified to realize a large hole had formed around her. A hole she was beginning to realize she couldn't see the bottom of. Dirt and pavement clattered into the widening gaps as it bounced off the sides.

Chris, Liam, Melissa, and Annabelle skidded to a halt at the edge of the hole. They gawked at her across the five foot gap. Behind them, she could see Dani and Luther gathered at the edge of the store, watching in horror as the earth gave another mighty heave. Cassie stumbled and fell as she lost her balance. A small cry escaped her as her hand fell into one of the ever growing pits, and her leg skidded off the side.

"Cassie!" Melissa screamed.

She knocked more rocks and pavement away as she scrambled to the middle of her small shelf. "Cassie!" Chris knelt before her and stretched his hand across the breach. "Grab my hand!"

She leaned forward as she grabbed for his questing hand across the gap. Her fingertips were just centimeters from his as she stretched herself as far as she could. Frustration filled her;

helplessness consumed her as her small plateau began to shrink. "Jump!" he shouted at her.

Desperation seized her as she lunged for Chris's hand. Air and space rushed up to meet her as she tumbled toward the large chasm. A small scream worked its way up her throat, but it lodged there as Chris's hand grasped hold of her arm. His fingers dug into her skin, his grip was bruising, but greatly welcome. Cassie's breath froze in her lungs; her body braced itself as she waited for the impending impact of the wall of dirt and rocks. The collision with the wall threw her off balance and spun her in midair as Chris held on to her.

Arms wrapped around her and grasped her so tightly the air exploded from her lungs. A startled cry escaped her, Chris's hand was ripped away and the crater rushed away from her. She would have panicked against the sudden hold, but she recognized Devon's smell and solid embrace instantly.

She allowed herself a moment to melt against him, to savor him and take comfort in the strength and reassurance of his embrace. Then, they were on solid ground again. His legs bent at the knees as he absorbed the impact of their landing. He held her against his chest, his nose buried in her hair as he inhaled her scent deeply. A shiver raced down her spine. She allowed herself to forget everything as her fingers dug into his thickly muscled arm. His lips touched briefly against her ear, then her neck, before he lowered her to the ground.

His hand encircled hers as he lifted her to her feet. His eyes were remorseless as they met hers, his jaw locked, and his shoulders stiff. This Devon was different than the one who had fled the store. That one had been terrified he would hurt her, and take her against her will. This Devon looked prepared to go to war.

He kept her behind him, his arm braced in front of her as he turned to face the strange man with the frightening ability to make the earth split apart. The man was grinning at them; his eyes alight with mischief and amusement. "There you are!" he cried as he clasped his hands before him. "I was so hoping you would join us!"

"Here I am," Devon grated.

Cassie found herself unable to move as she watched the exchange with fascination. Standing across from each other, the similarities between the two were even more noticeable, as was the immense hatred they had for one another. Devon blocked her even more from view as the stranger's gaze slid toward her, and his smile broadened to reveal his fangs.

"She's a fine little piece."

A low snarl escaped Devon, his muscles rippled beneath his shirt. Cassie thought he was going to lunge forward, but instead he pushed her back a step. "I'll destroy your mind and rip your throat out before I *ever* let you near her."

The stranger's amusement didn't wane at the threat. Instead, he seemed even more intrigued by the notion as his head tilted to the side, and he tried to get a better look at her. Cassie stared in disbelief at the back of Devon, even against Patrick he had been reluctant to use his ability. But now, not only was he threatening to wield it, he was also threatening to destroy this stranger with it.

Cassie jumped when Julian appeared beside her; his arm was firm against hers as he boxed her in, the hatred in his gaze left her breathless. She knew that hatred wasn't for her, even when he'd tried to kill her he'd never looked at her like that. There had always been an air of amusement, curiosity, and admiration about him when it came to her. There had *never* been hatred. Even when he'd claimed to hate Devon, she had never seen *this* look in his eyes.

"And if it isn't the venerable sidekick," the man purred as his eyes lit upon Julian. "I thought you two had parted ways when Devon went vegan on us. Imagine my disbelief when Matthew informed us you two had reunited, and for this *girl* no less. Our enemy." Devon stiffened even more at the name Matthew, while Julian muttered a curse. Cassie sensed the name, and this man's presence, was far worse than she'd even begun to fathom.

"How are you not killing each other over her?" The man continued. "Or are you sharing her like you've shared so many others before?"

The words were a stabbing reminder of Devon's past that she didn't want to hear. A past she'd just recently come to terms with. "Enough!" Devon roared. His hands fisted as he took a step forward.

"Easy," Julian cautioned and grasped hold of Devon's arm. "Your reaction is what he's looking for Devon."

Devon didn't lunge forward, but his tension didn't ease either. "Still a good sidekick I see," the man commented as he pinned Julian with a disgusted look. "Always second best, especially now."

Julian quirked an eyebrow, the amusement flitting over his features didn't reach his eyes. "Oh Robert, even after all of these years your jealousy hasn't eased up even a little bit has it? You were never best, second best, or even third, how pathetic and sad."

The smile slid from Robert's face, his eyes narrowed. Julian's words had rattled him. But even more than that, the name Robert rang a bell in Cassie's memory. She'd heard it before, she couldn't recall where, but she believed Devon had been the one to mention it. Her mind spun as she ran through everything Devon had ever told her.

"What are you doing here?" Devon demanded.

Robert's mouth pursed, his eyes raked her from head to toe. Cassie felt as if her skin had just been flayed from her body and exposed to the very marrow of her bones. Devon growled as Julian stepped closer to her. Her hands trembled, her spinning mind finally placed the name. She knew who this strange man was now. Her eyes landed on Devon's broad back, betrayal spun through her, but she couldn't bring herself to be angry, just dismayed.

Why hadn't he told her about this? What had happened between them to cause such animosity and hatred?

She glanced back at the strange man, but even before he spat the word with such vehemence, she already knew who he was. "You know why I'm here, *brother*."

DEVON COULD FEEL the turmoil rolling off of Cassie. He didn't feel disbelief from her though when Robert revealed what they were to each other. So, she had already figured it out, he realized. She knew his worst secret now, the worst part of him, the one thing he hadn't been able to bring himself to reveal to her. The one *person* he had never wanted her to meet.

Now he wanted her out of here before Robert came at her again. Robert would do everything he could to destroy her in order to destroy Devon. "Matthew sent you here?" He was barely able to get words out through the constriction in his chest.

Robert's grin, and the wicked gleam in his eyes should have alerted him, but he was still unprepared for what he said next. "Oh no, Devon, Matthew *escorted* me here. We all had to see that there were Hunter s still alive, and one of our *own* fancies himself in love with one of them. Plus, from what I've been led to understand, we are standing in what is now a ghost town, with a bunch of miscreants that never should have existed running around. All of our lives are on the line if they escape here; *all* of our safety is in jeopardy. Do you think any of us would miss this fun?"

Julian swore loudly and grabbing hold of Cassie, he shoved her roughly in between him and Devon as he stepped firmly behind her. Devon bristled at her startled cry, but he didn't protest Julian's action, nor did he react to Julian's protective hold upon her. It was where she ought to be, and he was grateful Julian would protect her with his life also.

Devon took a step back to push her more firmly in between them. Her hands curled into his back, her breath was warm even through the layers of clothes he wore. "I love you," she whispered as her head briefly dropped to his back.

Devon shuddered as raw emotion swirled up to choke him. She had put her absolute faith and trust in him, and even though he had omitted a big part of his life, she still loved and forgave him. He would do everything he could, do whatever it took, to make sure she walked away from this. Even if it meant doing things he had sworn he would never do again.

His gaze fell back to his brother; it wasn't Robert he sought, not Robert he could *use*. But where were the others?

Sensing Devon's gaze, Chris turned toward him, but he simply shook his head in response to Devon's silent question. Chris didn't know where they were either. Devon's hands clenched, his fingers fisted in frustration. They would avoid Devon for as long as they possibly could. They thought if they revealed themselves together they would be able to protect themselves from him.

However, they didn't know he'd been feeding on Cassie, a

powerful Hunter, who had Julian's Elder blood inside her also. They couldn't know the power she possessed, the strength flowing through her veins and into his. They may have a vague inkling about it, or at least Matthew might have foreseen it, but Devon didn't think they would be here if they knew it all. No matter what Robert said about the Hunters, or the creatures in this town, they still wouldn't be enough to entice The Elders out of hiding if they thought there was any chance they could lose this battle. No matter what, above even risk of exposure, Elder's valued their own lives far more than they valued anything else. The survival instinct in them was far deeper than in younger vampires.

Devon suspected the reasons for that were partly because they had seen and caused so much death themselves. They had a far better understanding of just how tenuous life truly was, even an immortal's life. He suspected the other reason was The Elders had caused so much destruction they feared death, and the afterlife they may have to face. There would be no heaven for them, or even for himself, but a fiery pit of Hell none of them wanted to experience.

No, The Elders had come here fully expecting to win this battle. Which meant Matthew's visions hadn't revealed everything, and that gave them an element of surprise The Elders wouldn't expect. There *was* still a chance he could get Cassie out of here. He didn't kid himself into thinking he could get them *all* out of here.

Shifting his arm behind him, his fingers entangled with hers. He allowed himself to take pleasure in the feel of her skin against his and the peace she brought to him. The beast inside was too focused on the upcoming battle, and the necessity to keep her alive to allow himself to drift into her too much. The man was terrified he would lose her, and could barely bring himself to release her hand. His fingertips lingered against hers before he let her go.

Bile and hatred rose up in crushing waves as he focused on his brother. They had never gotten along in life; in death it had been even worse. Robert had come here specifically to take Cassie from him, he was certain of it. But it wasn't Robert who Devon was looking for right now, and Robert knew that, as did the others.

Then he saw them, shadows emerging from the woods, but not all of them came forward. It didn't matter though; they were close enough now he could feel the edges of their minds. Close enough to seize them. He drew on Cassie's blood, and his Elder strength and powers. He subtly shoved forward with his mind, careful not to make waves that Adon could pick up on and alert the others to.

Slipping around their barriers, he slithered as stealthily as a snake in the grass to seize hold of two of their minds. Taking control, he twisted them to his will so smoothly their facial expressions didn't even flicker, their eyes never even moved. With subtle coercion, he instructed them to remain the same, to continue to act as they normally would.

He didn't need them now, but he would soon, and when the time came they would have no choice but to join his side and help him protect Cassie. With just one of the minds he could bend the most powerful amongst The Elder's to his will. He seized the other mind only as a precaution, but it was a precaution he wasn't willing to let go of.

With firm control over that *one* mind, Devon turned toward Zane, the man who had been a mentor of sorts to him. A mentor filled with nothing but hatred, vengeance, and bloodlust, and at one time Devon had relished it all. Devon had spent a fair amount of time with Zane many years ago, but unlike Julian, they'd never grown to like each other. They had *never* been friends. The two of them had simply learned from each other and savored in the ability of the other to one up each other in savagery. Devon hadn't seen Zane in nearly four hundred years, but his capability for cruelty and torture was still fresh in Devon's mind.

Anger and hatred blazed through Devon at the thought of what Zane would do to Cassie if he got his hands on her. He would make her time with Patrick beneath the school look like a vacation. Zane would torture her until there was nothing left of her, bleed her almost to death before bringing her back to do it over and over again. He would make sure she stayed alive for years in order to continue doing so.

Devon gazed upon Zane, the oldest Elder, and the one who ran the show. The one who mistakenly believed he still possessed more power than Devon. A small, cruel smile curved Zane's mouth as he turned his gaze from Devon to Cassie.

"Delicious," Zane purred.

Devon squashed her more firmly between him and Julian. Between the two of them, Zane would never get at her. Hopefully.

CHAPTER SEVENTEEN

CASSIE COULD BARELY BREATHE against the two rigid bodies pressed against her. But then she thought she wouldn't be able to breathe anyway. She was no dummy; she knew who these people were, knew what they represented. She knew what they had come here for, and what they would do to all of them. Devon and Julian may be Elders, and there may be two other vampires, four Hunters, and a Guardian present, but she knew they wouldn't be a match against eight Elders.

They were no match against eight of the monsters that had killed her parents. Hatred tore through her; she trembled with the ferocity of it. Ever since she'd learned the truth of what she was, and that The Elder's had organized a large group of vampires to destroy the Hunter line, she'd craved revenge. Now was finally her chance, but there were so many of them, and they were *so* powerful. At least they would be able to take a few of them out, because *she* would be sure to do so, before they were completely overrun.

"Delicious."

Cassie's eyes narrowed on the one who had uttered the word with such reverence. She studied the man carefully. He radiated power and maliciousness even more so than the others. He also sported a bit of a tan. She recalled Devon telling her that he'd known one other vampire who could walk about in the sun; this was most definitely *that* man.

His eyes were an ochre brown, so light they appeared almost golden in the moonlight, like honey. His dark blond hair was streaked with natural paler blond highlights. He looked like a Californian golden boy with his wavy hair falling over his forehead and his clean cut good looks. He wasn't as tall as the other men about him, but he bore an aura of power that made him appear larger, more formidable, and intimidating.

"Zane," Devon murmured his beautiful eyes hooded and dark as he stared severely at the other man.

Zane, somehow that name fit the man perfectly. He appeared a little older than Devon, as if he had been turned in his mid to late twenties, maybe even early thirties instead. Not like it mattered when they had been turned, they were all over five hundred years old now.

Devon's gaze was drawn toward the others as they shifted amongst the shadows. They moved together like one eerily smooth, flowing unit. They had been together for so many years, they didn't have to speak in order to communicate with each other, but simply picked up on the others motions and movements. Cassie's skin began to crawl, but she would *not* give them the satisfaction of knowing they had unnerved her. Cassie met their gazes, refusing to back down from their ravenous, nerve racking stares.

"Devon." Zane's full mouth curved into a half smile and his fangs flashed in the dim moonlight. Cassie briefly wondered where all the Halflings had disappeared to; they almost would have been handy to have around right now. She had a feeling they would go after this crew with a vengeance.

A cool breeze drifted through the trees, the clicking of their skeletal branches was spine-chilling in the oddly hushed night. No one moved as each group sized the other up. "Sleeping with the enemy?" Zane inquired.

Devon's muscles rippled as he bristled with anger. "You know I won't let you near her."

"Then we have a problem," Zane said. "Their kind kills ours. Their kind was never meant to walk this earth; they're an abomination that should have been eliminated years ago. It is only fate and misfortune that spared a small percentage of them." Zane's head tilted to the side as he studied her like a bug. "We cannot continue to allow these creatures to roam the earth."

Cassie's breath froze in her lungs. Julian's hand brushed reassuringly against her waist. "It doesn't matter what you want Zane. It never has, not to me, not to *us*, in case you have forgotten. You never ruled over us."

A red flash briefly encircled Zane's honey eyes. "You think you're all grown up, but you forget you're playing with the big boys again now."

"You think there aren't enough of us to take you down, Zane?"

Zane's gaze slid disdainfully over everyone. "No."

Cassie's pride prickled, her shoulders straightened. She went to step out from around Devon, but Julian grabbed her shoulder and held her firmly in place. "Stay," he commanded in a low voice.

She turned to glare at him, but he wouldn't meet her gaze as he remained focused upon the strangers still half hidden within the shadows of the forest. "You know there is a good chance I can take *you*, and we will take at least some of you with us. Are you willing to risk losing a few of your cronies?" Devon demanded.

Zane's mouth quirked in a small smile. "Temper, temper Devon, you never learn. You would think a half a millennium might have tempered that tendency a little. It will get you killed one day."

Cassie bristled over his words. No one was going to take Devon from her. *No one.* "What do you want, Zane?" Julian inquired.

"I would like them all dead, like they deserve to be, but we are not here to fight you. Not unless or until, it becomes necessary." Zane's gaze came back to Cassie, his head tilted to the side as he studied her carefully. "Without her, there is no you."

Devon's hand snaked back; he seized hold of her arm so fast she didn't see him until he had already grasped her. She blinked at his broad back, the only thing she could see now that her nose was smashed against him. "You'll never touch her!" His tone was so vicious, the hairs on Cassie's neck stood up at the same time her blood turned to ice.

A trembling took hold of her. She wasn't frightened for herself, or even for her friends right now, she was scared Devon would crack and do something reckless. "Devon," she whispered. Her fingers curled into his shirt as if that would stop him from attacking Zane.

His only acknowledgement of her was a small tensing upon her arm. "Easy Devon," another murmured from the shadows. "Though Zane is not making it clear, we are not here for that."

Cassie turned toward the man who had spoken. She could only imagine what people had thought about him back in his human lifetime as this man was *massive*! He stood over six and a half feet tall, with shoulders so broad they blocked out the trees behind him. His legs were the size of full grown tree trunks, his arms nearly as big.

His unruly brown hair curled around his broad, heavily bearded face. Though his hair was brown, his beard was red. His eyes were some strange mixture of his hair and beard, a deep brownish red that shone in the moon. Those eyes looked almost kind and impish. Though she knew what he was, and what his presence here meant, she couldn't envision him being cruel. If that hair and beard ever went gray, and despite his massive size, she could easily picture children sitting on his lap telling him what they would like for Christmas.

"Then what are you here for?" Devon demanded.

The giant of a man glanced at Zane disapprovingly. "To make sure the Halflings within this town do not escape, and they do not become known to the rest of the world. They'll endanger us all if they do."

"We are also here for the girl," Zane interjected as he shot the giant a dark look. Cassie's fingers dug into Devon's shirt, but she knew she couldn't stop him if he went after them.

"Zane!" the giant said brusquely.

"Enough Bernard," Zane ordered briskly. "Devon must know the whole reason why we are here, and what must be done."

Devon's one hand fisted, and though he still held her arm, she was able to twist herself away from his back. His eyes were a fiery red as he glanced toward her while trying to push her behind him again. Before Devon could successfully shove her aside, she managed to turn and meet Zane's amused expression head on.

"And what must be done?" she demanded.

He grinned at her. "You must be changed, of course."

Cassie's breath exploded out of her; she nearly fell over as her legs went weak. The quiet that followed was so profound she could hear one of the few rabbits left in the woods scurry back into its hole. Even Devon, who had seemed so close to the edge, remained paralyzed by the words Zane had just issued.

Cassie was the first to recover enough to respond. "Ok."

Whereas Zane's words had stunned everyone into silence, her single word caused an explosion of reaction so intense she almost covered her ears to block out their protests. The only ones who didn't start shouting their disapproval were Julian and Devon. They remained wordless as they stared at her like she were some alien from the Planet Jupiter.

The Elders watched as everyone who had been standing near the store completely forgot about The Elders and stalked forward. Their voices jumbled loudly together in their urge to be heard over everyone else. The only one who held back was Luther. His gray eyes were sad; the expression he wore was resolved.

Cassie couldn't tear her eyes away from his. She couldn't look away from the man who had been like a father to her for the past four years. He looked as if he'd lost her, or was terrified he was about to. Cassie knew what her decision meant, knew what the consequences of it could be, but she didn't care.

She had always known they would come to a crossroad, that one day the choice would be forced upon them. Lately she'd begun to think it would happen because Devon couldn't control himself and took her by force. If that happened he would always hate himself, even if she did come through the transformation unscathed. But if the choice was taken from them, if they were *forced* into it, then he couldn't blame himself and the instability he'd been living with would be eased.

It would be ok, *she* would be ok. She firmly believed that, no matter what anyone else said. She had survived far worse, and she was still intact. She *would* make it through this.

"It is settled then," Zane declared. He folded his hands before him as his eyes gleamed with approval.

"No, it isn't!" Devon exploded.

Cassie flinched from his flash of anger, but she didn't back down from it. "Devon…"

"This will *not* happen!" he interrupted fiercely.

"This *will* happen!" she retorted. "It *has* to happen Devon. It finally *has* to happen. The choice has been taken from us. We can do this, I *can* survive this."

His black hair fell across his forehead in a tumbled mess as he shook his head. "No, I will not take the chance…"

"The chance you will snap and do it by force. The chance I'll be killed and it will destroy you anyway? The chance I'll just grow old and die? What chance are you unwilling to take, Devon?"

"The chance I will turn you into a monster!" he shouted.

Cassie's heart broke, pieces of it scattered about her feet. She understood his anguish, but he didn't understand this must be done now. She turned toward Zane, hating the smug look on his face. "If this happens, will you leave us all alone?"

"Of course," he purred.

"You can't trust him, Cassie," Devon told her.

She knew that, she wasn't a fool. She also knew The Elders would need them as much as they needed The Elders, if they were going to take down the Halflings. No matter how powerful The Elder's thought they were, they would not *all* survive the creatures in this town. They would lose a few of their own in the process, and that was a chance Cassie didn't think they were willing to take.

"I know that," she whispered. "But we can't trust you anymore either." Devon looked as if she'd slapped him. She hated to hurt him by driving the knife deeper in order to get her own way, but it had to be done. He had to realize this was the end of the road, there was nowhere else for them to go. "You can't keep taking off whenever you feel yourself unraveling. I need you Devon, and if this continues on, I *am* going to lose you."

His eyes flickered, but she saw an easing in his features. "Cassie..."

"There is no choice, the decision has been made," Zane said firmly. "She will join us."

Cassie shot Zane a brutal look as resentment flitted over Devon's features. She'd just been starting to get through to him, but now she could feel his stubborn streak surging to life to deny Zane's words. She wanted to tell him she would *never* be on their side, but she bit her tongue.

"Wait..."

"There are details to iron out of course," Zane continued over Devon's protest. "We will have to make a decision on what will happen to her if the change is not successful. We also must discuss what our relationship amongst each other will be when this is done. There must be a truce struck."

"I will not let this happen," Devon grated.

"If it does not happen we will fight, because she cannot remain the way she is. We cannot allow a Hunter to exist who can turn into a monster. Apparently her kind used to have the decency to take care of them, but that doesn't happen now."

"Zane," Devon hissed.

"Why would you want to change me, and not kill me?" Cassie ignored Devon's censuring look.

Zane's head tilted back and forth like an owl scoping its' prey as he studied her. Though she was a trembling mass of nerves inside, she kept her shoulders thrust back and her chin lifted defiantly. "A battle would be fun, but some of us would unfortunately be lost in the process. You also know *most* of you will not survive. Is that a chance you're willing to take?"

"No," Cassie answered when Devon remained quiet and brooding. "No, but you must promise you will not hurt them."

"Of course I won't," Zane murmured.

"Cassie," Chris whispered.

She disliked the sadness and resignation in his eyes. "It will be ok," she promised.

"Their promises mean nothing," Julian informed her in a low, disgruntled voice. "Nothing, Princess, do you understand that?"

She swallowed heavily before nodding. "Do we have a choice?"

"We have a choice," Devon told her.

"Do we?" she whispered as her hand entwined with his. "Do we?"

Devon pulled her against him. His hands wrapped around her face and his lips descended upon hers. She could feel his fangs against her lips, but she didn't care as his tongue plummeted into her mouth with a desperation that left her breathless and shaken. Melting against him, she forgot about every rotten, evil thing surrounding them.

She needed this moment and this man, no matter how short lived it may be. He pulled away and kissed her lips, nose, and finally her forehead. "It will be ok," she vowed.

His eyes were emerald once more as he met her gaze. His fingers stroked her face before he bent to kiss her once more. He didn't turn to look at the others before speaking again. "We will go inside and discuss this," he said bluntly.

"Magnificent!" Zane announced happily.

Cassie closed her eyes against Zane's joy; she knew her time as a human was running short, but she wasn't terrified by the prospect. Not if it meant spending eternity with the one person she loved most in her life.

Anger flashed across Devon's gorgeous features, but he took hold of her hand and turned toward the store. His gaze briefly met Julian's, who hung back, waiting for The Elders to come forward. Cassie held her head high as Devon led her past the others, but she could feel the sadness radiating from them.

CHAPTER EIGHTEEN

Devon was braced for an attack but he kept his posture as casual as possible. He had tried to keep Cassie behind him but she refused to stay there and instead stood by his side. He could sense her curiosity, her questions, especially about his brother, but she didn't ask them.

His brother was a man he had cared for a little, but had never been close to in life. He had grown to despise Robert in death. Robert stared back at Devon, an amused quirk to his mouth as he leaned against the wall with his arms folded over his chest. Every once in a while, Robert's gaze would wander to Cassie and stay far too long for Devon's liking.

It didn't matter what Zane said, they were not here for a tenuous truce. If they had come here looking for a truce, they would have left Robert behind, no matter how many reinforcements they felt they may require. They all knew what Robert desired more than anything was to see Devon miserable, not dead because that would be too quick, but completely destroyed.

Julian's shoulder brushed against Cassie's; his lip curled into a sneer as he glared at Robert. A fierce amount of hostility radiated between Robert and Devon; there was even more between Robert and Julian. Especially since Robert had once tried to kill Julian, and would have succeeded if Devon hadn't intervened. That had been the last time Devon had seen Robert, and he thought it had been the last time Julian had too.

Devon had left his brother broken and bleeding, and near death. He'd been brutal and ruthless at the time, had savored in the blood and the power, but he'd been unable to bring himself to kill his own brother. He regretted that decision now. Cassie tilted her chin as she glared back at Robert.

Robert broke into a grin and his eyebrows wiggled suggestively as he tilted his head to the side. "You know I was always the better looking, more sought after brother. You could always switch; many a woman has."

Devon's hands fisted as he fought the urge to punch the smug look off of Robert's face, but he knew Robert wanted that. "They obviously lied to you," Cassie retorted.

Robert's grin widened. "I would enjoy draining you dry."

"I'd like to see you try."

"Cassie," Julian warned.

Devon remained quiet and unmoving. He wanted Cassie to stop baiting Robert, yet he hoped Robert would rush him and give him the excuse he so eagerly sought to kill him. "Enough," Zane held up a hand as Robert stepped forward. "She *will* be one of us."

"Why are you so determined about that?" Cassie inquired.

"To join forces of course. Hunters and Vampires have fought for over a thousand years; it is time to end that war. If you are both a Hunter and a vampire we can guarantee this batch behind you will stay clear of us."

Cassie glanced behind her as her mouth pursed. "You killed our parents."

"Bygones," Zane replied flippantly.

Cassie's head snapped back around; her eyes narrowed. Devon braced himself as her fury beat against him. He didn't want them to see what she could be capable of, didn't want them to see what was inside of her. Not now anyway, he didn't need them to attack right now, and he feared they would if they realized just how much power she possessed. "Bygones!" she retorted. "They were our parents you son of a bitch!"

Devon took a defensive step forward. Zane was not one to mess with, but instead of becoming irritated, true amusement lit Zane's eyes. "She's a feisty one, I like it."

"You don't know how feisty I can be!" she spat back at him.

"Cassie," Devon cautioned. "Enough."

She glared up at him. Folding her arms over her chest, she focused her hate filled look on Zane again. Her foot tapped on the floor, but for once she held her tongue. "The change will occur tonight."

"No." Devon's shoulders slumped as he turned back to Cassie.

"What do you mean *no*?" Zane demanded as his amusement vanished. "This *will* be done."

"Yes, it will," Cassie agreed. "But not tonight, not until these creatures have been taken care of. You will need Devon and me in this fight, if something goes wrong with the change you won't have either of us. You and Devon are the only other vampires here who can walk about in the daylight, and we know that some of the Halflings can too."

Zane was thoughtful as he pondered Cassie's words. "And how do you know I share Devon's ability?"

Cassie rolled her eyes. "You're the only other one sporting a tan."

Amusement returned to Zane's features. Devon wasn't fooled though, Zane may be entertained and impressed by Cassie, but Devon knew Zane would still kill her in a heartbeat. "Very true my dear. The change will wait until this ordeal is over, but the moment it is over the change *will* occur, even if I have to do it myself."

Devon's lip curled in a sneer. He may not agree with this, but no one else was *ever* going to touch her. "That won't happen," Devon told him.

"Then make sure the change does occur," Zane informed him coldly.

"I'm not one of your little followers Zane, I never have been." His gaze raked disdainfully over the people gathered around him. "Do *not* think you have any control over me."

"But I do," Zane replied. "You will do anything not to have her hurt, in any way. If you insist upon pushing this into a fight you both may survive it, but not everyone will. You wouldn't like her heart to be broken would you?"

Frustration filled him; he would love nothing more than to beat the smug look from Zane's face. Cassie touched his arm as she sought to soothe him. "How do we know we can trust you not to turn on us anyway?" she inquired.

"How do we know we can trust you not to turn on us once the change is complete?"

She glanced nervously around before her gaze settled on Devon, seeking help. "You don't."

"And neither do you."

"You could allow Julian to touch you," Devon suggested. "To learn the truth."

"Then you would know the truth, and we wouldn't, that would put us at a disadvantage," Zane responded.

Devon glanced toward Julian. His jaw was set, his hands fisted. His eyes burned with his desire to grasp hold of one of them and learn the truth, but he remained restrained and unmoving. "Bernard can tell if we are lying to you or not," Devon answered.

Bernard glanced over them, his gaze briefly settled on Chris before he nodded his agreement. "Yes, the boy will not block my ability, he is not strong enough."

"Excuse me?" Chris inquired harshly.

Bernard turned away, apparently deciding Chris wasn't worth talking to. Chris continued to glare at the massive giant of a man. "Bernard's ability is the same as yours; he can sense people's emotions and what they are truly like inside. He will know if we are lying," Annabelle told Chris.

Chris looked even more exasperated and insulted by this response. Unfortunately though, it was the truth. Bernard was far more powerful than him, and if they weren't facing off against each other, Chris wouldn't block his power. It would be a brutal battle between the groups, but the outcome would more than likely favor The Elders. Zane didn't want to lose any of his group, but Devon still didn't understand why they would be willing to back down, or choose for Cassie to be changed.

"Then you will allow Julian to touch you," Devon commanded.

Zane's eyes flickered with hostility and resentment. He didn't like being ordered around, it was why Devon had made it more of a command than a question. He preferred Zane rattled and irritated, it may let some of his defenses drop enough for Julian to slip in.

"Fine," Zane finally relented.

Julian's fangs flashed as he was given reign to set his powers free. Devon seized hold of Julian's arm before he went any further. He expected for Julian to grab hold of Zane and see what he could learn from him. But Devon knew there was a possibility Zane had become powerful enough to keep Julian blocked from anything he didn't want him to know.

Holding Julian, he tried to make sure Julian understood there was someone else he had to touch. Someone Devon now controlled, and who would be unable to keep anything from Julian while under Devon's command. Julian's eyes filled with amusement and admiration gleamed in his gaze. Devon was starkly reminded of how things used to be between them, how close they had been, how devious and cruel they had both been at one time in their lives.

He was reminded of the fun they had once shared, not only while killing and hunting for women, but also just with each other. They had been closer than brothers, far closer than Devon and Robert had ever been, and that was one of the reasons Robert hated Julian so much. A twinge tugged at Devon's heart; he actually found himself wishing they could share that bond again. Julian's eyes glimmered briefly, something slipped across his features as he sensed Devon's change of thought.

"I would like to know why they want her to change so badly too," Devon said aloud to explain his halting of Julian to The Elder's.

Julian's gaze slid to Cassie, longing bloomed briefly in his iced eyes. Then, to Devon's complete and utter surprise, he grasped hold of Devon's arm with his free hand, squeezed it, and nodded to him. Julian didn't say the words, but Devon knew he'd just released any resentment toward him. He had his friend again, and he could rely upon Julian once more.

Cassie turned toward him as Julian strode across the room.

Tears glimmered in her eyes as she slid her hand into Devon's and squeezed it reassuringly. He studied her, amazed by her strength and beauty. Touched by her unwavering love and understanding, no matter what he kept from her or did to her. She was too good for him; she deserved better than this life.

One day he would make this up to her. When this was over, he vowed he would give her everything she deserved, and more. His hand tensed around hers as he clasped it within both of his.

Julian grinned savagely as he stopped before the oldest Elder. They were the golden boys of The Elders, both fair and stunning with disarming good looks, but the similarities between them ended there. Zane was refined, elegant, and thin with expensive clothes and even more expensive tastes. There was never a hair out of place, never a speck of dirt upon him. Julian was unruly, preferred beer to champagne, had never worn anything more expensive than cotton, and was never happier than when he was rolling around in the dirt getting drunk and causing a raucous. Their completely different personalities were only some of the reasons they hated each other. One of the main reasons being that like Devon, Julian had never fallen into line with the rest of The Elders. He disdained their way of life, much preferring to be out in the world, reveling in it, instead of hiding and slinking through the shadows.

Zane had never allowed Julian to touch him before; he had gone out of his way to avoid it every time they'd met. From the look on his face, he wouldn't allow it now if he had a choice. "This is to be quick. You get one brief chance to find what you are looking for and that is all," Zane sneered.

Julian's mouth quirked as distaste flashed through his eyes. "Don't be afraid Zane, it doesn't hurt. Much." Julian taunted.

Anger sparked from Zane, but before he could retort or react, Julian grasped hold of his arm. Zane jerked back instantly as his arm flew up to knock Julian's hand aside. "Thanks for the insight," Julian murmured.

Zane's eyes flooded red, his jaw clenched, but he didn't swing at Julian. Julian moved down the line of Elders examining each one of them before stopping before Adon. Though Adon had one of the strongest abilities, he was also one of the two younger than Julian, and therefore unable to resist Julian's probing. He was also under Devon's firm control.

Before anyone could stop him, Julian seized hold of Adon's hand. No one moved. Everyone remained frozen until Devon instructed Adon to react as he normally would have. Adon jerked his hand free of Julian's grasp and delivered such a speedy round house that Julian didn't have time to dodge it. His teeth clattered loudly together as blood exploded from his inner cheek and sprayed across the floor.

Releasing Cassie, Devon jumped forward. Julian wiped the blood from his mouth with his sleeve, but he didn't attack Adon. "That's one, you won't get another," Julian promised him.

Adon glared at him with his hands fisted at his side. Devon didn't tell Adon to back down, he couldn't. Adon had to appear normal; they couldn't suspect Devon now had complete control over one of their own. "No Adon," Zane said. "We are not here for that."

Adon remained unmoving, his slender five foot four frame as taut as a bowstring. Aside from Annabelle, he was the smallest person in the room, and had what was now commonly referred to as little man syndrome. His temper was infamous and fiery, but it had supposedly been in check ever since he'd nearly been lynched by a mob two hundred years ago. The humans had discovered what he was after he'd gone on a drunken rampage in a tavern. It was only the interference of Zane, and Robert, that had kept Adon alive.

Devon was amazed Adon had survived so many years, but he supposed living away from society for extended periods of time had probably attributed to that. Although Adon looked as if he still considered pouncing on Julian, his eyes returned to their dark mocha color as he took a step back. His dark hair fell across his cheek. Adon was of Greek ancestry, but years spent out of the sun had faded his olive complexion.

Julian turned away and nearly bumped into Devon. "Wasn't expecting that," he muttered as he wiped away the remaining blood trickling down his lip.

"Nor I."

"Did you find out what you wanted to know?" Zane demanded, obviously irritated with the situation.

"I think we can trust them," Julian told him. "They don't like this union, but they are accepting of it because they feel Cassie will be a powerful ally, an asset."

"Asset?" Cassie inquired sharply.

Devon disliked the rebellious fire in her eyes. "The Elders," Julian said disdainfully. "Mistakenly believe *every* vampire created belongs to them, and is meant to do their bidding, and to serve them. They think they will have ultimate power over you."

Zane smiled coldly at Julian. "We may not control you, but we do have ultimate power over you. We all serve the same purpose; we all want to keep our own kind safe. Cassie will be a great aid in that."

"And if things go wrong?" Cassie demanded.

"Everyone in this room knows you will have to be dealt with if it comes to that."

Cassie's eyes were hopeless and lost. Devon ached for her, but he couldn't disagree with Zane's statement. If something went wrong, they would have to both be destroyed.

"Every one of your *friends* is to agree to this arrangement, aloud and separately so Bernard can read them. If there is no agreement, and if he feels any kind of betrayal or lie from you, there will be consequences."

Panic flickered through Cassie's eyes, but before she could protest, Julian seized hold of her arm and bent low to her ear. Though Devon couldn't hear what he said, Cassie's mouth clamped shut. Around the room people began to respond. Julian continued to hold her arm as Cassie bent her head and listened to everyone's yeses. Devon remained a few feet from them, his eyes focused on Bernard as he read each response and nodded afterward.

Chris's silence was profound within the crowded room. Cassie finally lifted her head and turned to look at her best friend. "Chris?"

"I agree with the change, but I will not help to destroy you." His gaze flickered to Devon. "Either of you."

Devon tilted his head as he studied the boy who had come to be his friend. "Understandable," Devon said.

The scent of Cassie's tears was acute in the room as she hurried to Chris and enveloped him in a hug. "Odd," Zane murmured.

Devon despised the tone of his voice. "What is?"

"I would never allow Anastasia to hug another man."

"No dear, you allow me to do so much more," Anastasia purred as she licked her lips eagerly. The last time Devon had seen her, her black hair had been floor length. It was now cut into a sleek bob just beneath her ears that showed off her refined, aristocratic features. Her dark blue eyes stood out starkly against the pallor of her skin, and the midnight of her hair. "Because I love it when you catch me."

Devon's stomach twisted in disgust. The two of them had been together for over four hundred years. Their love was strong, turbulent, and completely sick and twisted. They did things to each other, and other people, that had repulsed him even when he'd been at his absolute worst. There had been a time when he'd thought what they shared was the only kind of love a vampire could have. A time when he believed if he *did* find a mate, their relationship would be exactly like Zane and Anastasia's. He was thankful he'd been completely wrong. Their relationship was twisted and dark, because *they* were twisted and dark.

He glanced behind him to make sure Cassie wasn't watching; he didn't want her to witness this sick exchange. She was still hugging Chris, Luther and Melissa had joined them; they spoke quietly as they clung to each other.

"What is your assessment Bernard?" Julian inquired obviously just as sickened by the exchange as Devon was.

"They tell the truth," Bernard stated. "They may not like this arrangement, but they will agree with it. If we do not betray them, they will not betray us."

"Wonderful," Zane said as he clasped his hands before him. "Now we must decide how to proceed with these creatures, but that can wait till tomorrow. We are all tired, it was a lengthy trip."

"You will *not* be staying here," Devon told him when Zane looked around the room.

"Oh?"

Devon folded his arms over his chest as he faced off against the lead Elder. "We may have a tenuous truce, but we will not pretend to like or respect each other. You will *not* be staying here."

"But we must discuss plans."

"Tomorrow."

"Hmm," Zane nodded. "I suppose you are correct, we should not push our boundaries."

"No, you should not."

"Where is safe around here?" Octavia inquired. Her liquid brown eyes were rapt as she studied Devon with distaste. She had once tried to pursue him, but he'd spurned her advances as she'd also been with his brother at the time. Devon wanted nothing to do with anything Robert had touched, ever. Octavia was not a pretty girl in the classical sense, but she was one of the most sensual, curvaceous women he'd ever seen. She was also one of the cruelest and most vindictive.

"The bank has a safe; you will be fine inside there. No sunlight will get in, and there is a way to let yourselves out from the inside," Devon told them.

He could feel Cassie's gaze upon his back, but he didn't turn to look at her. He wasn't going to tell her he'd attempted to lock himself in there in order to stay away from her. The discovery of the release handle inside had prevented him from being successful however. "And what will we do if they come for us during the day?" Octavia asked.

"They will not," Matthew answered. "The battle does not begin today."

Everyone focused their attention upon the slender man with his hands folded peacefully before him. His shock of orange hair puffed out around his face in unruly wisps. The orange freckles spattered across his face stood out against the deathly pallor of his skin. Matthew had been fair in life, but in death it seemed all of the color had drained from his body, and into his orange freckles and hair to make them stand out far more vibrantly than they had before. Though the rest of his features were perfect, sculpted even, the orange color around his head completely detracted from them.

"When *will* it begin?" Julian inquired.

Matthew shrugged his slender shoulders and unfolded his hands as he spread them wide. "Your guess is as good as mine; you know my visions do not reveal everything. Just as I do not know who will win, or what her change will bring. There are some things the world keeps me in the dark about. These are a few of those things. Though perhaps, if I was allowed to touch the girl…"

"Absolutely not!" Devon interrupted harshly. Matthew would take too much pleasure in being allowed to touch Cassie, and Devon would be *damned* if he let any of them get close enough to touch her.

"Well, then," Matthew continued in his melodic voice. "We will have to remain in the dark about those things, unless the young seer has anything to tell us." Melissa shook her head in response to the inquisitive looks cast her way. "It is best to have some secrets in one's future anyway, makes life all the more exciting."

The last time Devon had seen Matthew, he'd suspected the man was losing his mind. But now, listening to the cadences and nuances within his tone, Devon was certain of it. He didn't know what had finally driven Matthew over the edge, whether it was his numerous visions, his knowledge of things that weren't supposed to be known, or his unending cruelty and malicious-ness. Whatever had caused it, it now appeared Matthew had more than just a few screws loose, but a few hundred of them.

"But the battle will come to us during the night, not during the day," Matthew continued.

Julian shook his head. "I guess they aren't as smart as we were giving them credit for."

"And why do you say that?" Matthew's brown eyes were inquisitive.

Julian seemed unable to figure out the strange creature across from him as he studied him. "Because they would know to attack during the day, when we are far more vulnerable."

"Perhaps they are too; perhaps though they can walk about in the day, they prefer the darkness of the night to hide the evil inside them. Perhaps they feel it best not to expose themselves to the good of the sun's rays as they feel undeserving of it. That is the way it was always intended. In return for immortal life, we are denied the pleasure and warmth of the sun's rays, it is the way things are supposed to be. Then the abnormalities rose up amongst us to taint this earth with their presence during the day."

Devon lifted an eyebrow. Yep, Matthew had finally flipped his nut, and apparently he wasn't as enamored with Zane as he'd once been. Now it seemed Zane was an abnormality tainting the earth and so was Devon. Julian cast Devon a sideways glance.

"If our kind were meant to walk amongst the light, then we would not burn upon entering it. Their kind, even the ones who roam the day, may still feel the sting of redemption upon their skin. As they should. For us to not feel the sting of the warmth is a disgrace, an affront…"

"Enough Matthew!" Zane spat.

Though Matthew grew quiet, the tick in his jaw indicated he'd had more to say. Julian circled his finger beside his temple and mouthed the word, *cuckoo*. Devon nodded his agreement. They both received dark looks from Zane, but Matthew seemed oblivious to them as he piously refolded his hands before him.

"We'll see you at nightfall then," Elspet said.

Devon's eyes were drawn to the slender girl standing behind the other Elders. She was the youngest amongst them at barely over five hundred years old. Devon had met her a few times many years ago, after she'd first been changed. It wasn't until recently, when she'd attained the prime age of five hundred she'd been drawn into the ranks of The Elders. When Devon had known her, she'd been a pretty girl with delicate features and fine brown hair flowing down to her shoulder blades. She'd worn simple dresses and stayed mostly in the background. She hadn't displayed overt acts of cruelty, but had simply fed when the need struck her. At the time he'd thought her lack of cruelty would eventually get her killed. He'd never imagined she would be an Elder, let alone fit in with the elite group she was now a part of.

The girl before him now was nothing like the girl he'd known. She had shaved her head, and on one side had a beautiful angel tattooed on her skull, on the other side was a snarling devil with blood dripping from its mouth and its claws curved over. Her lip, eyebrow, and nose had been pierced, and she sported metal all the way up both sides of her ears. She was dressed all in black spandex that hugged her lithe figure. Though he couldn't see the tattoos on her arms, he could see the tail ends of them curling around her hands and wrists.

Devon held her gaze as he nodded briskly. He would have agreed to almost anything to get them out of this store, and as far away from Cassie as possible, for now. They said nothing more as they filed out of the store. He was a little amazed they were actually leaving. He was even more amazed they were hiding Matthew amongst them, when he'd obviously lost his mind. Though Devon had never met an off the rocker vampire, he couldn't imagine they would be much fun to deal with, or keep under control.

"Does Matthew think he's a freaking preacher or something now?" Julian demanded when they disappeared into the night.

Devon shook his head as he ran his fingers wearily through his hair. "He thinks he's something now."

"They only keep him alive for his visions," Julian told him. At Devon's questioning look he elaborated. "I saw it through Adon, Matthew has been crazy for a while now, but Zane needs him."

"What made him that way?" Melissa was pale; her hands folded before her as she twisted them nervously.

Julian shrugged as he shoved his hands in his pockets. "Some people are just not cut out for this lifestyle, no matter what. Matthew was always a little off. You mix that with Zane's constant torture and mental abuse, and apparently it made him crack. Matthew was Zane's puppet, his play thing, and he has broken him. But he still likes to pull his strings once in a while."

They all gaped at him, horrified by his description of what Zane had done to Matthew. "It is not the worst thing Zane has ever done," Julian murmured.

Devon wished Julian would stop talking. "Can we really trust them?" Luther inquired.

Julian nodded as he folded his arms over his chest. "Yes. They will abide by this truce because it suits their needs. I can't guarantee they will stick to it if Cassie doesn't survive the change, and we lose Devon. They will have no need for you then. I can't guarantee any of us will survive if such a thing happens."

Devon ignored their curious stares; he was determined not to think about that right now. He held his hand out to Cassie; relief filled him when she clasped hold of it. Her hand was warm and reassuring as she squeezed his. He bent to brush his lips across her forehead.

CHAPTER NINETEEN

CASSIE WATCHED Devon make the bed with startling speed and agility. Robert had been wrong when he'd said he was the better looking brother, he had been very wrong. Devon fluffed up the sleeping bags, before unrolling them on the floor. Cassie realized he was stalling as he set everything up, biding for time before facing her.

There were a million questions she had, the foremost of which concerned his brother. She knew there were things he tried to keep her sheltered from, and she understood that. But unfortunately, some of those things had walked into their lives today and thrown them even more upside down. However the questions could wait, right now all she desired was Devon.

He finished fluffing the blankets/pillows. She could tell he was looking for something else to do, some other way to stall, but unless he planned on fluffing the down right out of the blankets there was nothing left for him to do. His shoulders were stiff as he turned toward her, his body braced for the onslaught he suspected was coming. His beautiful emerald eyes were wary as they hesitatingly met hers.

"Are you ok now?" she inquired. "Can you stay around me?"

Guilt and anguish surrounded him as his gaze darted away. "Cassie..."

"It's ok Devon. I understand more than you think I do, but I have to know."

"And why is that?"

Cassie braced herself for rejection as she readied to hand herself over to him completely. "Because I would like to spend the night with you, and I mean *really* spend the night with you."

She fought back the red blush of embarrassment creeping up her cheeks and heating her skin. She couldn't seem childish and insecure right now, she had to sound confident and determined, but she couldn't stop the flush in her face.

She could feel the need radiating from him, but she could also feel his hesitance. "Cassie there is nothing I want more, but not here, not now..."

"Then when?" she interrupted quietly.

"When this is over..."

"We may not survive this."

He recoiled from her words. "I will *not* allow anything to happen to you."

Cassie squeezed her hands in her lap. "I know you will try Devon, but there are some things you can't control. There are some things you cannot stop. No one knows what will happen to me when this change occurs; no one truly knows what the outcome of this battle will be. All we know is we have right now, and I have to know what it is like to be with *you*."

Devon shook his head, but she could feel his defenses crumbling. He glanced around the dusty, cobweb filled attic. Shaking his head he turned back to her as his arm swept around the room. "You deserve better than this, you deserve *so* much more than this."

"It's better than the backseat of a car," she replied, trying to sound airy, but knowing she'd failed miserably. "It doesn't matter *where* Devon, as long as it is with *you*."

His eyes burned into her with an intensity that shook her. "This may be our only night," she continued to push at his weakening defenses. "I'm not going to pass it up because you feel this is not good enough."

"I may hurt you."

"You won't."

Red fire filled his eyes, it startled her but she didn't react. If she did she knew he would shut her down completely. "How can you possibly know that?" he demanded. "After yesterday, after what I wanted to do to you, what I still *want* to do to you, how could you possibly know I won't hurt you?"

"Because you love me," she whispered. "You left so you wouldn't hurt me; you cared nothing for your own safety when you left, only mine."

"I left you unprotected," he said.

"You left me in a building full of fighters, strong ones too. I hardly feel that is unprotected. You were the one who was out there alone, exposed and vulnerable. You are too tough on yourself Devon. You're a good man."

"You have no idea what kind of a man I am, or was. No idea what goes through my mind when it comes to *you*."

Though she knew he was trying to push her away, she didn't back down. "I know *you* Devon. I may not know everything about your past, but I don't have to know it all. There are things I may never know about you, and I accept that because I love *you*! I know who you are. I know what you want from me far more than you think I do, because I want the same things from you."

His eyes were hooded like a snake's as he studied her. Beneath his lowered lids, they shone as clear as rubies in the dim illumination of the room. And then he was on top of her, moving so fast she only caught a blur, before he seized her. His hand wrapped around her neck as he pulled her head to the side. Cassie gasped, her heart leapt as his finger trailed over her frantic pulse.

She could sense the wildness in him, the instability, but she didn't move. She knew if she did he would withdraw from her. He would leave her within this room, alone and lost if she reacted in any way. She didn't care what he did to her, or what he needed from her now, because she would give him anything he asked for. No matter what it was. She knew it was for the best to wait for the change, but if he lost control and it happened now, then she wouldn't regret it, and she wouldn't fight it.

"Right here." His voice was hoarse and grating as his finger stilled upon her vein. She could feel his struggle for restraint battling against his ever present, driving hunger. She remained frozen, her eyes half closed as she fought against the trepidation and excitement tearing through her. He was unstable right now, but he wouldn't hurt her, no matter what he thought. His touch was thrilling, enchanting. Her heart danced, her body quaked with the urge to touch him, but she remained immobile. "Right here is the pulse of your life, and I crave it."

Cassie's eyes closed, she had to fight back the tremble working through her. It was not a tremble of fear, not anymore. Her heart didn't leap in terror, but in anticipation of what was to come. He brushed her hair aside as he pulled her closer. His lips pressed to her throat, his fangs skimmed over her neck before pressing briefly against her throbbing artery. She couldn't stop the low moan of pleasure that escaped her. She waited breath-lessly for him to bite down and take what he wanted from her.

To her surprise, he kissed her softly. His lips pressed against her vein, his fangs receded as he touched upon her neck. Cassie's head spun, her legs quivered as his arms enfolded her and pulled her against him. "You foolish, foolish girl," he breathed in her ear.

Her trembling increased, tears burned her eyes as she melted against him. Maybe she was foolish, but she didn't believe so. No matter what he thought she had absolute faith in him that he would never hurt her. That the man in him would always win out over the demon when it came to her.

The tender kisses he placed across her skin left her completely weak. Her legs gave out when his tongue swirled over her ear. He held her up as her heart leapt as crazily as a bird trapped in a cage. "Cassandra," he whispered. "Are you sure?"

"I've never been so sure of anything in my life," she managed to get out through the constriction in her throat and chest.

He lifted her effortlessly; his hands skimmed under the baggy flannel she wore. His touch upon her bare flesh was almost her undoing. She was trembling as he carried her to the makeshift bed he had created. Laying her down, he followed her as his mouth seized upon hers. Though Cassie had expected his kiss to be desperate, frantic, it was surprisingly gentle and achingly loving.

Her whole body reacted as he leisurely pulled her shirt from her. Cassie's mind swam with pleasure; she forgot everything and everyone else as her entire world became focused upon him, and the joy he brought to her. The beautiful new sensations he created in her, sensations that might have been frightening if they had been with anyone other than him. However, with him, there was only joy and a sense of awe she'd never thought to experience.

All of her concerns and doubts from the past, all of the things that had held her back completely faded away. She never thought of the women of his past, never wondered if he would compare her to them and find her lacking in the end. For she knew now, he would never find her lacking, never cherish anything more than her.

When they finally joined together, she knew true bliss. She knew what it was to belong and fit. She knew nothing of misery and uncertainty as she clung to him, riding out the storm of their love. She didn't know she was crying until he kissed away her tears and whispered words of love as he touched her reverently over and over again.

Later, when she offered him her vein, she knew she'd been right. He never thought about other women with her, and he could *never* find her lacking. For him, when he'd met her, it was as if every other woman had ceased to exist. It wasn't that he didn't think about them, they had simply faded from his mind. He didn't compare her to them because he couldn't recall them. She lacked experience but she'd brought him more joy and pleasure than he'd ever known, or ever thought to experience in his extensive life.

Cassie drifted to sleep, blissfully content within the strong embrace of his arms.

DEVON PADDED DOWN THE STAIRS, trying to be as soundless as possible so as not to waken anyone, especially not Cassie. After what they had just exchanged, he didn't want her to awaken alone, but there was something he had to do. He moved through the empty front of the store. Joey and Patrick had been placed in the back room, untied from their chairs, but retied to some of the wooden beams.

He reached the open cellar door and rapidly moved down the stairs. Julian was standing by one of the windows. The sun wasn't bright enough for him to move away from the glass yet, but it would be soon. Devon knew Julian had retreated here hours ago; before Cassie had offered Devon the greatest gift he'd ever received. He was still awed by her openness and willingness to trust him, especially when he didn't even trust himself. She had far more faith in him than he deserved, far more love and understanding than he had ever thought to receive, and it humbled him. There was nothing he wouldn't do for her; nothing he wouldn't give her.

The faint light filtering through the windows lit Julian's ice blue eyes and warmed them to an almost ocean hue. Julian's face was blank, but his eyes flickered when he scanned Devon quickly. "Is she ok?" he demanded, his voice oddly hoarse.

Devon nodded as his hand clenched on the thin railing of the stairs. Devon had known Julian would be aware of what had passed between them, he still didn't like it. Not only would Julian smell it upon him and Cassie, but a simple touch would reveal all to him. That was why Julian had retreated here when Devon had taken Cassie upstairs. "You knew what she intended."

Julian nodded. "I saw it when I touched her, yes."

"Why didn't you tell me? Why didn't you stop her?"

Julian tilted his head. "Why would I?"

"Because you knew there was a chance I could lose control and hurt her."

"Was there?"

"Julian," Devon growled, not in the mood to deal with his friend's cavalier attitude.

Julian moved away from the window as the rays became too much for him to stand. "I admit I worried for her safety, but she didn't. The amount of faith and trust she has in you is staggering."

"You know what we have done to other human women," Devon whispered. He didn't like to think of those atrocious acts while the glow of what had just happened still surrounded him, but he needed to hear what Julian had to say.

"I may not like to remember, not anymore, but yes I know. However, this was something that she *had* to do, and I couldn't bring myself to stand in her way. I believe she's right. You both needed this night; she *deserved* this night. Her love for you, your love for each other..."

Julian broke off and shook his head as his gaze drifted away. Devon could sense the emotion welling up within him, the hurt, and yet the awe flooding him. "It is staggering Devon. Believe me, if I thought there was any chance you would hurt her, I would have warned you. I would have stopped it, but I *knew* you wouldn't. The demon inside us is strong, but no matter how close you get to snapping, it is always *her* you put first and protect. You may not have faith in yourself, but she does, and I do too."

Devon was staggered by Julian's confession and absolute belief in him, which Devon now realized was just as much as Cassie's. "Julian..." his voice trailed off as Julian turned toward the growing daylight. "You really do love her, don't you?"

Julian turned back to him. "Yes, I do."

"Then how, why...?"

Julian shrugged as he ran a hand through his disordered hair. "You know when you first met Annabelle I understood your obsession for her, understood you loved her because I'd been there once before too. I got it, I really did. I even sort of understood why you stopped feeding from humans because of her. I *never* understood how you could just hand her over to Liam like you did. I thought you were crazy, weak, a complete and utter fool.

"But I understand it now. You loved Annabelle enough to let her go. You loved her enough to realize you didn't love her enough. That you didn't love her the same way she loved Liam and that he loved her. I love Cassie enough to realize the same. I love her enough to know what I feel for her is a pale comparison to what you feel for each other. I would die for her, but I would not die *without* her. I do want her happiness more than I want my own, and you are her happiness."

Devon was staggered by Julian's admission, rattled by the keen insight his friend had developed. "I see."

"I guess I'm the crazy, weak, fool now."

"No, you're simply more of a man than a monster once again."

Julian's eyes sparkled with amusement. "Is that what this feeling is? Humanity?"

Devon laughed as he slid down to sit on the stairs. "It's a bitch," he muttered.

"It is," Julian agreed. He moved over to sit on one of the crates stacked in the basement. "We can't trust them you know. I may not have seen any plan for betrayal in them, but we can't trust them."

"I know."

"Especially not Robert."

Devon's hands clenched as anger shot through him. Julian's hatred toward Robert was apparent in the rigid set of his shoulders. "No matter what the others believe, or what they plan, he *will* try to kill her."

"Yes," Julian agreed.

"I'll kill him first."

Julian's eyes grew distant and thoughtful. "No Devon, if he goes for her, I will take him out. I owe him for the last time we met, but this time I'll be prepared for the battle, and not ambushed."

"Julian…"

"You can't kill your own brother, Devon. Even back then, you were unable to destroy him, though you knew he would kill you in a heartbeat."

"If he goes for her…"

"I will take care of him. I owe it to him."

Devon thought over Julian's words before nodding. Julian was right, Robert would kill him if given the opportunity, but Devon had never been able to kill his brother, until now. But Julian would take great pleasure in destroying Robert, in paying him back for the ambush he'd executed on Julian all those years ago.

"Brother," Devon said on a snort of disgust. Growing up they'd never been anything close to brotherly, but once Robert had been changed, he'd grown to hate Devon more. Devon had never understood his brother's hatred of him. Robert had always been the favored son, the one who had stood in the spotlight while Devon slunk through the shadows hoping to go unnoticed at home. "He must be kept away from her."

"Yes." Folding his legs before him Julian leaned forward. "Are you going to go along with their plan?"

Devon's head slumped as his hands folded before him. "I don't want to condemn her to this life," he whispered.

"It's what she wants."

"I know that, but the consequences…"

"Are something that can be dealt with after. You know this has to be done, Devon, if you fight it they may kill us all."

"What if things go wrong?"

Julian folded his arms across his chest. "We all know that is a possibility, but this is something that *has* to happen Devon. Whether they make it happen or you do it willingly."

"I know."

They sat together as they listened to the odd hush of the deadened town, interrupted only by the small snores or shifting from the sleeping people upstairs. Devon rose slowly; he had to get back to Cassie before she woke. He wanted to hold her and find the solace only she could bring to his tormented soul. Julian's eyes were oddly alight in the warm glow of the sun.

"You will find your Cassie one day," Devon told him.

Julian's mouth quirked, he shrugged as he rose to his feet again. "Maybe, but I'm not going to start looking for her anytime soon."

"I didn't either, but one day she'll just be there." Julian looked as if he was going to argue, but he remained quiet. "You really have changed."

"So have you. I actually like you again."

Devon grinned at him. "Same here, but if you kiss her again I'll rip your throat out."

Julian laughed loudly as he shifted on the crates. "It was a moment of celebration only."

Devon wasn't as amused as Julian about it, but he didn't blame him, Cassie was irresistible, and Julian loved her. He also knew that, to Julian, the kiss had been a way of expressing his love and saying goodbye to her. To Cassie, it had simply been something sweet and celebratory. It had also been a way of sorting her feelings out, of knowing where she belonged, and that was with *him*.

"She told you about it?"

Devon shook his head as he leaned against the thin rail. "I saw it."

Julian's forehead furrowed. "During the blood exchange?"

"Yes."

"I've never opened myself up to another person."

"Neither had I, until her."

Julian's electric eyes were back on him, a small smile curved his mouth. "No, you hadn't."

"I have to get back up there." Julian nodded, but he didn't look back at him. Devon padded up the stairs, leaving his friend to his sorrow, while he returned to his greatest joy. Guilt tugged briefly at him, but he forgot about it as his eyes landed upon Cassandra curled within the blankets. Her golden hair spread around her, and her tiny hands were folded beneath her cheek. She was so astonishingly beautiful, sweet, and loving.

She was so wonderfully his and always would be.

CHAPTER TWENTY

CASSIE BLINKED against the light filtering around the old blanket Devon had hung over the window. Shadows filled the attic, but a small amount of illumination played over the boxes stored there. Devon's arm was wrapped securely around her, his bare chest pressed to her back. A thrill of excitement shot through her as memories of the night came rushing back to her. She hadn't known anything could be so amazing, and she wished they could just stay in this room for the rest of their lives.

But, unfortunately, their lives would allow no such thing to happen.

His hand caressed her arm. "Are you ok?"

Suddenly she felt shy, they had shared something so intimate and special last night, but now she wasn't quite sure how she was supposed to act, or react. Her voice caught in her throat; she couldn't get words out. He rolled her over as he tenderly brushed the hair back from her face. His emerald eyes were troubled as they searched her face.

"Did I hurt you?" he demanded.

Cassie forgot her shyness in the face of his obvious distress. "No, of course not."

"I tried not to cause you too much pain, but I know I lost some control. I'm sorry Cassie…"

He broke off when she rested her hand against his cheek. "I'm fine Devon, really," she assured him. "It only hurt for a moment, and then it was over."

He frowned at her. "Are you sure?"

"Positive." His fingers stroked over her cheeks as he kissed her nose. "It was amazing Devon." She was barely able to hear her own words over the increased beat of her heart.

He smiled as he kissed her again. "It was more than amazing."

"Yes," she breathed. She lost herself to him as his delicious kisses deepened and all of the many problems existing outside of here drifted away. In here, with him, there were no problems. There was only love and utter bliss as she lost herself to his body and the passion only he could make her feel.

It was a while later before she roused again. The room was more illuminated, and it appeared to be mid morning. Below her, she could hear people moving about as whispers of conversations were exchanged. Her hand and head rested upon Devon's chest; he didn't make a sound, but she knew he was awake.

"We should go down," she muttered.

Devon's hand rubbed over her back and ran up to her shoulders before entangling in her hair. She lifted her head to look at him and propped her chin on her hands as she studied him. He was magnificent, amazing, and completely hers. She didn't feel shy now, she felt loved, and so unbelievably secure in this small room.

"Not yet." She frowned at him as he brushed back her hair;

his fingers brushed against the marks on her neck. A thrill shot down her spine; she couldn't stop her toes from curling against his solid legs. His eyes sparked with amusement as a smile curved the edges of his full mouth. He touched her lips with his fingers; he traced them briefly before reluctantly withdrawing from her and biting into his wrist. "You must have blood, and strength."

"I'm fine," she assured him. She longed to share the experience with him again, but she didn't like him thinking he'd hurt her.

"I took a lot from you Cassie, and there are shadows under your eyes."

Her eyes latched onto the glistening drops of blood pooling on his wrist. For a disconcerting moment hunger tore through her. The prospect of his blood didn't repulse her as it should. Instead, it excited and enticed her in a way it never had before. She suddenly wanted it for more than just a stronger bond with Devon, but because she craved it like a man in the desert craved water.

Confusion whirled through Devon's eyes, but before he could question her, she grasped his arm and bent her mouth to him. She knew once the bond was sealed, all doubts and questions would fade away as their minds mingled together. His hand wrapped around the back of her head as he held her close.

Cassie closed her eyes, a low moan of ecstasy escaped before she could stop it. His blood was delicious and filling in a way it never had been before. She could feel his turmoil over her reaction to it, but he didn't pull away. Instead he held her closer as her own dread began to build. This wasn't normal, but she couldn't bring herself to care.

She fell into him, allowing his thoughts and love to entwine her in a warm cocoon of security and adoration. His mind opened to hers, she had experienced a similar sensation the last time they'd exchanged blood, but this was far different. She tried to revolt before she was ensnared completely in the whirlwind of his mind.

"It's ok," Devon whispered. "It's ok, don't fight it. You must see."

Cassie didn't know what she needed to see, but as he pulled her closer she knew he needed this from her. Pushing her doubts aside, Cassie allowed herself to drift and mingle with his mind more intensely than she ever had before. Suddenly she was in his life, feeling what he wanted her to feel, living what he wanted her to live.

She stood with him as a young child with black hair and big green eyes. He was skinny and gangly, but amazingly adorable with his dimples and two missing teeth. He was so full of hope, mischief, and exuberance. Until his father's drinking started to get out of control, and his father's wrath turned on him. Until his mother was beaten while trying to protect her youngest son, and his brother turned his back on Devon's frightened cries. Until all of his hope and mischief were destroyed beneath his father's heavy fist, and resentment was all that festered within him.

When Devon escaped the cruelty of his home, he never looked back and never expected to step foot on the property again. Eager to be free, he explored the world, and lived the life of drudgery he swiftly adopted instead of going to the university. When Elizabeth changed him, he'd never been happier. He now had an outlet for all of the rage and hurt festering inside of him, now had a way to bury his despair in the joy and thrill of the hunt and kill.

Though he'd vowed never to return home, and thoroughly enjoyed his new life and all of the power it gave him, he found himself inexplicably drawn back to his family's massive country manor a few years later. His father's mind was rotten from his many years of heavy drinking. His brother however was young, healthy, and thoroughly enjoying his life as Lord of the Manor.

Devon watched him from the shadows of the early night as Robert moved about ordering this servant here, and that servant there. He was aware how alike they looked, but he was keenly reminded their personalities had always been opposites. He'd never enjoyed ordering people about. In the eyes of his father and his brother, he'd never been anything more than a servant amongst those walls anyway. Never been anything more than the *disposable* offspring, and they had reminded him of that on a daily basis.

He didn't know what had drawn him back to this hated place after all these years, but he found himself oddly fascinated by it. He'd been unable to get inside to see his father, but he found himself peering into the windows at the weak and feeble man who had once terrified and brutalized him. The man had beaten him to within an inch of life more than a few times, but Devon could now kill him with a flick of his wrist. His father had ruined his childhood, but in his old age he was paying for his excessive alcoholism and brutality. Devon had never put much stock in God, but he felt the cosmic hand of fate at work here, and he was satisfied with it.

Devon withdrew from the window and moved through the night to the front of the manor. The windows were lit with candles; inside he could hear the melodious music of a violin. His brother was having a small gathering, coaches and horses were gathered out front. Liveried footmen stood silently by them.

He was hungry, but he wouldn't hunt or feed here. He'd never come here again, and he would leave it the way he'd found it. He wouldn't sink to his father or Robert's level with spiteful acts of vengeance, they weren't worth it. He slipped through the gardens, so lost in his own thoughts he didn't notice the couple stealing time amongst the shadows until he was on top of them.

The woman gasped and jerked away from the embrace of her lover. "Devon!" she blurted.

Devon nodded to her. "Jane."

His eyes scanned over his brother. Robert had always been bigger than him, thicker through the shoulders, and broader in the chest. But either because of what he'd become, or just the normal process of adulthood and genetics, Devon was now a little taller and broader in the back and shoulders. Robert looked anything but happy to see him as he studied him with open disdain and his arms folded firmly over his chest.

"Devon, is that really you?" Jane whispered. Her hand covered her mouth now; her surprise had turned to keen interest. They'd once had a fling, but apparently she'd moved onto his brother when Devon had left.

"We thought you dead," Robert remarked.

Devon's mouth curved into a harsh smile. "Not even death could keep me down."

Robert shook his head as his eyes narrowed. "What are you doing here?"

Devon shrugged and held his hands out before him. "I was simply hoping to see my loving family once more."

Jane took a step back as her survival instincts finally rose up to bury her astonishment over seeing Devon again. Her head turned back and forth between them as she sensed the growing animosity between them. "Will you be staying?" Robert inquired, ever the gentleman.

"No."

"Will you see father?"

"No."

Robert frowned in confusion. He expected Devon to be here for something, money, vengeance, shelter, anything. That he'd come for nothing was something Robert couldn't grasp. "Where have you been?" Jane asked.

He shrugged as he slid his hands into his pockets and his mouth curved in a cruel smile. "To hell and back, but I greatly enjoyed the trip." Jane took another step back from him. "I must be going now," Devon told them.

"Will we see you again?" Jane asked eagerly.

Devon shook his head. "No, I will not be returning here. Have a good life."

"Wait! Devon *wait*!" He turned back at Jane's hurried cry. "Where will you be going?"

Devon couldn't stop the large grin that flashed over his face. "That's the beauty of it. I'll go wherever the world, and time, can take me."

They both looked completely baffled, but he expected them to be. Unlike him, they didn't have eternity to travel the world and experience the wonder of life, and especially the joy of death. Devon slipped away, unaware Elizabeth had followed him to the manor where she had spied upon him, and been witness to the dislike amongst the brothers.

He didn't know she would approach Robert that night, and as vengeance for Devon leaving her, she would also change Robert and set him lose upon the world, and Devon.

Cassie clutched him as his fingers twined through her hair. His memories poured rapidly into her; it was as if he was trying to purge himself of everything as rapidly as he could.

After his change, Robert had slaughtered all of the servants at the manor, and their father. He'd burnt the home to the ground and effectively severed all of his ties with a life that had been kind to him, but he'd despised it all the same. Devon hadn't known of Robert's change, or the slaughter, until fifty years later when they'd run across each other again in Venice.

Devon had been beyond stunned to see his brother alive, and untouched by age, but Robert had been prepared for the meeting. He'd been searching for Devon for years. Robert had been the favored child of their father, and he had inherited his father's malicious streak and ingrained hatred for Devon. Even at his cruelest, Devon didn't have the depth of psychosis inside of him Robert possessed, and always would. Robert may not have been beaten throughout his childhood, but he had longed to be the one doing the beating.

When he had come across Devon though, Robert had expected to come across the weaker brother Devon had once been. Robert had thought he would come across a man he could torture and brutalize to his endless pleasure, before finally destroying him.

He'd been sadly mistaken. Devon only had eight years on Robert as a vampire, but he was inherently stronger, faster, and far more vicious than Robert had ever fathomed. Robert had tracked Devon down in order to abuse him; he hadn't expected to be the one getting beaten. He hadn't expected to find his weak younger brother stronger than he was.

His hatred for Devon grew even more after the encounter, and when Julian entered the picture Robert became even more infuriated and volatile. There had been no stopping Julian and Devon together; there had been no way Robert could get to Devon, until now.

Now Robert knew the one way to destroy his brother was to destroy Cassie, and he would do everything in his power to make sure that was done.

Cassie pulled away from Devon and wheezed in a breath as the memories pounding against her ceased. Tears burned her eyes, her heart broke for the innocent boy he'd once been, and for the man that boy had been turned into, for the monster the man had become, and for the man who lay beneath her now, terrified he was going to lose her.

"Devon."

He brushed the tears from her cheeks and wiped his blood from her mouth. "I won't let him hurt you."

"I know," she whispered. "But *why* does he hate you so much? He's your brother, he should have protected you. He should have helped to defend you. You were a helpless child."

Devon's eyes were dark and distant. "Robert was always twisted, like my father. I didn't see it as a child because I couldn't see anything past my father, but Robert was always cruel too. It was a while before I thought back on those days with a different eye and suddenly realized the things I had missed. The servants were frightened of Robert. At the time I thought it was because he was going to be the future master, but he brutalized them. He beat them as he saw fit, took the women whenever he chose, as my father did. But I never saw the joy, the absolute *ecstasy* he took in it, not until after.

"My mother was also afraid of him. She tried to protect me, to shelter me from them, but I recall times when she would tremble in their presence. Tremble in the presence of her *own* child. She wanted nothing more than to get me out of that house and as far from them as possible. Unfortunately, once I was free I ran wild with it. I should have taken more time for her, should have opened my eyes sooner to what was going on in that house, but I could see nothing past my own torment. When I finally did it was too late for my mother. She withered away once I was gone."

Cassie choked back a sob as she shook her head. "That's not

your fault. You couldn't have stopped it; you couldn't have stayed there. If you had..."

"They would have killed me," he said when she couldn't finish. Cassie recoiled from his words; no child should have to go through what he had. No wonder he had kept the truth about his brother hidden from her and had tried to keep her shut out of his past.

"I'm glad you did, but you didn't have to show me," she managed to choke out.

He played idly with a strand of her hair as he twirled it around his finger. "Yes, I did. You must know Cassie, no matter what they say, we cannot trust them. Especially Robert."

Her fingers absently caressed his bare chest. "I know."

"If they had truly come in peace, and for the reasons they say, they wouldn't have brought Robert with them."

The thought of Devon's brother was enough to make her blood boil. If she got the chance, she knew she would kill Robert. Just as Robert would do the same to her. "The change, what is it like?"

Devon's hand stilled on her hair. "Cassie..."

"It has to be done Devon, whether they force it or we choose it, it must be done. I think I should be prepared for it."

"The pain is very intense, but hopefully I will be able to take some of yours onto myself by keeping hold of a piece of your mind." Cassie shook her head in protest. "Yes, Cassie, that is going to happen no matter what you say. It doesn't last long; the longest I've seen is an hour. Mine was only twenty minutes."

Cassie could handle the pain, no matter what she wouldn't allow Devon to take it on for her. "That's not bad."

She managed a wan smile for him. Though she was looking forward to joining him completely, to being with him forever, she didn't relish the thought of dying. "I will make it as easy as possible for you."

"I'll be fine," she replied.

She knew he wasn't giving into her wishes, but she allowed herself to be lost to him when he kissed her.

CHAPTER TWENTY-ONE

CASSIE TRIED to peak out from behind Devon, but he stood firmly in front of her and had no intention of moving even a little bit. She bit back a sigh of impatience. The testosterone level in the room was running high, and she was frightened one of the strong, super powerful men in this room would crack.

She suspected it might be Devon as Robert had nearly sent him into a rage the minute he walked into the room. Robert had taken one look at Cassie, and his eyes had lit with maliciousness. "Don't you smell interesting. Looks like someone is a woman now, does that finally make you a man, Devon?" he'd inquired flippantly.

Cassie's face flooded with color; her body burned with the heat of embarrassment suffusing her. She'd been unable to meet any of the startled gazes directed her way. Julian had grabbed hold of Devon, holding him back when he'd been about to pounce on his brother.

Devon had held back from destroying Robert all these years

because Robert was his brother, and to Devon that meant something, but it didn't matter anymore. Not if it meant her safety, and her life. Nothing mattered more to him than that. Robert was now fair game, and it seemed Robert had finally realized that as he'd remained blessedly quiet ever since those first few comments.

"How do we draw them out?" Zane inquired.

"They'll come to us," Devon answered. He thrust his arm behind him when Cassie tried to move to get a better view. She frowned at his back, but he didn't bother to look at her in order to get the full force of her displeasure.

"They'll lay a trap if we allow them to."

"Outside will be better," Luther said. "In the open where we can see them coming, and where they will have less of a chance to divide us."

Zane's gaze slid over the boarded windows, and then around the store. "Yes, perhaps you are right. There is no room for movement in here. We draw them out into the open and with all of us…"

"They will not be a part of this. There is no reason for them to be," Devon interrupted.

Anger spurted through her as Chris, Melissa, Dani, and Luther spun on him. "You can't leave us behind again!" Cassie interjected. Devon turned toward her; his emerald eyes blazed as his jaw clenched and his nostrils flared. "Not after last time, and you *will* need us."

"I'll make sure you are kept somewhere safer…"

"Absolutely not!" Chris interrupted Devon sharply.

"There is no need to discuss this. They *will* be involved. I intend to see what they can do, what they are capable of." Zane's honey eyes landed upon her, and a spark of amusement filled them. "I especially would like to know what your little sweet-heart is capable of."

Cassie glared at him as she folded her arms over her chest. Devon's hands fisted; the corded muscles in his arms stood out. "I do *not* want them involved in this!"

"It doesn't matter what you want. We had an agreement, and this is going to be part of it. No matter what happens these creatures must be destroyed, and I will take all the help we can get on this. Also, I *must* know what she is capable of, how strong she is. She killed Isla; we have to know if she is capable of killing us too."

Devon glanced back at her. He'd told her they couldn't trust them, but she'd still been holding out hope everything would work out, until now. Julian bristled beside Devon, his ice eyes were troubled as they met hers. "That wasn't part of the arrangement," Julian replied coldly.

"It was an unspoken part," Zane replied flippantly. "And it is a part that will be carried out. Now, where should this battle take place?"

Cassie's heart thumped loudly, she stared at Devon's back as Zane and the other Elders hatched a plan. She was acutely aware her side remained completely quiet.

"It is settled then."

Cassie's head shot up; she peered around Devon's back as Zane folded his hands before him. The pleased look on his face caused a chill to slide down her back. Devon remained stiff before her, his back ramrod straight. His gaze remained ruthlessly upon Robert, who smiled back at him. Julian's shoulder brushed briefly against hers as he stepped closer to her. She'd worried he would hate her, or at least avoid her after what had happened between her and Devon. Instead, he stood beside her loyally, his faith in her absolute.

When he glanced down at her, she saw an understanding in his gaze that left her breathless. Without thinking, she seized hold of his hand and enfolded it within hers. She knew what he might see, but she also knew he would see how much she loved him and appreciated everything he'd done for her.

His hand tightened around hers as a small smile played across his mouth. How he understood and still cared for her was something she didn't understand, but she knew he did and he wouldn't abandon her, or Devon. She held Julian's hand as she turned back to the others.

The Elder's gazes were fixed upon their joined hands. "This is far more entertaining than I had imagined," Robert purred. Anger and hatred boiled through Cassie. Devon glanced briefly back at them, but he showed no signs of a reaction as he spotted their entwined hands. "Maybe we should just allow them to kill each other over her."

"Now, now, Robert, what fun would that be? Come along, we have some disdainful creatures to hunt." Anastasia's mouth curved into a cruel smile as she sneered at Cassie.

The Elders exchanged a small smile before they slipped outside to stand by the door. Cassie found herself able to breathe easier as their revolting presences left the room. Devon turned and grasped hold of her shoulders. "You are to stay near me; for once in your life, do *not* do anything foolish. For once in your life, please listen to me Cassie. Please, for me, do this."

She bit on her bottom lip as she fought back the tears clogging her eyes and throat. "I will," she vowed, knowing she would do anything to ease his troubles.

Julian squeezed her hand before releasing her to Devon. She stepped into Devon's arms and buried herself against his chest as she savored what may be their last moments together. She didn't see Matthew until he was upon them, a tall shadow of a broken man, a wraith who had soundlessly moved away from the others. A hiss escaped Devon; his fangs sprang free as he swung her away from Matthew. But Matthew didn't come at them; instead he seized hold of Julian's arms. "My son, you should not covet another man's mate. They haven't sealed the bond, but you know it is wrong to do so."

Julian threw up his arms to dislodge the man. Matthew stared at him, his hands folded before him and his eyes distant. "I am sorry my son, but you must walk a different path than the one you have chosen."

"Don't touch me again you crazy freak," Julian snarled as his eyes flashed a ruby color.

Matthew bowed his head as he nodded briefly. "Julian," Cassie whispered. She reached for Matthew, a man who had been beaten and broken by the cruelty of his fellow vampires.

Julian seized hold of her hand before she could grasp the wraith. "Don't touch him!" Julian barked. "You do *not* want to take the chance of him learning anything about you, Cassie."

Cassie recoiled; Matthew retreated toward the others. Zane's gaze was focused and questioning, but he said nothing as Matthew rejoined them. Julian watched them go, his eyes troubled and distant. He didn't turn back to them though as he stiffly moved toward the door.

"Devon…"

"I know," he said.

They both watched Julian as he slipped out the door. The slump to his shoulders revealed something had just passed between him and Matthew. Whatever it was, Julian didn't like it.

She glanced over as Chris, Melissa, Dani, and Luther moved to join them. Annabelle and Liam hung back, hugging each other as they whispered to one another. "They're going to turn on us," Luther stated.

Devon's hands constricted on Cassie's back. "The first chance they get."

Cassie shuddered, her eyes closed as she hugged Devon. Her heart was breaking, terror filled her, but she shoved it all fiercely aside. If she started to break now they would never survive this, and they had to make sure the creatures in this town were destroyed before they could wreak havoc upon the earth.

"All of you have to be prepared to defend yourselves as soon as this is over. You also must be prepared to run, to flee, when this phase of the battle is over," Devon told them.

Though Cassie didn't protest, there was no way she was leaving him behind.

DEVON KEPT Cassie behind him and Julian. He knew she resented it, but he was going to make sure she survived this night. Beside him, he could feel Julian itching to reveal what he'd glimpsed from Matthew. Julian glanced back at Cassie. She met his gaze, her beautiful eyes troubled as she watched him. "It was about me, wasn't it?" her voice was so faint Devon barely caught her words.

Julian turned away as his hands fisted at his sides. Small tremors shook Cassie's delicate frame. He had to know what Julian had seen. He couldn't take the chance of losing her. "Julian." Julian remained unmoving. "Julian!"

"Shh." Julian's gaze flickered toward where the others were gathered, not far away.

It took all he had not to grab hold of Julian, drag him from here, and demand to know what he had learned. But he couldn't do so. It was obvious Julian had no intention of letting The

Elders know what he had learned. A shadow amongst the woods drew Devon's attention away.

He wasn't fooled into thinking this would be an easy battle, even with The Elders on their side. He wasn't fooled into thinking the remaining creatures would all come at once, or that they wouldn't have a plan of their own. Devon was certain Zane's only true plan was to attempt to lure the creatures out and slaughter them as best he could.

Devon turned suddenly. Dani issued a small cry as he roughly pulled her forward. Bending close to her, he pressed his lips to her ear. "There isn't a Grounder amongst them, they might not know what you are, don't use your power until they are the only ones left standing."

Dani's gold flecked eyes flitted toward the group of Elders. Devon released her abruptly and met Zane's curious and amused gaze with defiance. The head Elder was far too smug for Devon's liking. Another shadow moved rapidly amongst the trees as it hunted them.

He turned his attention to Cassie, who was watching the woods attentively. "Remember your promise," he reminded her.

Her attention remained riveted upon the forest as she nodded. They stood upon the street in front of the mercantile, away from the area Robert had destroyed. They were exposed to the stalkers in the forest. The first one burst from the woods and five others emerged behind it. They barreled down on The Elders who were closest to them. Melissa spun toward the building as ten more of the monsters emerged from inside. Devon didn't know how they'd gotten into the building, but he was certain they'd always known how to do so.

"I love you," Cassie whispered, seconds before they were besieged.

CHAPTER TWENTY-TWO

POWER FLOWED THROUGH HER; Cassie relished in the influx of it as the thrill of the fight, the eagerness for the kill descended upon her. The fear inside of her was buried as adrenaline pulsated to the forefront. She felt the change come over her, knew when her eyes turned red. She braced in preparation to launch herself at them. The others had already descended upon The Elders who eagerly embraced them in battle. Before the monsters could reach them, before Cassie could leap into the fray, Julian spun on Devon. Grabbing hold of his arm, he roughly pulled Devon toward him.

"Matthew is insane," he rushed out. "He has seen what could become of Cassie, but he hasn't told anyone yet because he almost hopes it will happen." Cassie's mouth went dry, her heart thumped riotously in her chest. Julian looked crazed as his gaze latched onto her. "It's not good, *none* of it is good, we have to get out of this somehow. We have to get Cassie away from them."

Cassie briefly forgot about the creatures rushing toward them as Julian's words sank in. The broken, crazed man had seen something that had to do with *her*! Something that had terrified Julian, something that put *all* of them in peril.

They had finally gotten here; she was finally going to join Devon. But now, whatever Julian had seen from Matthew had left him so torn and horrified he was shaking before them. Cassie wanted to assure him Matthew was wrong, that not all premonitions came true. Melissa was living proof of that, but she couldn't do that when they were about to be attacked.

"Julian..." Cassie broke off as Julian's ice blue eyes swung toward her. She could see the love in his steady gaze, but his pouty mouth was pinched as his platinum blond hair fell around his chiseled features. "Oh," she breathed.

"We will discuss this later," Devon interrupted. "Now is not the time."

Cassie was torn away from the horror of what Julian was saying, and back to the horror of what was rapidly unraveling before them. Watching the rushing horde barrel toward them, Cassie decided to sheathe the stake and go immediately for the crossbow. She loaded it with the ease of someone who had done it hundreds of times before. Lifting it high, she took aim at the one in the lead and closest to Chris.

She squeezed the trigger. The arrow let loose with a reassuring rush of feather and air that sped it toward its target and hit home with a reassuring thud. The kill would have made her smile, if it hadn't been for the monsters scrambling easily over their fallen brethren.

Cassie swiftly reloaded as the first one leapt at Annabelle and Liam. They fell back from the weight of the creature clawing and spitting at them. Cassie had attributed more reason to them, but they appeared to be in the midst of a blood frenzy that made them crazed and unpredictable.

Raising the crossbow, she took aim at the one barreling toward Luther. She fired, but was off target as it slammed into the creature's collarbone and knocked it back. The injury hindered its progress but didn't stop it. Cassie swore as she scrambled to grab another arrow, but it was too late. They were already on top of them. She tossed the crossbow aside and grabbed hold of her stake.

But the attack didn't come from the way she'd been expecting and was prepared for. Instead, it burst free of the woods on their left hand side. Cassie caught the flurry of movement at the last second. No matter how prepared they were, or how strong they were, they were outnumbered and nowhere near as frenzied as these creatures were.

Red eyes filled her vision; the stench of putrid flesh assaulted her nostrils. Hands seized hold of her, claws curled around her upper arms as it jerked her forward. Years of training took over as she managed to rip one arm free of its grasp. She drove her fist straight into its nose, knocking its head back as its nose shattered beneath the force of her forceful blow. Blood sprayed over the both of them, but it continued to come at her until she slammed her fist into its cheek forcing it backward.

Taking advantage that it was off balance, Cassie leapt forward and knocked the creature back further. She twisted the stake in her hand and spun it around as she drove it forward. The creature howled as its fingers clawed at the wooden protrusion jutting out of its chest. Cassie ripped it free and shoved the creature back. It writhed and made strange gurgling noises until all its movements finally ceased.

She didn't have time to study the creature, didn't have time to take in what she had just done as another one grasped hold of her and knocked her back. She stumbled beneath the force of its weight and nearly fell over. Devon's shout filled her ears as the creature managed to claw one of her arms open and spill her blood. Its nostrils flared as the scent of her blood agitated it.

Its misshapen jaws snapped together eagerly as it pulled her closer. There was flesh clearly visible within its teeth. Cassie fought to keep her balance against its anxious, frantic aggression. She didn't find much satisfaction as her foot connected with its shin. There hadn't been as much force behind the blow as she would have liked. Devon appeared behind it; his eyes were a fiery blaze as he seized hold of the thing's head and roughly jerked it to the side. The loud crack of its neck echoed through the night. Its arms flailed as it tried desperately to claw at its distorted head. Devon's ruby eyes briefly met hers; she turned away, unwilling to watch what happened next. She tried to block out the sickening sounds of bones breaking further as flesh was torn from the creature's body.

Her friends were being herded further away from the store. Chris's nose was bleeding, his shirt was torn open to his belly button, and more blood marred his chest. Melissa's hair had been ripped free of its braid and hung in a tumbled black mass around her shoulders. Liam and Luther were fighting off three creatures, Luther was bleeding from a cut on his cheek, and Liam was losing ground. Annabelle and Julian were just finishing off two of more of the Halflings.

Cassie looked rapidly around, but none of them seemed to have noticed her standing alone. She spun toward Devon, he'd been swamped by three of them. He was the one who required her help most right now. She clutched her stake as she threw herself back into the battle.

A woman, or at least what had once been a woman, came charging out of the fray. Her jaws bit up and down so forcefully, her fangs sliced into her lower lips. Blood trailed down her chin and soaked the tattered remains of her shirt. Cassie swung her fist into the woman's cheek, but she dove forward and wrapped her arms around Cassie's waist.

The force of the thing's momentum carried them both backward before they tumbled to the ground in a scattered heap. Cassie's breath rushed out of her; she barely managed to keep her head from slamming off of the pavement. For the first time all of her confusion was burned away as the comforting swell of rage rushed to the forefront. Blood sprayed across Cassie's face as the woman's teeth clacked loudly, and she clawed at Cassie.

Clinging to her stake, Cassie used her anger and strength to brace her legs. The woman tried to cling to her, but Cassie was able to toss her off. Cassie's wrath escalated as the scent of her own blood hit her. Using her arms and legs, she sprang easily off the ground. The woman hadn't quite recovered yet, and she was just getting back to her feet.

Cassie leapt on her and drove her down to the ground. There was a time when Cassie's guilt over killing something, even if it was a monster, would have made her hesitate, may have even cost her own life. Those days were gone. There was no remorse anymore. She had people to protect; she had Devon to think of. No matter that this creature had once been a woman, she may have even had a family, Cassie didn't hesitate.

She drove the stake into the woman's back. Bone shattered, the woman screeched an inhuman mewling sound that caused Cassie to recoil slightly. She felt a tug of pity for the poor creature, but she didn't regret her actions. If this woman had been allowed to run free, the destruction she would cause to innocents would be on Cassie's hands.

Cassie jumped to her feet and spun quickly. She leapt forward as another creature leapt onto Devon. They seemed determined to take him down. Panic tore through her, she couldn't lose him. She would *not* lose him.

Arms suddenly wrapped around her. A strangled cry escaped her, the arms squeezed forcefully enough to knock the breath out of her. Cassie panted for air as she struggled against the iron hold crushing her against someone's chest. Her legs flailed but came up against nothing as whoever held her stood with their legs braced apart.

"I'm going to enjoy this."

Hatred tore through her as she recognized Robert's voice. She swung her head back but came up with nothing as he moved out of her way. She was preparing for a different method of attack when she felt it. Whatever breath she had left rushed out of her, as the stabbing pain tore through the center of her stomach, just beneath her rib cage. She choked as she tried to get some air into her lungs but received none as fiery agony tore through her.

"Robert no!" Zane bellowed.

Cassie was briefly confused by his command. Weren't they all going to turn on them anyway, and just what had Robert done to her?

A rush of something warm against her skin suddenly punctured the agony. Her mouth dropped as she stared in dismay at exactly what Robert had done. A silver dagger handle jutted out from her belly, the warm rush she'd felt was her own blood oozing from the wound.

Her pain was forgotten as the battle for her life was renewed. "Such a little fighter," Robert purred. To her utter disgust, he leaned forward to brush a kiss against her cheek; his tongue flickered lightly over her skin. Though he had just stabbed her, this was a far worse atrocity as she shrank away from his hideous touch. He chuckled in her ear as he ran his tongue over it. "Oh what I would have loved to have done to you, what I would have loved to make my brother *watch* me do to you. Just in case I was never able to get that opportunity, I'm taking this one."

Cassie grasped hold of the handle of the knife and tried to pull it free. His hand remained locked around the handle. Her hands clenched as she tried to keep her blood inside of her body, tried to keep her life from rapidly flowing out of her. Robert spun suddenly with her in his arms. A new wave of fire scorched through her entire body as her legs swung out around her.

"Look up!" Robert hissed in her ear. Cassie couldn't look anywhere but at the hideous knife causing so much torment inside of her. "Look up!"

At this command, Robert shook her violently. She gasped; her head came up as tears filled her eyes. She would do anything to make the torture stop, anything to make it better. Then she realized exactly what he meant for her to see, and she knew instantly she would have taken the pain a thousand times over rather than have listened to him.

Her gaze locked on Devon's fiery red one. He'd frozen, oblivious to the battle that continued to wage around him. Hopelessness tore through her as she fully realized she wouldn't be walking away from this. Robert was going to kill her.

Devon's eyes flickered briefly, their beautiful emerald green shone through as love blazed from them. Tears, that had nothing to do with her agony, spilled down her face. "Don't worry; you'll see my brother again, in Hell," Robert whispered in her ear before kissing her again.

Her body bucked as Robert ripped the knife upward. He broke into the bones of her ribcage, tearing through her organs and skin before roughly tearing it free. A gurgled scream ripped from her, her hands clawed at her gouged flesh as she uselessly tried to close the gash.

Robert released her and shoved her roughly away. Cassie stumbled before falling to her knees and slipping forward. This was it, this was the end, and though she'd always known it would come at a young age, she hadn't expected it to be this young. All she yearned for now was more time with Devon. She wished she could have been there for him, and her friends; they wouldn't take well to this.

Devon's roar of fury filled the air. She managed to turn her head enough to see him amongst the creatures. He tried to get free to reach her, but they had taken his inaction as an excuse to pounce upon him. His eyes were more than on fire, they were pure molten lava as rage buried him within its grip of insanity.

She suddenly understood why Zane had yelled at Robert, why he hadn't intended for her to be killed just yet. They hadn't planned for her to go down until they at least had Devon under control in some way.

But now... Now, he was going to kill them all. Including her friends.

The thought caused her to tremble, but she couldn't move as weakness seeped into her muscles, and her life poured out of her veins. "Cassie! Cassie!" Chris skidded across the ground toward her.

Grasping hold of her shoulder, he pulled her attention away from Devon. Chris's face drained of color as he gazed at the blood spilling from her battered body. The sapphire depths of his much loved eyes bloomed with tears as knowledge slammed into him. "It's ok, I think this was meant to be," she managed to whisper.

Determination blazed through his eyes. "No it isn't."

He was bending over to scoop her up when Julian swooped

down upon them. He grasped hold of her and easily pulled her into his arms. Cassie groaned as the movement caused fresh fire to burn through her body. "Hold on, just hold on," Julian commanded.

He curled Cassie against his chest and used his shoulders as battering rams against whatever creatures came at them. Chris shoved and punched his way through the crowd as they ran through it. Cassie could feel the weakness seeping into her, and the hurt wasn't so bad anymore. "Annabelle!" Julian bellowed. "Annabelle I need you! Now!"

Cassie caught a glimpse of the small girl fighting to get free of the crowd. "Julian." His ice blue eyes came down to hers. "Julian it's ok."

"Yes, you will be ok," he barked as he broke free of the melee.

"No, Julian, it's ok. I always knew..." a rough coughing spree broke through her; suddenly the pain was back in shooting waves. Julian's eyes widened, and though he was tormented at the thought of losing her, his pupils dilated at the sight of her blood. "I wouldn't live long," she finished on a hoarse whisper.

He tore his gaze away from her as he bolted across the street. "You'll be fine, you'll be fine. Annabelle!" he bellowed again.

Sensing the impending end of her life, Cassie touched his arm. "Julian, you can't let him die. Promise me you won't let him die, not because of me."

"Cassie..."

"Please Julian," she pleaded. "Please. My life is not worth his too."

This time when his eyes met hers, there were tears spilling down his cheeks. He may want to deny it, he may still hope Annabelle would be able to help her, but she saw now that he knew the truth. She would not survive this. "I will do everything I can to keep him alive," he vowed.

Tears spilled down her cheeks. "And yourself too?"

He hesitated before nodding briskly. "And myself too."

"Thank you."

Cassie's head slumped against his chest as he shoved into the store door. Darkness seeped over her, a strange sense of peace embraced her. She'd thought she would be scared in the end, but she wasn't, not for herself anyway. Warmth seeped into her outer limbs to replace the cold chill that had taken up residence there.

It wasn't ok she was leaving everyone; she would have loved to stay with them forever, but she wasn't afraid. There was something else waiting for her, and in the end she'd always known fate would never be denied. It could never be changed, and this *was* her fate. It always had been.

She heard Julian screaming for Annabelle's healing ability again, and then she heard nothing more.

CHRIS WAS numb as Julian burst into the store. He nearly broke the door off its hinges as it slammed against the wall with enough force to shatter the plaster behind it. Chris had heard Cassie's whispered words; he could feel the strange sense of comfort and peace settling over her, and he hated it.

He couldn't lose his best friend, he could *not* lose her, and she was ready to be lost. Please, he begged silently. Please just hold on.

"Annabelle!" Julian's voice was so loud the windows in the store rattled but Annabelle was already racing through the door. Her strawberry colored curls were a mess, blood smeared her cheeks, but she appeared unharmed as she bolted toward Julian.

Chris shut the door and propped a chair against it as its bent frame wouldn't allow it to close properly.

"Hurry," Julian pleaded in a hoarse whisper.

Julian knelt on the floor and placed Cassie gently upon the ground. Her hands slid limply away from her stomach to fall upon the ground. Chris got his first good look at the hideous injury. Bile rushed up his throat as he stared at the brutal tear in his friend. The strong pulse of her blood had slowed to a near stop. Her shirt was torn open and her flesh was covered by the deep red color of her life's blood.

A small moan of despair escaped him. Cassie was a fast healer, but even with Annabelle's powers he couldn't see how they could do anything to heal *that*. It was too deep, too brutal and cruel to ever be healed. They were going to lose her, he was certain of it; he was going to lose his best friend.

Tears clogged his throat and made it almost impossible for him to breathe. "What are you waiting for? Do something!" Julian snarled at Annabelle. She remained frozen, her hand over her mouth as she gazed at Cassie. "Annabelle!" Julian barked.

Annabelle shook her head and turned toward Julian; her shoulders slumped in defeat as she huddled in on herself. The hollow look to her eyes made her appear somewhat shrunken. "I cannot heal the dead Julian," she whispered forlornly.

Chris felt as if he'd been punched in the gut; pain clutched at his chest as tears instantly sprang forth. "No," he moaned.

He took a step toward Cassie, unable to believe she could be so savagely ripped from their lives, that her inner light could so easily be doused. He froze though, unable to go forward as his gaze landed upon her face. Cassie's eyes were halfway open, her pupils dilated and unseeing as she stared at the ceiling. Her mouth was parted, her face lax. Knowledge strangled him with its intensity as he turned away. He choked for air as loss engulfed him.

Julian and Annabelle remained unmoving, but he could feel their sadness and loss even through his own sorrow. Julian swore loudly; turning away, he slammed his fist down on one of the metal shelves. It crumpled beneath the blow and spilled its contents across the floor. Before Chris could even blink, Julian lifted up one of the cases, and heaved it across the room as if it weighed no more than a feather. Glass and materials shattered across the room. Chris wrapped his arms around himself as he took a step away from the cans rolling toward him. Julian bellowed before lifting another shelf and heaving it across the room.

Fresh misery swamped Chris, but this time it was so intense it knocked him to his knees. He couldn't breathe, couldn't see as his vision blurred, and his head pounded with the torment pulsing through him in never ending waves that nearly caused him to pass out. His forehead almost touched the floor as his heart shattered into a million pieces, and destroyed everything good and right inside of him. His humanity burned away to leave only scattered pieces of nothing that were quickly buried by rage. The blood in his ears was a loud rush blocking out nearly all other sound. A thirst for vengeance, for destruction and brutality, swamped him. Both of the emotions were so intense he labored to breathe as tears rolled down his cheeks.

"Julian stop," Annabelle pleaded.

Julian's shoulders heaved as he stared at the back wall. His hands fisted at his sides, his body shook, but he'd regained some control over himself again. "Devon can't know about this, not yet. Not until we can contain him in some way. I promised her I wouldn't let him die, and I *am* going to keep that promise," Julian said.

"How are we going to do that?" Annabelle whispered.

"I don't know."

Chris tried to find his voice, tried to rise up against the tidal wave of emotions crashing over him. He was certain if he couldn't get control, he would be buried beneath the debris of Devon's wrath and grief. Forever caught up within the whirlpool now controlling the vampire. For Chris was keenly aware there was nothing left of the man within Devon. The man had been destroyed by Cassie's death; the monster inside had finally burst free of its cage to take Devon's place.

The End.

**The fifth and final book, *Phoenix Rising*,
is now available.**
***Phoenix Rising* on Amazon:** http://bit.ly/PhRsAmz

Stay in touch on updates and new releases from the author by joining the mailing list!
Mailing list for Erica Stevens & Brenda K. Davies Updates:
http://bit.ly/ESBKDNews

FIND THE AUTHOR

Erica Stevens/Brenda K. Davies Mailing List:
http://bit.ly/ESBKDNews

Facebook page: http://bit.ly/ESFBpage
Facebook friend: http://bit.ly/EASFrd

Erica Stevens/Brenda K. Davies Book Club:
http://bit.ly/ESBDbc

Instagram: http://bit.ly/ErStInsta
Twitter: http://bit.ly/ErStTw
Website: http://bit.ly/ESWbst
Blog: http://bit.ly/ErStBl

ABOUT THE AUTHOR

Erica Stevens is the author of the Captive Series, Kindred Series, Fire & Ice Series, Ravening Series, and the Survivor Chronicles. She enjoys writing young adult, new adult, romance, horror, and science fiction. She also writes adult paranormal romance and historical romance under the pen name, Brenda K. Davies. When not out with friends and family, she is at home with her husband, dog, and horse.

Lightning Source UK Ltd.
Milton Keynes UK
UKHW02f1837150518

322661UK00031B/886/P

9 781478 131816